HER ACCIDENTAL
HIGHLANDER
HUSBAND

CLAN MACKINLAY SERIES

HER ACCIDENTAL HIGHLANDER HUSBAND

CLAN MACKINLAY SERIES

ALLISON B. HANSON

This book is a work of fiction. Names, characters, places, and incidents are the product of the author's imagination or are used fictitiously. Any resemblance to actual events, locales, or persons, living or dead, is coincidental.

Copyright © 2020 by Allison B. Hanson. All rights reserved, including the right to reproduce, distribute, or transmit in any form or by any means. For information regarding subsidiary rights, please contact the Publisher.

Entangled Publishing, LLC
10940 S Parker Rd
Suite 327
Parker, CO 80134
rights@entangledpublishing.com

Amara is an imprint of Entangled Publishing, LLC.

Edited by Nina Bruhns
Cover design by Mayhem Cover Creations
Cover photography by romancephotos/DepositPhotos
Rod Hill/GettyImages

Manufactured in the United States of America

First Edition September 2020

In memory of my Aunt Nan

Chapter One

Looking down at her hands, covered in her husband's blood, Marian Fletcher Blackley, Duchess of Endsmere, felt surprisingly calm. She'd known for the last five years this was the way it would end.

With blood on someone's hands.

She'd expected it to be the other way around. Many times during the duke's rages she'd thought he would kill her. There were times, after being kicked repeatedly, she'd almost wished he had killed her so the pain would end. So her torment as his wife would be over, and she would no longer have to live in constant fear.

But tonight, something deep inside her—an intense will to survive—had taken over. He was angrier with her than she'd ever seen, and she'd known it would happen tonight. He was going to kill her. She had seen it in his eyes. He wouldn't have been able to control himself and she would have died.

When he'd raised his fists, she'd reached out in defense. Her protection had come in the form of the fireplace poker. Her palm had grasped it unerringly and her first strike along his temple had downed him.

It would be unladylike to mention the second, third, and fifth strikes that had ended her fear and pain from this man indefinitely.

Lucy, her lady's maid, knocked frantically at the door, having heard Marian's screams. "Your Grace, are you all right? Do you need me to call a doctor?"

Lucy knew all, having had to dress Marian's injuries in the past. It was no surprise that tonight Lucy expected to need to piece Marian together once again. Only it wasn't Marian who was injured. In fact, for once, Marian didn't have a mark on her.

The duke, however, was clearly dead.

Opening the door, Lucy gasped. "Oh, Your Grace! What has he done? I will fetch Dr. Simmons. He cannot expect me to tend—" Lucy's rambling stopped abruptly when Marian allowed the door to open wider so the maid could see the carnage spread out on the rug.

"'Tis not my blood this time." Even Marian's voice was calm.

Surely this wasn't normal. She should have swooned or launched into hysterics by now. But all she felt was peace with what she'd done. What she'd been forced to do to save herself.

Marian's gown was covered in blood, as were the rug and a good part of her bedchamber.

"I see." Lucy swallowed, her voice just as calm as Marian's. "Well, he's dead," she announced after checking the body. "Now what?"

The fear and panic that had previously been kept at bay swarmed in now, chilling her bones. Marian's hands trembled as she tossed the poker to the side.

"I— I don't know. I guess we call for the magistrate."

Lucy shook her head. "You've not a mark on you, and with your Scottish accent they'll see you're hanged for killing a peer of the realm."

Marian tried to swallow and found it impossible. "What should I do?"

"You must leave. We'll get you changed out of that dress and I'll burn it. You must leave London immediately before word gets out. I can go with you."

"You can't come with me. Your daughter is expecting any day. You're needed here." Plus, Marian would never implicate her maid in her crimes.

At five and thirty Lucy was ten years older than Marian, and the only friend the duke had allowed. Mainly because he was unaware of their friendship.

"Where will you go?" Lucy asked.

"I won't tell you. That way you can answer honestly when you're questioned."

Lucy grasped her arm to stop her as she moved toward her wardrobe. "You cannot go to your family home in Scotland. They will surely track you there and bring you back to hang. You need to stay clear of your clan lands. It's certain death."

Marian nodded in agreement, though that had been her plan. Her father had passed a few years ago. Her older brother would take her in and keep her safe. But she would be bringing trouble to her brother's home. She could only imagine what he would do to keep her safe. She would be putting him in danger by going there.

She needed to find another place of refuge. Somewhere she wouldn't be expected to go.

Thoughts of her younger sister came to mind, but she pushed them away. Her relationship with Kenna had always been strained. Her father and stepmother had been a constant wedge between them, saying things to make sure Kenna felt like she had less worth because, to their standards, she wasn't as pretty as Marian.

After their mother died, Marian had been raised for one

purpose only, and that was to be wed to an English nobleman. Every moment of her youth had been spent primping and practicing for her debut at London court. Her Scottish tongue had been twisted until she was able to form her words with the correct English flair.

She'd done everything that was expected of her. Forgone the fun her younger sister and brother seemed to have running wild in the Highlands with nothing but mischief on their minds.

Yet, despite being the well-trained, obedient daughter, she'd been tricked into this nightmare of a life with a man who'd despised her very existence.

A man she'd killed.

The thought fired her into action.

If she wanted to live she needed to flee London, and the only place she knew was Scotland. She'd head for the border and figure out the rest if she made it that far.

Now that she was free of the horror her marriage had been, she wanted to find a safe place to live where no man would ever have control over her again.

...

Cameron MacKinlay heaved another large rock into the cart, making the horse snort and shy. Letting out a breath, he frowned at the blisters across his palms and wiped the sweat from his brow.

"Damn, Lachlan." Cam shook his head and picked up the shovel to loosen the next rock so it could be loaded.

Despite the cursing, it was his own fault he was loading rocks. If he'd not refused to follow his laird's orders, he would be back at Dunardry Castle sitting down at the midday meal. Instead, he had hard bannocks and ale to look forward to.

Still, he'd rather face hard labor and poor fare than be

forced into marriage merely to satisfy a clan alliance. Aye, it was done all the time in the Highlands. In fact, Lachlan himself had married his wife, Kenna, because of such a thing. But Cam didn't want to marry.

War chiefs did not always come home to their families after battle. He knew it well enough. When he was nine, his own father—the war chief of Clan MacKinlay at the time—had not come home.

His father had been a good man, but duty called for him to take risks. He'd been a war chief first and foremost, a husband and father second. As his position demanded.

Now Cam was in that same position, and he didn't want to see the worry in a woman's eyes, as he had his mother's. He didn't want to abandon a family if death claimed him.

When he became the war chief of Clan MacKinlay at the age of nineteen, he'd made that solemn vow. Having a family would make him weak, causing him to delay when forced to take risks, and the entire clan could be put in danger because of it.

Lachlan knew how Cam felt, yet he had still ordered Cam to marry the McCurdy lass. It was true, such an alliance with the McCurdy clan would mean access to the sea and what lay beyond for his clan. But he just couldn't do it.

He'd rather face his punishment in the fields collecting rocks.

Besides, even if he were of a mind to marry, he'd not risk such an alliance unless he was very certain it would result in his clan having access to the sea. Marrying into the McCurdy clan was no guarantee of that. The word of a McCurdy was not something Cam would ever put his life on.

He'd much rather take what they wanted from the other clan by force. Dougal McCurdy couldn't be trusted. Cam felt the relationship between the clans was far too strained to build a reliable alliance. Lach didn't agree. Thus the impasse.

So, instead of being at the castle training his warriors for a takeover that would grant the MacKinlays access to the port and all trading that came with it, Cam was out here in this desolate field gathering rocks.

As he bent to lift the next stone he caught movement in the trees. A woman bolted out of the forest and ran straight for him, as if he'd wished for a lass and the fairies had delivered her right out of the glen.

"Help me, please," she rasped, her breathing labored from running. He could barely hear her over the sound of loud barking. Three hounds sprinted from the woods with two horsemen directly behind.

Taking in the woman's tattered gown and shoeless feet, he would expect her to be a wench from a nearby village, but her speech sounded rich and cultured.

English.

When she reached Cam she didn't stop. She grabbed hold of him and shimmied up his body as if he were a tree. Her bosom heaved right in his face.

A better man might not have noticed, but Cam was not a better man.

"Help," she repeated. "Sister. Kenna," she managed to get out between gasps of air.

Cam hadn't gotten a good look at her, but she surely didn't look like Lady Kenna. Kenna's hair was fiery red and curly, where this lass was golden-haired...under the dirt.

"Hey there," one of the men on horseback called as they drew up in front of Cam where he held the trembling girl. The hounds continued to bay as they circled him. "Turn the girl over to us and we'll leave you to your work."

The man was also English. Some kind of guard, Cam guessed by his dress.

"I'll do no such thing," Cam said stiffly. He didn't like being ordered about by a scrawny Englishman on his own clan's lands.

"She is a criminal, a fugitive from the Crown's justice, and I have orders to bring her back to England where she will be hanged for the murder of her husband, the Duke of Endsmere."

If this was indeed Kenna's sister—and he believed the lass—Kenna would not appreciate him handing her over to certain death.

"Call off the dogs," he said when the woman had made it to his shoulders in her effort to get away from the snapping jaws.

A Scot wearing MacDonald colors moved his horse closer and called the hounds back.

"I am afraid ye have the wrong woman," Cam said with a look of disgust. "This canna be the wife of the late Duke of Endsmere, because she's my own wife, Mary." He wrapped an arm around the woman and set her on the ground next to him. She gripped his hand and hid behind him. "Isn't that right, love?" He squeezed her hand, silently telling her to comply.

The woman nodded emphatically. "Aye. This be my husband," she said in a Scottish brogue that would do her clan proud.

The English twit snorted and shook his head. "Trust me, friend, you do not wish to be caught up with the likes of her."

"I'm afraid I'm already caught up, *friend*. You'll not be taking my wife from me."

The Englishman let out a huff and turned to the Scot for help.

"You say this is your wife?" the Scot asked.

"Aye. She's my wife. And I am the war chief of Clan MacKinlay. You have no right to take her off clan lands without an order from King Charles *and* permission from our laird."

The Scot nodded once and turned to the other man.

"Whether or not she was his wife a moment ago, I assure ye they are now wed. They stood before witnesses with hands bound and declared themselves married. Under Scottish law they are hand-fasted, and it is a binding marriage."

Cam glanced down at the woman's hand in his, her fingers clenched as tight as her small hand could grasp his larger one. A tattered piece of her dress had been tangled around their wrists as she'd scrambled up his body. She was holding on to him now as if preparing to be bodily pulled away.

He played through the past moments and realized what the MacDonald arse had said was entirely true.

"This MacKinlay has the right of it," the MacDonald man continued. "You may not take her without retaliation from the clan. You will need an order from the crown to get the laird to give up one of his clan without a battle. A battle I'm not willing to walk into, especially with just you at my back."

"This is ridiculous. What kind of barbaric land allows people to wed in such casual fashion?"

Cam assumed the man didn't need an answer to his question. Besides, he was too stunned to speak at the moment. He and this woman, whose name he didn't even know, had declared they were wed while holding hands in front of witnesses.

She was, indeed, his wife.

Bloody hell. Cam swallowed and picked up his sword from the cart behind him with the hand that was not being clutched by his new bride. Whether he'd planned or wanted this didn't matter. She belonged to him and his clan now, and he protected what was his.

"If you wish to try to take her, let's get on with it. If not, be off with you."

The Englishman puffed and slapped his leg, scowling

down at them. "I will be back with an order from the king himself if I have to, and she will be returned to England to stand trial for her actions. No Scottish witch kills a peer of the realm and gets away with it."

With that, he spun around and took off. The Scot held for a moment with a smug grin on his face.

"Congratulations on your wedding. I hope she doesna kill you as she killed her last husband." He laughed and followed after the other man, the dogs trailing behind.

Cam turned to face his wife.

Chapter Two

When the danger was gone, the large MacKinlay man let out a breath. Marian slipped her hand from his, shaking loose from a part of her dress that had become twisted around their wrists. Surely this man didn't plan to allow handfasting law to shackle him to a woman he'd never even met.

A woman who, admittedly, may have launched herself at him indecently to get away from a pack of savage dogs.

Her cheeks burned as she looked up...and up. He was as large as a tree. He'd seemed sturdy under her physical onslaught. Clearly no dandy, as her previous husband had been.

But the last thing she wanted was another husband. Especially one as large and imposing as the giant beside her. He'd said he was a war chief, which meant he was bred for violence and destruction.

She could never be married to someone like that. Despite his warm brown eyes—the color of aged whisky—that seemingly held kindness and patience.

He'd saved her life. She owed him her gratitude, but

nothing more.

"Thank you, truly." She offered him a curtsy, which seemed rather foolish considering her breasts had been in his face earlier and they were now possibly wed. Her cheeks heated again at the memory.

"Did you kill the duke?" His voice rumbled as he watched her. He probably thought he'd be able to spot a lie. He would be wrong. After five years of living with a monster, she'd become adept at hiding all emotion behind a blank expression.

She swallowed, trying to block the images and memories of that night or the weeks since. It had been a trying journey as she'd made her way from London to her sister's home.

She'd traveled at night so as not to be seen. When she had the opportunity, she'd stolen a horse, which she'd later left at an inn so it could be returned to its owner. She might be a murderer, but she was no horse thief.

The money she'd taken from Blackley House had helped ease her way. It was amazing how much loyalty and silence could be purchased with coin. Up until it had been stolen. But she must have been betrayed at some point if Sir Ridley had tracked her this far north. Or maybe he'd made a pact with the devil.

However, the man standing beside her had protected her, so he deserved the truth. She lifted her chin. "Yes. I killed him."

Her would-be husband simply nodded and tossed his shovel in the cart. "What happened to your shoes?" He frowned at her feet—bloody, blistered, and covered in filth.

"I took them off to soak my feet in the stream. When the dogs came after me, I didn't stop to put them back on."

Another nod, and then he scooped her up. She was working herself up to be indignant about his manhandling when he plopped her up on the seat of the cart. She didn't think there was enough room for him beside her, but he managed to fit. With his side pressed up against hers, he flicked the reins to get the horse to move.

"We should get you up to Dunardry. Your sister will be pleased to see you, I think."

"That's it?" Marian stared at his profile as he turned the horse and steered the cart in the opposite direction. "I tell you I killed my husband, and you're still willing to take me to your mistress straight away? How do you know I'm truly Kenna's sister?"

"It wouldn't make sense to lie about that while telling the truth about murdering someone."

He had a point. How annoying. "Both things are true," she said.

She just hoped her sister didn't hate her. She didn't know where they stood. It had been years since they'd had any contact at all. Kenna had sent her a letter written in her own hand a few months after Kenna left Fletcher Castle to marry the MacKinlay laird. Marian had beamed with pride for her sister and shared the letter with all who would listen. Then she had written back to tell Kenna about the plans for her beautiful wedding. But she'd never heard from her sister again. Marian had sent many letters after that, with no reply.

Many a day after the post had been brought to her with no word from home, she'd wondered what she'd done to deserve their silence. Maybe they'd thought her too English to associate with. Which would be almost comical since many of the women in London thought her accent too rough. She was a savage from the wilds of Scotland, after all.

Apparently she belonged nowhere.

"What's your name?" the man sitting next to her asked.

For a moment she considered giving him her alias, but there was no reason for that at this point. He knew she'd murdered the duke, and her sister would doubtless call her

Marian.

"I'm Marian Grace Fletcher Blackley, Duchess of Endsmere." She held out her hand awkwardly since he was holding the reins. He took it in his and squeezed it before pressing a kiss across her fingers. She felt a twinge of excitement at his lips touching her bare skin. She pulled her hand away at the same time he released her.

"So I hadn't lied when I called ye Mari."

He could call her whatever he wanted as long as he took her somewhere safe.

"Pardon the correction, Your Grace," he said after a few moments of silence. "But it would be Marian Grace Fletcher Blackley *MacKinlay*." He gave her a wink. "Since we're wed."

"Blast and damn," she muttered and clenched her teeth. It appeared he *was* planning to hold her to this sham of a marriage.

Did he think to get money from her? She almost laughed at the thought. She had nothing. Even the dress she wore—tattered and dirty as it was—didn't belong to her.

"And you would be?" she asked, thinking it was time he introduced himself as well.

"Cameron Michael Callum MacKinlay. Call me Cam."

She shivered at the way his name rolled off his tongue. It was a good Scot name.

"Feel free to be pleased with yourself for besting me on having more names and impressive titles." He winked, then smiled, and she couldn't help the smile that came to her lips at his jest. She wasn't expecting a sense of humor from someone so large and imposing.

"Please, just Marian. I've no need for fancy titles."

"You don't look much like Lady Kenna, except maybe when you smile," he said, glancing at her, then turning back to focus on the path in front of them.

She shrugged. "I know. My father used our looks as a

wedge between us. The pretty one and the wild one." She shook her head, once again angry on her sister's behalf.

"Don't worry, lass. You're bonny too," he said with sympathy in those warm brown eyes. The sun glinted off his brown hair, showing strands of red and gold mixed through the sable.

She couldn't help but laugh. It amused her that he'd confused them. "Actually, I was supposed to be the pretty one," she told him, still smiling.

"Truly?" His surprise caused her smile to falter. He didn't think her pretty at all? She looked down at her ratty gown. How oddly freeing not to have her looks define who she was.

She nodded and said, "I guess I don't look very attractive at the moment. But my looks were the reason I was chosen by the Duke of Endsmere as his bride. It's been five years. Perhaps I've lost what beauty I once possessed after having to endure such a hideous farce of a marriage."

He shot her a glance. "As I said, you're bonny. I just assumed you were the wild one, as I've never seen Lady Kenna tear out of the forest looking like a wood sprite, launch herself into a man's arms, and force him into matrimony."

Marian laughed again. He spoke the truth. It was probably the most daring, adventurous thing she'd ever done, to flee London on her own.

"Perhaps Kenna has mellowed with age. She was once a hellion who ran around in breeches and only cared about riding her horse and hunting with our brothers."

Cam snorted, a grin playing at his lips. "She hasn't done so lately."

When they were young, Marian had teased Kenna about her hoydenish ways, when really it was jealousy. How nice it would have been to go off without a care and do whatever she'd wished. As the oldest daughter, Marian had been primped and polished to perfection. She was enslaved to her duty to the family and was not afforded the luxury of fun.

She'd been paraded around at court and forced to attend tedious parties and dinners. The men who'd flirted had not been like the men she'd known in Scotland. They were all rather foppish. But despite their shortcomings, none of them had wanted to make an offer for a half-English woman from the Highlands. They'd teased her about her accent, which in fact barely remained, thanks to her tutors.

Only the Duke of Endsmere had been interested, having lost his first wife to a fall. It wasn't until after Marian was married to him and had suffered her own first fall at his hands that she realized the true reason he'd chosen her. He'd been so desperate for a match he'd been willing to take a Scot.

How silly she'd been to think she had won the affections of a duke. Instead, she'd earned the attentions of a man with an evil reputation even in his own circles, and who had no other options. Hadn't he told her time and time again how lucky she was to have been brought to London as his wife when she was only one step above a whore or a beggar? Most times when he'd said this, she'd been in such pain she knew it hadn't been *luck* that had brought her into his lair.

She'd prayed to God for escape, vowing never to care about such trivial things as dresses and hair or making a noble match, if she could only be safe.

Years ago, she'd been told she was beautiful, a sight to behold. Now she was nothing, and she didn't care if a man ever fancied her again.

Her blond hair was loose; some fell to the front, covering the long scar along the side of her face. In London the fashion was to have only a few curls cascading down, which put her scar on display. Though, only the very brave or most vulgar people dared ask her about it. As with all of her injuries and scars she'd lied, knowing no one wanted to hear the truth…or could do anything to help her even if they'd wanted to.

And no one had wanted to.

...

Cam studied the lass in quick glances as they made their way to Dunardry. He avoided the village, not wanting to be stopped and asked who she was. He wasn't sure what he'd say just yet.

It was quite a situation.

They were legally married, but would Lach allow it when he'd wanted Cam to marry someone else?

Cam looked at her again and thought she might be lovely once she was cleaned up and smelled better. He cringed at her bare feet, glad it was August so she hadn't lost her toes to the cold.

"If you thought Kenna was the pretty one, does that mean my sister has blossomed?" she asked with a tender smile. "I always expected she'd grow into a lovely woman one day."

"She has indeed bloomed," Cam said and then coughed to cover his smile. He and Kenna were dear friends. He was happy for Lach to have found love with her. And while Cam might at times have felt a twinge of envy and wished he'd had a woman of his own, he knew love wasn't wise for a war chief to indulge in.

Love made a warrior think too much. As a single man, Cam could rush into the heart of a battle, knowing no one would be shattered if he never came home. Well, except maybe Kenna and Lachlan, and his other cousin, Bryce, who was coming out to greet him as he pulled the cart to a stop in the bailey.

Bryce eyed the half-empty cart and then the lass in the seat next to Cam. "Did you dig her up out of the field?" he asked with a crooked grin.

"Wise arse." Cam jumped out of the cart and came around to help Mari down. "Mari, I'd like you to meet my cousin, Bryce Campbell." He turned to the shorter man who still towered over Mari. "Cousin, I'd like ye to meet Marian Fletcher MacKinlay, *my wife*."

Watching Bryce's eyes go wide as he coughed and choked was worth admitting the strange course of events that had landed Cam with a bride.

"Your *wife*? Are you mad? You've only been gone three hours. How did you take a wife?"

"She simply ran out of the woods and we married," he said, enjoying himself a little too much. It was a funny story to tell, but he had a feeling it wouldn't be all that fun to live with the consequences.

Especially after Lach found out.

Chapter Three

Two little boys ran up and grabbed Cam's legs, squealing in delight. He picked up the one on his right and held him up to inspect his face. Damn if he could tell them apart, even though Kenna and Lach knew at a glance.

"Are ye wee Douglas or the other one?" Cam asked.

His only answer was laughter. The lads were a little over a year and didn't say much yet.

"You guessed it right. 'Tis Douglas," Lach said, following behind. "What is this?" He scooped up Roddy and then took Douglas.

Cam didn't know how the man managed to hold two squirming boys and still look imposing and in charge, but he'd mastered it when his sons were but wee babes.

"I thought I told you to gather rocks until nightfall."

"Aye, but I had a run-in with an English tracker, a MacDonald, and a fugitive from the crown's justice, whom I married."

As with Bryce, Lachlan's response was amusing. He looked from Cam to Mari and then over to Bryce who shrugged and made another choking sound.

"I don't know where to begin," Lachlan finally said.

"Perhaps with introductions," Cam suggested and turned toward his wife.

"Mari, I'd like to introduce the laird of Clan MacKinlay, Lachlan MacKinlay. Lach, my wife and your sister by marriage, Marian Fletcher MacKinlay."

"My lord," Mari said with a curtsy. "We've met. I was present at your wedding to my sister."

Lachlan's eyes went wide before narrowing in close examination. His appraisal seemed to land on her bare feet. "You married a duke, as I recall."

"Yes. However, as Cameron mentioned, I murdered him and have fled London to end up here."

Cam's lip twitched at her casual explanation. He nodded and added his part. "She was being chased by the tracker and the MacDonald I spoke of. I had to stop them from taking her back to England where they planned to hang her. I thought Lady Kenna would not like that overmuch, so…"

"You married her," Lachlan said flatly.

"Aye." Cameron nodded. "Though not intentionally. It just worked out as such."

"Of course." Lach turned to Bryce. "Would you please fetch Lady Kenna from the kitchens?"

Bryce hurried away as Lach turned back to face Cam. "Your order for the day, if I recall correctly, was to gather stones for the curtain wall until nightfall. I do not remember telling ye to save damsels in distress by wedding them. As you may remember, you were contracted to wed the McCurdy lass at the end of the summer to secure an alliance with their clan."

"I do remember, but I canna marry her now as I'm already wed." He held out his hands innocently. He hadn't wanted to marry anyone; however there was some enjoyment in not being forced to marry someone merely for a questionable alliance. "We still have the chance to take the McCurdys by force so ye can gain the port you want. While I'm not available to wed the lass, I am capable of training your men to take over their clan."

"And how many MacKinlays will we lose in a battle of that size? Do ye think our enemy will just scurry off and give up their lands because we wish it?"

"Nay, but with training, and a good plan—"

Lach groaned and rolled his eyes.

"Surely there is some way to correct this misunderstanding." Mari came forward with an elegant smile on her lips. It might have even looked regal if not for the dirty hair and ragged dress.

"*Misunderstanding?*" Lach raised a brow at Cameron. "Are you wed or not?"

They were legally wed, though Cameron was determined it would be in name only. It wouldn't matter to him that a woman shared his name to stay out of a noose. So long as she didn't carry expectations of him being a true husband.

In fact, this would be the best thing for both of them. He could go on about his life as the war chief, and she would be safe on MacKinlay lands. It was clear by fact of her having murdered her first husband that Mari didn't take to marriage well. So this union would be just the thing to keep them both happy and free.

Cam waited for Mari to respond. She swallowed, then answered, "It appears that we are, based on Scottish law, my lord."

"And we are in Scotland, aye?" Lach shifted and shushed the squirming children, who settled with their heads tucked on either side of his neck.

"Yes, my lord."

"Humph." Lachlan turned toward the door as Kenna

stepped through it—though waddled was more accurate. Kenna was expecting another babe in a month or so.

"Hello, there," Kenna said to the woman at his side.

Mari took a step forward, her eyes wide in surprise. "Sister?"

After a moment of shock, Kenna gasped and her eyes filled with tears. "My God! *Marian?*" She rushed to her sister. "Is it really you?"

• • •

Marian stood frozen as her taller sister hugged her. Or tried to. It wasn't easy with her large belly in the way. Kenna pulled back to look at her, and Marian saw the confusion clear on her familiar face.

Marian now understood why Cameron would have thought her the wild one and Kenna the pretty one. Kenna was absolutely radiant. Her coppery hair was pulled up in a tidy bun with curls erupting in a perfect way. Pregnancy definitely agreed with her. It had given her lovely curves, and her dress was new and fashionable.

"Are you well?" Kenna asked, taking another step back and resting a hand on her belly.

"I am better now I've seen you." And with that Marian broke down in tears. "I didn't think I'd make it."

She'd managed to keep her wits since leaving London. Her focus had been on getting somewhere safe. With that task finally accomplished, she was able to give in to the fear of what might come next. From the time she'd been a young girl and her father had made his plans to improve his standing with the English through her, she'd known what her future held. She had no idea what to do with this new feeling of uncertainty.

"Mayhap we should allow her to clean up," Cam said. "She's come a long way. Might ye have a clean dress that would fit her?"

"It would be a bit long, but I think we can manage," Kenna replied.

"She'll need a room," he added.

The laird laughed once without humor. "Nay. She's your wife now. She'll stay in your chamber."

It was clear her brother by marriage was using the situation to punish Cam—her husband. She'd been hoping this marriage could be one in name only. In truth, she didn't want to give up a chance of freedom, but the MacKinlay name would protect her if Ridley or others showed up wanting to secure the bounty on her head.

"Wife?" Kenna looked between Cam and Marian with a startled expression.

"Aye," Lachlan said bitterly. "Cam's been gone for the morning. Doesn't he always come back from such a task with a bride?" She could see the laird's simmering anger at his war chief lurking underneath the amusement.

Instinctively, Marian took a protective step between this man and her younger sister. She wasn't sure what to think of the laird. He looked ready to launch into violence at any second…and yet the children clung to him without fear.

"Mama," one of the boys said while reaching for Kenna.

Kenna was the mother of these children? And the one still in her belly. A familiar twinge of jealousy sparked in Mari's chest and she quickly brushed it aside.

She was happy for her sister. And it was clear Kenna was happy and loved here. Something Kenna hadn't been at Fletcher Castle.

The jealousy twisted into shame. How many times had she and her parents tried to force Kenna to conform rather than accept her as she was?

"Stay with Papa, Roddy. I must see to Auntie Marian." Kenna kissed the children and then her husband before looping her arm through Marian's and tugging her toward the keep. "Come. We have much to catch up on."

That much was true, though Marian didn't know where to begin.

She was taken to a sparse room with a large bed taking up most of the space. Kenna settled on a chair and rubbed her belly as a tub was carried in and filled with hot water.

How Marian longed to slip into the bath and allow the warmth to soothe her aching body. Perhaps this would be the last time she need call on the healing properties of a bath. She hoped to be safe here.

Except she knew better than to think her past could be so easily washed away. Kenna was clearly excited for them to be alone so she could shower Marian with questions. When the last steaming bucket was dumped and the servants closed the door behind them, Kenna gazed at her expectantly.

"Do you mind stepping out while I undress?" Marian asked, feeling her cheeks heat.

Kenna laughed. "We've seen all our parts since we were wee lasses. You're much skinnier than before, but I'm sure everything's the same as I have."

Marian stared down at her dirty feet. It wasn't the nudity that bothered her. It was that Kenna would see more of her story than most people knew. She had planned to tell her sister the hell that had been her life the last five years. But telling was different than seeing.

"I'll turn around if it suits you, but I don't want to leave. I'm so excited you're here, and I think it will take several days to catch up. I don't want to delay."

Marian laughed at her sister's eagerness and stripped off the filthy gown while Kenna faced the wall.

She hadn't been certain of her reception, since her sister had never reached out with so much as a note in the last years. But she couldn't deny Kenna appeared happy she was here.

Perhaps she'd been too busy with her life and children to write.

"Just toss that dress over by the door to be burned. I'm afraid there's no saving it."

Marian let out a sound of bliss as she slipped into the warm water and dunked her head. Picking up the soap, she lathered and began washing off a month's worth of dirt and grime.

"So, where should we begin?" Kenna asked as she turned around.

Most of Marian's scars were hidden beneath the surface of the water, so she allowed herself to smile and enjoy the start of her healing of body and soul.

For the first time in years, she felt safe and cared for.

Chapter Four

When Mari had been dragged away by Kenna, it left Cam alone with Lach and the boys. Cam figured he was safe for the moment. Lach wouldn't yell or draw his sword with the wee ones present.

But it was only a moment before the nurse came for the boys and Cam's cowardly grasp at protection was whisked away into the castle.

"I didn't expect such a thing from you." Lach's voice remained level. It may have been worse than yelling. He was disappointed in Cam.

Cam knew well enough how much his laird had wanted this alliance. It had once been Lach's plan to wed a McCurdy himself and seal their clans together so the MacKinlays would gain access to the sea. It had been Lach's father's wish, and now that the old man was gone, they'd all wanted to see it through to honor the former laird's legacy.

"In my defense, my laird, I didn't expect such a thing, either. What would you have had me do? Let them take the lass back to England to be hanged for merely defending herself?"

"Nay. I am glad you claimed her and brought her home. I'm just angry with the situation. You know how much I've wanted this alliance. I was so close to making that happen, and now..."

"I ken you're disappointed, but a marriage doesn't have to be the only way. I can train the men to take the castle before they've even seen us. I've drawn up plans of their hold, and I know how we—"

"It's too risky. If we fail, not only would we lose the chance of an alliance, but we could very well lose Dunardry and our clan."

Cam wanted to fight him on this, but it was no use. Lach had the weight of his people holding him back from such an aggressive tactic.

Lach nodded as if coming to some conclusion. "We'll just have to get the marriage annulled so ye can marry Dorie McCurdy."

"What?" Cam hadn't expected this. "The hell, you say. I'm not getting an annulment." He had no idea why he was so adamantly against such a thing. He grasped for reasons. "She would be ruined."

Lach laughed. "She's a murderess who's been traveling alone for over a month. She'll not grace a London sitting room ever again."

"She's my *wife*." Cam stated the fact firmly. Defending it with a glare.

"You said yourself, you don't even know the lass. What do you care if it's Marian Fletcher or Dorian McCurdy? A wife is a wife to ye."

"It's Marian Fletcher MacKinlay, and it will stay that way. I'll sign no annulment."

Lach's eyes went wide with surprise. He looked toward the gate in confusion. "She's bonny enough, but have you become besotted with the lass on the trip back to the castle?"

"Of course not. I'm the war chief." War chiefs didn't become besotted—at least successful ones didn't. They needed to be focused. There was no time for the dealings of a wife when there were men to be trained and plans to be laid.

Lach sniffed. "You think a war chief canna be besotted with a lass? I remember your da looking googly-eyed at your ma."

"Aye. And it made him weak."

"You think me weak for loving my wife and children?" Lach asked.

"Nay." Cameron looked away. He hadn't meant to offend his cousin. It had been the opposite for Lach. He'd gained many things with his union to Kenna. "It's different for me. A war chief is expected to take risks and make decisions to protect this clan. I can't do the duty justice if I'm worried over getting myself skewered and bringing sadness to a wife."

"I see." Lach frowned.

He didn't see. He couldn't. He hadn't witnessed the grief and melancholy that took over a wife when she'd lost her love.

"It appears the duty of being war chief is in truth a curse. If you never allow yourself to love anyone within these walls, what drives you to protect it with your life?" Lach asked, his head cocked to one side. For once in the bloody conversation, Cam didn't feel his laird was mocking him.

It was easy to speak his answer. "Honor."

Cam hadn't wanted to marry, but now he was wed and he would honor his vows, spoken purposefully or no. The best he could do was make sure he and Mari didn't fall in love. He wasn't at risk for such things, and Mari had been wed to a monster. It was clear she wanted no part of a true marriage.

This union would be perfect for both of them. They would protect each other from the things they didn't want. And have all the freedoms they desired.

"I'll not have an annulment," Cam repeated and walked away.

...

Marian chastised herself for spilling everything to Kenna in one sitting. Her pregnant sister was still pale from hearing the tale of how Marian came to be sitting in a tub in Dunardry Castle.

The water had long gone cold when she'd finally finished her story.

Kenna dashed a tear from her cheek and offered a watery smile. "Your poor skin must be wrinkled. Let's get ye out of there before you become chilled."

Forgetting herself in the comfort of their reunion, Marian had stood. It wasn't until Kenna gasped that she realized what she'd revealed.

Fresh tears filled Kenna's eyes. It wasn't normal for her sister to cry, and Marian accounted it to the emotions brought on by pregnancy.

Pressing her lips together as if to steel herself, Kenna handed over a linen so Marian could dry her scarred skin. "You are safe now, sister. No harm will ever come to you as long as you are here."

Marian trembled at her sister's vehemence and allowed herself to relax.

Kenna helped her with her hair, pausing briefly upon seeing the scar across Marian's face. She frowned and continued brushing. "I can't help but become furious every time I see your scars. I wish the man was alive so I could kill him with my bare hands for what he did to ye."

Marian smiled. "I thank you for your allegiance; however, I would not see you anywhere near that man."

"Why didn't you write to tell me? I would have sent a

dozen warriors to retrieve you."

Coming from another's lips, it might have sounded like an empty promise. But Marian could tell her sister wasn't wasting her words.

"I did write to you, but you never wrote back." Marian somehow managed to keep the accusation and hurt out of her voice. Kenna froze and looked at Marian in the mirror. "I understand. You have a busy life here as the laird's wife." Marian glanced away.

Kenna dropped onto the bench beside her and took her hand. "Marian, I wrote to you nearly every week for years. And only finally gave up when the boys were born and I was truly too busy. You never answered my letters, but still I kept writing, hoping you'd tell me how you fared. I thought ye hated me still."

"Hated you? Never have I hated you."

"When I ruined your dress."

"Oh, Kenna. I was angry with your recklessness, but I have always loved you. You are my sister. It's natural to pester one another, but under that is love, always." Marian cleared her throat. "I must apologize, for it seems my husband did us both a disservice by interrupting our correspondence. For I wrote to you, begging you to answer. I was alone in London, and despite all the training, I was an outcast. A barbaric heathen from the north. And when dinner or tea was over and my rudimentary upbringing disgraced my husband, he made his displeasure at my existence quite clear."

Kenna wrapped her arms around Marian and squeezed tight. At the odd angle, they were able to cling to each other closely.

"We shall have time now to share all the words in those letters. That bloody cod might have stolen a few years from us, but we will not let him destroy our bond. He canna."

Marian smiled at Kenna's intensity. "I will like that very

much."

Kenna stood and took up fixing Marian's hair again. "You'll be happy here. I know it. The clan is filled with good people. I have a lot of friends here. I'll introduce you to them. And your husband is second in command of the clan. You'll not be a duchess, but you'll hold a place of respect as his wife."

Marian caught a smile on Kenna's lips.

"Do you know him well? What is he like? He's so…large."

"He's one of my best friends. He's protected me many times."

Marian nodded. His sheer size proved him a formidable warrior and one prepared for providing protection.

She blurted out the thing she most needed to know. "Do you find he is quick to anger?"

Kenna gripped Marian's shoulder, then softened her hold when Marian jumped at the contact.

"You couldn't have married a more gentle man than Cameron MacKinlay. From what I hear, he's a beast in battle, as expected from a war chief. But he's able to leave that behind when he steps back inside the castle walls. I trust him with my wee boys. You can be assured he'll never touch ye in anger."

Marian must have looked skeptical, because Kenna pushed on.

"I've seen Cam come into the hall, still dripping with loch water where he'd washed the blood from his skin and clothes, pick up one of my boys, and sing them to sleep. He'd not hurt a soul unless it was his duty to do so."

Marian nodded. "I'm glad it was him out in that field."

"Aye. Now, let's get you into a dress so you can get to know him better yourself."

When Marian glanced up at her hair, she saw Kenna had finished and it had all been pulled back away from her face.

"I like to have curls at the side." Her hand fluttered near

the scar on her cheek.

"You are a beautiful woman. You've no need to hide behind curls."

"But—"

"This is your home now. You do not need to hide."

Kenna helped her into a dress that would have been lovely if she'd had her sister's assets to fill it out. How things had changed. It used to be Kenna who lacked the curves necessary for certain fashions.

Marian had not been allowed large meals. The duke often embarrassed her publicly when she ate, so she picked at her food. At home, she was given a very small portion per the duke's orders. This practice had left Marian quite spindly. And being on the run had been hard, so she was even thinner than before. The result was disappointing. The gown drooped and sagged, making it clear it was not made for her.

"We'll get the ladies working tomorrow to make you proper clothing. Until then, let's eat. I'm starved," Kenna said exuberantly.

With one hand on her belly and the other clutching Marian's, Kenna led them into the great hall. The hum of conversation quieted only briefly as the seated clan members took her in. She was granted a few nods and smiles as she made her way to the front where Cameron was sitting and speaking to Lachlan.

Marian reached for curls that weren't there. It was a habit. Her way of hiding what happened in her home.

But this was her home now. She dropped her hand and stepped forward to greet her husband.

Chapter Five

Cam sat at the head table next to the laird and did his best to ignore the jests regarding his accidental marriage.

"Aye, I'm surprised after he stumbled into the marriage, he didn't also trip and end up with his cock in her, too. He might have come back to the castle with a wife *and* child." Angus laughed at his joke while Cam scowled at the old coot.

The other men at the table chuckled and Cam decided this was how it would be for some time. He might have thought the situation funny, as well, had it happened to someone else.

He was about to come back with some comment that would no doubt get tangled and make him look more the fool when he looked up and saw Kenna approach the head table with an angel at her side.

"Dear lord," young Liam said solemnly from the end of the table. The other men fell silent.

Cam thought Liam's words were well chosen. He stood and bumped into Lach when he rose as well. They walked side by side to meet their wives.

Lach bowed to Mari and then held out his arm for Kenna.

Cam did the same, but he couldn't take his eyes off Mari. She was stunning.

"You're beautiful," he whispered and noticed her smile waver. He remembered then that her beauty had turned out to be a curse. Perhaps it was a compliment she no longer enjoyed hearing. "That is to say, you look much better cleaned up."

Her smile picked up slightly, and she leaned closer to him. "I could say the same of you. You surely smell better."

He laughed. "As I recall, no one would have confused ye with a rose when you stuck your bosom in my face."

When her smile fell, he realized he'd gone too far with the jest. He was such a dolt around women when conversation was involved. It was why he only ever took them to bed. He didn't talk to them first.

Kenna was the only exception, and mostly because she didn't act all that much like a woman. But Mari was completely feminine. He'd need to do much better.

"Pardon." He coughed. "Your fragrance was not as off-putting as I made it seem."

She merely blinked at him for a moment.

"That was no better than what you said the first time," he muttered to himself as she blinked. Unable to help himself, he tried once more. "Having your breasts in my face was a pleasurable experience no matter—"

"Thank you," she interrupted. God bless her for stopping him before he made it even worse. But when the silence grew on, he fell victim to discomfort.

"I didn't hate it, is all I'm saying." Not at all. He helped her to her seat, allowing his gaze to linger on the curve of her breasts. He noticed how dainty she was. A few inches shorter than Kenna, and smaller too. The gown she wore hung loose on her tiny frame.

He'd heard that thin women were the thing in London. However, in the Highlands, a frail woman wouldn't survive the harsh winter without putting some meat on her bones. He'd work on feeding her until she was healthy.

He noticed a thin red scar on the cheek facing him. It traveled from the corner of her left eye down to her jawline. He swallowed and let out a steady breath. The scar could have been a result of an injury or accident, but he could see how perfectly shaped it was as it mirrored the line of her face and doubted it had been made without intention.

The bloody duke.

Cam clenched his fork too tightly. The monster was dead and no longer able to hurt Marian.

He smiled at his wife, wondering what other horrors she'd experienced and how he'd ever be able to sit quietly and listen if she chose to tell him. She'd been forced to kill in defense of her own life. Her stories would be unsettling for sure. He'd have to remain calm if ever she shared her past with him.

She caught him looking at the scar, and as if by instinct she reached for her hair, tugging a few strands from the twist.

When he raised his hand to stop her, she winced, eyes closed as if waiting for a strike.

"Settle, lass," he whispered and glanced out at the hall to see if others had noticed.

"I'm sorry. I told Kenna this style wasn't at all the thing, but she insisted."

Moving slower this time, he took her hand and stopped her from destroying Kenna's handiwork.

"It's lovely. *You* are lovely. There's not a one of us save the little ones who doesn't bear scars. Wear yours with honor, lass, for only a survivor is able to wear scars."

She swallowed, and after a moment she nodded and turned back to her food.

As they dined she took tiny bird bites of her meal, then pushed it away when she hadn't finished half.

"Are you not hungry or is the food not to your liking?"

he asked, thinking it odd. She'd been on the run with little money. Surely, she hadn't had easy access to food. But maybe her palate had grown used to London cuisine and their rough meal of venison and greens wasn't setting well.

"Truth be told, I am famished. But it's considered unladylike to eat everything upon one's plate." She pressed her lips together and looked longingly at the plate.

He didn't understand women's logic, but he did know how to fix a problem when one arose.

"That may be. What do I know?" He pulled her plate closer and dumped more food on it. "There. Now ye may eat only half again."

She looked up at him with surprise and gratitude, then turned back to the plate, eating what he'd added. This time she left only a few small bites behind.

"That was delicious. It's been so long since I've enjoyed good food." When she smiled at him he lost his breath. "Thank you, Cameron."

He swallowed and managed to nod, thinking he'd gladly give her his last morsel and waste away into dust if she asked it of him. How could anyone look into those smiling eyes and treat her harshly? He couldn't imagine it. Clearly the duke hadn't had a soul.

He cleared his throat in an effort to dislodge the anger rising in him. "I believe we have entertainment tonight. Would you like to stay, or are you too tired?"

She bit her bottom lip for a moment. "I'd like to stay. If you would."

He pushed away his disappointment, not exactly sure why he was disappointed.

He doubted she would invite him to her bed—make that his bed—after they'd married by accident. It wasn't that they were truly man and wife, except in the legal sense. Then again, the legal sense was all most marriages started with.

And technically, the marriage wasn't officially legal until it was consummated.

They stayed throughout the evening's entertainments, and then she excused herself to go to their room. When he offered to escort her, she refused his offer and nearly sprinted from the hall for the stairs.

Cam might have considered sleeping in the great hall, except the other men would know it. Their joking didn't bother him, but he wouldn't let Lach think he was put out of his own room.

When he'd given her ample time to get ready for bed, he went to his chamber and knocked on the door. He waited for her to answer before entering.

She was sitting in bed, her golden hair braided over one shoulder. The fire had died down, making the room dim, but he could see enough to know her gaze was intent on her lap where she twisted her fingers. It looked painful, and he wanted to go to her to make her stop, but when he took a step toward her, she gasped in fear.

He changed direction toward the fire and stirred the logs to give more light.

He thought briefly of what it might be like to sleep next to her, or even to consummate the marriage they had stumbled into earlier that day. But when he saw her anxiety, he tossed thoughts of that possibility aside.

She'd been married to a cruel man and probably expected even worse from a large Scottish brute. He'd give her time to acclimate to their situation and get comfortable with him.

When he stepped closer to the bed to take the extra blankets, she flinched.

"Be calm. I mean you no harm. I'm just going to put these blankets down by the fire so I have a place to sleep tonight."

"You won't be sleeping in your bed?"

"Nay. I think you've had enough excitement for one day."

He waited until she glanced at him and winked so she'd know he was joking.

She only looked slightly relieved and glanced away as quickly as she'd met his gaze. She was as skittish as a beaten horse.

He settled by the fire and frowned into the darkness when his back settled against the hard floor. His bed was built for someone of his size. She looked like a wee mouse in a ship.

There was enough room for both of them, but he'd not cause her distress. He'd give her time to adjust to her new home. And a husband. Small steps covered just as much ground—it just took longer.

"Thank you, Cameron." Her voice barely moved the air in the room.

"For which part, exactly? Marrying you by accident, bringing you safely to the castle, or sharing my food with you at dinner?"

"Everything, actually. I had come so close, but if you hadn't scared off the tracker it would have been all for naught. I would be on my way back to London to face my sentence."

"Not to worry. I was looking for a way to get out of my work anyway."

She laughed softly at his jest. The warm sound calmed him.

Maybe this would work after all. Lachlan hadn't wanted to marry Kenna, but now they were happily in love with one another. Who was to say the same couldn't happen for him and his new bride?

Nay, not the love part; he didn't want that. But having someone to share his life with would be nice. As would the physical aspects. His wife was bonny, and he hoped he could convince her someday soon they'd be good together in that way.

"You haven't asked me why I killed him," she said,

changing the course of his thoughts.

"I saw the scar on your cheek, and I'm certain there are more. I have no doubt you had your reasons. I can't imagine you would have willingly given up a soft life as a duchess for one on the run, married to a man you don't even know, without cause. When you want to tell me, you will, and I'll listen." And hopefully remain calm for the telling.

"You're not worried to sleep in a room with a woman who killed her first husband?"

"Nay. Not at all."

He heard a slight sniffle and then a louder sniff. The sounds of a woman crying. He wondered if he might have misunderstood the situation. Had she loved the duke and killed him by accident? Did she mourn his death?

"Do you miss him, lass? Your husband?"

"God, no." The answer came quickly in a voice rough from tears. "He was a monster. I'm glad he's gone."

"Then why are ye crying?"

"I never thought I'd feel safe again."

She was sleeping in a room with him—a near stranger—and yet she felt safe.

"Welcome home, Mari."

At his words a sob broke out, and he had to force himself to stay put. Eventually, she quieted and fell asleep.

He had just fallen asleep himself, when she woke him with her screams.

Chapter Six

Marian was sure it was a dream. After all, she'd already lived through this hell once. She couldn't possibly be made to live through it yet again.

But there she was, looking in the mirror as her new maid, Lucy, came in behind her. Marian looked back to her own reflection as she sat there in her gorgeous gown, a garment created specifically for her, for this day. The day she'd married the Duke of Endsmere.

She was a duchess, and as all had told her throughout the wedding party, she was a lovely one. And now, in a matter of moments, she would lie with her new husband and truly be his duchess.

"Don't be nervous, Your Grace," Lucy said as she undid the gown and drew the pins from Marian's hair. "It is not all that bad. Have you been told all that is expected of a wife on her wedding night?"

Marian felt her cheeks warm and saw the maidenly blush in the mirror.

"Yes. I'm aware of what I'm to do." According to the

letter Kenna had sent, they'd had things all wrong. The pain, according to her younger sister, was insignificant, and making sounds and moving were encouraged by one's partner.

Marian had to admit, she found this perplexing. Perhaps it was different with a Scottish laird than what she was told to expect from an English lord.

Nodding, she imagined she had the right of it. Her new husband was not at all like the men in the Highlands. While she'd tried her best not to be disappointed by his stature, she would have liked to have braw arms to hold her and a chiseled jaw dusted lightly with stubble.

But no matter, she was a duchess now and she would get through this night, whether the pain was insignificant or not.

Throughout her years of training, she'd mastered the art of fitting in and adapting to whatever environment she was exposed to. Tonight would be the same. She would follow along with her husband and make him happy. If it was truly pleasurable as Kenna had sworn, she would be happy in it as well. Though she couldn't imagine it as so.

The duke—Mathias, she could call him now that they were wed—seemed much too serious to *enjoy* the bedding. Certainly someone of his standing wouldn't fall victim to his baser needs. Dukes were beyond lust.

Throughout their wedding, and the meal that followed, he'd hardly looked at her. His thin lips stayed firmly in a straight line that appeared neither happy at the occasion nor displeased. He was simply there.

The few times she'd attempted conversation he hadn't said more than a few terse words. Eventually he'd frowned at her impertinence and she'd tried no more.

Theirs was not a love match. He'd checked her over during her visit at court like a prized gelding and had written her a few short notes to determine her willingness to marry him. Everything seemed rather cold, but she hadn't expected anything different.

She'd been prepared for this duty since she was a girl. With her nerves in check, she donned her fancy new night rail, frowning at the low cut of the neckline. It was obviously created to entice a man, with strategically placed areas where only lace covered her bare skin. One such place exposed her navel, and she placed her hand over it, feeling vulnerable.

Her maid brushed her hair, all the while praising her beauty. With her hair shining, she was helped into the high bed, where she sat with the blankets pooled around her waist, waiting for her husband to enter.

It seemed like hours passed. She had slumped back along the pillows and actually dozed off when she heard the door open. She popped up from the bed and pressed a smile to her cheeks.

"Good evening, Your Grace," she said, hearing the nervousness in her voice.

Her husband stumbled as he came closer. He looked her over and winced away as if she were a hideous ogre. She looked down at herself, seeing the neckline had shifted and one of her nipples was on full display.

"Your breasts are disgustingly huge," he said, obviously physically repulsed.

It was her understanding men liked large breasts. She remembered her brothers fighting over a lass solely for that reason. Yet, her husband didn't like hers.

Her earlier assumptions proved true. Scottish men were far different from English lords in their preferences.

"My apologies."

"Don't speak. Your rough tongue is nearly as distasteful as your figure. Come closer so I can see what I'm cursed to bear for my former wife's clumsiness."

On shaky legs, Marian moved around the foot of the bed and stood before her husband as he frowned at her with hatred. She'd expected pain on her wedding night. A quick thing, but this was different.

Her husband disliked everything about her. He didn't grope at her as she'd been told might happen. Instead, he drew back as if hoping his robe wasn't soiled by contact with her skin.

She was completely lost. Her skills of fitting in were of no help in this situation. Instead, she stood mutely with her eyes on her feet as he continued his appraisal. He pointed out how her hair was too light—he preferred brunettes. How she was too tall, which was almost humorous as she was the shortest fully-grown woman she knew.

He poured a glass of port as he continued telling her all the ways she had failed him. Ways she was unable to do anything to change. When it appeared he'd finished, she sniffed back the tears of disappointment and raised her head. She'd been reared for this duty, and she'd not fail.

"Perhaps it would be easier for you to lie with me if it were dark. If the candles were—"

Her suggestion was cut short when he struck her across the mouth to silence her. She felt the intense heat and tasted the coppery flavor of her blood as she stumbled back.

"How dare you suggest I'm incapable of performing my duties as a husband, despite how inhospitable the vessel may be?" He struck her again, this time hard enough she lost her balance and fell to the floor by his booted feet.

She remembered thinking how shiny they were when he drew back and kicked her in the stomach. Air left her lungs in a gush, and for a few moments she wasn't able to breathe in. Her vision fluttered on the edges.

She longed to go home. Except she was married to this monster, and this hell was now her home. There was no escape. She was trapped.

He turned toward the door, and she slumped in relief that

he was leaving. She'd have time to tend to her wounds and come up with a plan to stay clear of him. Except he hadn't left. He had just gone to the table by the door to retrieve something. When he turned she saw it was a knife.

"Mari, *Mari*," he said.

Except the duke had never called her Mari. Only Cameron used that name. "Wake up," he encouraged, and she opened her eyes to find the Scot sitting on the bed. She jumped back and he held up his hands, showing he meant no harm. "You were having a nightmare, lass. Are you well? You're soaked through."

She looked down at her thin shift, noticing how transparent it was in the low light. Covering herself, she looked up in time to see interest and appreciation in his eyes.

He was not disgusted by her. She'd seen the way he looked at her earlier at dinner. And then he'd slept on the floor so as not to scare her. Even now, he watched her with nothing but concern. She knew he would not hurt her, however her body responded instinctively.

When he stood she jumped away.

Again he made a calming gesture. "I think you should change into a new shift. Do you have one?"

She shook her head and shivered. She'd been given only the one garment and had been thankful for it.

He nodded and walked into the darkness. He returned with a clean shirt. "Here you go. It's much too big for you, but it's clean and dry."

He turned his back on her. When she didn't move, he looked over his shoulder. "Go on. Put it on. I swear on my honor, I'll not peek."

It was almost humorous. This giant was her husband. He had the right to peek, and much more. Yet, she didn't worry as she pulled the thin, damp shift over her head and settled the heavier fabric over her body. She sniffed the collar, noticing it smelled of him. A warm, earthy scent that brought a smile to her lips.

"Thank you," she said when she was covered and had regained her composure.

He turned and smiled down at her. Even with the menacing shadows cutting across his features, he looked kind. He grinned and turned to go back to his place by the fire. On the floor.

The ridiculousness of it struck her, and she reached for him. Her long fingers didn't encompass his wrist, but he stopped and faced her.

"This is your bed. There's plenty of room for the both of us. The floor can't be all that comfortable." She patted the mattress when it seemed he didn't understand what she meant. It was the middle of the night. She'd need to be clearer. "If you'd meant to ravish me, you would have done so by now. Stay here with me. I trust you."

He sniffed and rubbed his jaw. "I appreciate it." He bowed and slid in next to her.

She'd thought there was plenty of room, but once her large husband was settled, there wasn't much space left between them. While his shoulders and chest were immense, his waist was narrow. She was able to sleep on her side and curl her knees into the void left there.

"I hope ye sleep better now. But if you do have another bad dream. I'm right here to help." He patted her hand and she responded by lacing her fingers through his and holding tight. He let out a breath but didn't pull away.

In Cameron's shirt and with his warmth next to her, she thought she would drift off immediately. But despite being more comfortable than she'd ever been before, she wasn't able to sleep.

"Do you wish me to go back to the floor, lass?" he said into the darkness, startling her. She'd thought he was asleep long ago.

"No. I'm sorry. It's just...I've never slept with a man before."

He shifted to his side as if to look at her, but the darkness made that impossible.

"You never shared a bed with your husband? He just... and left?"

She nodded, and he let out an unpleasant huff. His question had been vague and her answer misleading, but she said nothing further.

He squeezed her hand. "Well, since it seems sleep has abandoned us, mayhap we could talk."

She smiled into the darkness as a tear ran down her cheek.

This night was so different from her first wedding night. There was no pain here with her new husband. Only comfort and understanding. Kenna had promised she would be happy, and it was already clear she was right. Marian had never been so content.

Maybe this marriage would work out, after all.

• • •

Cam wasn't sure if Mari truly wanted to talk, but he knew it was the only chance they had to better know one another. He went first, telling her stories of his youth. She laughed and gasped at the appropriate parts of his tales.

He made sure to tell the humiliating ones as much as the flattering ones so as not to make her think he was prideful. Besides, he might have run out of stories if he'd only told the favorable ones.

Occasionally she fell silent, and he thought she might have finally drifted off, but when he was quiet for too long, she would ask a question to get him talking again.

She fell asleep after what felt like hours. Her hand went slack in his and her breathing evened out. He lay there a while longer, drawing in the scent of her and stroking the soft skin of her hand with his thumb. She was so small, he worried of rolling over and smothering her.

Before that worry got too far developed, the lass shifted right up against him until he had no room to move. Her face pressed against his shoulder, where her warm breath feathered across his neck. Her knee slid over his thigh, resting inches away from his stirring cock.

Good God. How would he ever find sleep like this? With his wife entwined around him like vines on rocks?

She hadn't shared much of herself. She'd told a few stories he already knew from hearing Kenna's tales. Though it was interesting hearing them from Mari's perspective.

His new wife was not as reckless as Kenna. She'd been worried anew to tell the account of Kenna standing on her horse's back. Her indulgent laughter spoke of her love for her younger sister. In that moment, Cam had thought she'd make a wonderful mother.

Not that he hoped for such a thing.

Earlier in the day he'd planned not to bed her so he'd not get her with child. But then she'd come to the meal all cleaned up and looking like an angel, and he'd felt his body respond.

As it was doing now.

Damn. He'd need to be stronger.

He was a war chief, in control at all times.

Instead of remembering her soft curves pressed against him, or her warm breath, he thought of drills with his warriors.

Now that he was wed to someone who wasn't a McCurdy, he had a chance to convince Lach into a takeover. If the laird allowed him to go to other clans to recruit more men, he'd have a large enough army to guarantee success. There was still time for them to get things in place before the McCurdy found out their alliance was over. The man would see Cam's marriage as an insult.

While Cam had never met Dorie McCurdy, he had made arrangements to take her to wife. But instead he'd married a total stranger. Mari.

Mari snuggled closer against him and made a soft sound that roused him once more.

Despite his discomfort, he must have managed to fall asleep, because he woke in his bed.

His room was empty, and for a moment it was easy to believe everything from the day before had been a dream. Except his bed still smelled of Mari.

She was real. And she'd just slipped out the door.

He dressed quickly and hurried to catch her. When he got to the corridor, he found her hovering by the stairs. He stepped closer and understood what had caused her to pause. Lachlan and Kenna were arguing in quiet hisses.

"I'm just saying I have a responsibility to keep the clan safe, and your sister being here may bring down a battle with the bloody English."

"She is my *sister*. You canna turn her out. She has nowhere else to go."

"We can give her funds."

"Funds are not the same as having a home and family."

"I'm merely considering all of our options."

"Well, you can discard any *options* that end with sending Marian away. I'll not have it, Lachlan MacKinlay. If you put her out, I'm going with her. And I'm taking my boys with me."

"They are *our* boys, and you're not going anywhere. We'll come up with something everyone can agree on." With that, they quieted, and he heard their footsteps move farther away.

Mari looked mutely up at Cam with sad eyes.

"Don't worry. Kenna always gets what she wants in the end. Lach likes to play the one in charge, but he's happily wrapped around his wife's little finger."

"He's not wrong. I could be bringing great danger to the clan."

Of course Cam knew this, but he wouldn't allow the thought to take root. Mari was his wife now, which meant he had a duty to keep her safe and give her a happy life. He didn't know the unpleasant details of her former marriage, but he knew she deserved better than whatever she'd been through.

No duchess would up and decide to kill her husband and run off to the wilds of Scotland alone unless she had no other choice.

"Shh. Don't even think it," he soothed. "If the worst were to happen, I would keep ye safe. You're my wife now, and I protect what's mine."

When she frowned and looked away, he thought maybe she didn't want to be his. She hadn't chosen to be his. He hadn't asked her thoughts on the matter. Neither of them had a choice, so it seemed like a waste of time to discuss it.

He let it go and escorted her down for the morning meal. Kenna and Lach were still unhappy and silent when they got to the head table.

Mari slipped her hand from Cam's. "Please excuse me. I need a moment," she whispered, and left before he had the chance to stop her.

Chapter Seven

Cam hesitated, unsure if he should go after Mari or not. She'd asked for a moment and it seemed rude not to give it to her.

He wasn't the most knowledgeable of men when it came to a woman's feelings. He knew how to please them in bed, and how to make them laugh. But the serious things... He'd never had much occasion to know such things. But now he had reason. He had a wife, and she was upset over what his clod-headed cousin had said in her hearing.

That being the case, it should be his cousin who should fix things.

"What's wrong with Marian?" Kenna asked before Cam reached the table.

He pointed at Lach. "*He's* what's wrong with Mari. She heard the two of you arguing on the steps and she knows he wants to send her away. Could ye not have such discussions in your chamber so she'd not hear your stupid plans? Not that you'd get very far with such a strategy. If Kenna hadn't already ended the notion, I surely would have."

"I'm the laird. Why doesn't anyone listen to me?" Lach

complained. When Kenna tilted her head expectantly, he let out a sigh and tossed his bannock on the plate. "Fine. I'll see to her and make sure she knows she's welcome." He continued to grumble under his breath as he passed by Cam to leave the hall.

"Know this, laird. If you make my wife cry, I'll hurt ye during drills today." It was no empty threat. He enjoyed making his cousin work for it. The man had been a soldier for years, fighting for the French in Spain. Lach certainly knew how to evade and attack, but Cam gave him a good show.

When Lach was out the door, Cam took his seat. A serving maid brought him his food, smiling attentively. A day or so ago he might have winked and stirred up a conversation. But instead, he offered a brittle smile and turned his attention to the woman sitting next to him.

"Thank you," Kenna said.

"For what?"

"For protecting my sister."

"Your sister is my wife. Had ye expected I'd not keep her safe?"

Kenna smiled. "Nay. I ken you have a good heart. It's just nice to see there's a chance for more."

Cam wished he hadn't just taken a sip of ale, because his surprise had him spitting it out across the table. "*More?*" he choked. "What do you mean by *more*? Surely you don't mean love, Kenna MacKinlay."

"You'd be surprised how love can sneak up on people."

"It can't sneak up on me. I'm watchful and have a large sword."

Kenna only laughed louder. "We'll see."

"No, we won't see. I don't want it. I can't do it. You know why it's not for men such as me. I've spoken to you about these things in the past."

"You mean the part about how war chiefs don't deserve

love?"

"I dinna say they didn't deserve it. I said it was too risky. Both parties could be hurt."

"We all carry scars from our upbringing. I still worry I'll never be good enough." When Cam snorted his disbelief, she shrugged. "It's hard to convince someone of something they've been told for a long time. For you, it's clear you don't want to leave a family behind as your da left you and your mother, but are ye willing to give up on happiness on merely the chance it could happen to you the same way?"

"A *chance*? I'd say it's more than a chance, given my duty. And I'd rather not have to think about the people I could leave behind when I draw my sword in battle."

"That's ridiculous. You think of all of us when you go to battle. Otherwise, why would you bother? The people you love in this castle are the reason you are able to fight. Knowing we need you makes you fight harder. It makes you stronger."

"Mayhap. But it's different, I think, with a family. I fear I'd be distracted with making sure I didn't get hurt so not to leave them."

"Cameron Michael Callum MacKinlay, you'd best always make sure you don't get hurt, no matter if ye have a family of your own or not. There are many people here who would miss ye if you didn't come back."

"Aye. I do make sure." It wasn't something he could explain to Kenna. She wasn't a husband. She didn't know the responsibilities a man faced.

He could provide for Mari without engaging his heart. He wasn't in love.

And he'd make sure he stayed that way.

• • •

Marian had made it to the stables and was trying to reason with the surliest groom she'd ever met over a horse when Lachlan stepped in.

"What's going on here?" he asked. His voice—dripping with authority—gave her a chill.

She might have tried to steer the story from the truth if the curmudgeon holding the reins hadn't spoken up first.

"She asked for a horse, my laird, but couldn't say that she'd be able to bring it back."

"And what need do you have for a horse, sister?"

Sister? She laughed at his feeble attempt to win her over. Straightening her spine, she looked at a spot over his left shoulder. Making eye contact with men had become impossible in recent years. Except for Cameron. Even in this short time, she felt safe enough to look into her husband's honey-brown eyes. The way they seemed to warm over when he smiled gave her courage.

It was yet another reason she should go. She was too comfortable with him. She couldn't let down her guard. Men watched for such things and struck when a woman was unprepared.

She'd been wrong to come here. It was wonderful to see Kenna again and know her younger sister held no ill will. But this wasn't her home.

A pull of sadness twisted in her stomach. She had wanted Dunardry to be her home and her refuge. And she wished she had time to get to know Cameron better. For she had liked the feel of his arms around her last night. But it was best to deal with things at once and get on her way.

"I understand you wish I wasn't here. So I planned to take a horse and go."

"Just like that. In the dress you're wearing. No food. No money."

She looked away. "I made it from London to here with

less. At least I'm wearing shoes."

She hated the tear that betrayed her by falling down her cheek. She quickly wiped it away, but a few other tears joined their leader.

"I'm the laird—"

"As you keep repeating. I'm sure you're aware I used to be a duchess. And I can tell you, titles don't mean a damn thing when all is said and done. A duchess can wander the countryside with no shoes, and a laird—" *Can be an arse*, she finished silently, not wanting to anger him.

With that, she turned toward the gate. If he wouldn't allow her to take a horse, she'd leave on foot. She didn't know where she'd go, but she didn't want to lure the English to the MacKinlay clan.

Lachlan was justified in sending her away. He was responsible for the safety of his people. Harboring a fugitive of the crown was counterproductive to his duty.

"Marian, I'm sorry. Please stay," he said when he caught up to her.

"Ridley knows I'm here. It will only be a matter of time before he returns with soldiers. He won't leave without me. There's a price on my head."

Lachlan nodded and let out a breath. "My wife and children live within these walls. I'll not endanger them. But you are my sister by marriage, which makes you my family as well. I have a duty to you, and I canna protect you if you leave the castle. So you'll stay, and we'll come up with a plan if Ridley returns." When she didn't move in the direction of the hall, he added, "Please."

If he thought she was simply being dramatic, he was wrong. She wouldn't put herself through the trouble of such theatrics for no good reason.

"I'll not cause you to live in fear of an English attack because you helped me."

"There are worse things to fear if you leave," he said with a grimace, placing a hand on her arm. He didn't grasp or pull, but still the contact made her flinch away. He released her quickly, his brows pulling together.

Surely Kenna had shared the reason she'd killed the duke. To her surprise, the laird didn't look on her in pity. Instead, he lowered his hand slowly and let out a breath. "Please, stay."

Marian nodded and let him lead her back to the hall. She paused and turned to him, offering a half smile when she realized what worse fears he had referred to. "You're afraid of Kenna."

"When it comes to my wife losing the sister she's just gotten back, aye, I am." He winked at her. "God and all the saints help me if I turned ye away."

When they returned to the hall, she sat next to Cameron. He took her hand and gave it a squeeze under the table.

"Everything well?"

"Yes. Thank you," Marian offered, though it wasn't exactly true. Things were fine for now. But she did need a plan for when Ridley returned.

Lachlan thought it his job to protect the clan, but in this, she was the one who would need to save everyone when the time came.

Chapter Eight

Marian spent the day with Kenna talking about their childhood days and laughing. As the afternoon drew out, they turned to other topics.

"How was your first night in the castle? Did you sleep well?"

Marian could tell by Kenna's sly smile she was asking a quite different question than the one she'd voiced.

"I did sleep well. Thank you for asking."

"Can you not take a hint?" Kenna lifted her hands and let them fall to her lap.

Marian burst out laughing as she recalled how impetuous her sister was. Kenna's laughter joined in, and it felt like old times.

"I've missed you," Marian said sincerely.

"I've missed you, as well, but I have to say, despite your struggles to get here, I like that we know each other better now. We seem to have grown out of our differences."

"You mean that you don't spend your days swinging from the trees, and I'm not as focused on sitting properly and speaking without a brogue?"

"We're on more common ground," Kenna agreed.

"Aye." Marian let the Scot word slip from her tongue, causing them to laugh again.

Eventually their discussion turned to their husbands. She knew Kenna was trying to tell if Marian was satisfied by Lachlan's apology.

"I understand his position as laird," Marian said honestly. "I'd not think poorly of him for doing what is right for Clan MacKinlay."

"You make it sound as if you're not part of the clan."

She nodded. "My being a MacKinlay is born of a complication, not a choice by either party."

"Perhaps, but I dare say ye may have found yourself in this position at some point anyway."

Marian tilted her head in question, taking in Kenna's wry smile.

"Cam favors you. It's clear to see. And I'm still waiting to hear what happened last night. Don't you think you've made me wait long enough?"

Marian shook her head. "I'm afraid you've waited in vain, for the story is less than scandalous."

"Go on."

Marian explained how he'd started out on the floor. "When I woke from a nightmare, he helped me into a dry garment—"

"And ravished ye?" Kenna asked hopefully.

"No," Marian confessed. "But he did sleep next to me. Only to offer comfort," she added quickly when Kenna's eyes lit up.

"It's good for now. It won't be long before the two of you are comfortable enough for more to blossom between you," Kenna predicted.

Marian wasn't so sure. Even if she did find Cameron

attractive, he was a man. And men were too unpredictable.

"I know you find him daunting. It's true he is a large man, but he has a heart to match. He'd never hurt someone who did not deserve it. He has a tender soul."

Marian had seen evidence of that already. Yet she also remembered how charming the duke had been before she married him. He'd seemed gentle, as well, but later was revealed to be the opposite.

"A war chief with a tender soul?" Marian chuckled at the thought. "He must have something lurking deep within that can bring him to kill in battle." Marian swallowed. To think she'd shared a bed with the man the night before, and would probably have to do so again tonight.

How much longer before he dropped the charade and took what was his by force?

Unless she willingly gave it to him first... Would that be better? Heading off the battle before it was brought to her gates? It was a common strategy for clan wars. Could it work for her?

• • •

Cam wasn't sure what to expect when he got to his chamber that night. Would Mari allow him to sleep next to her as she had the night before, or would he be consigned to the floor again?

He hated to give up the ground he'd gained but knew he had to move at her pace or risk being put out altogether. His wife had been seriously wounded, and unlike those injuries of the physical nature, her inner scars would take far longer to heal. If ever. He couldn't risk reopening them and causing her more pain.

He found Mari in bed on the side she'd slept on the night before. The big space where he'd slept spread out in welcome with the blanket turned down. Dropping his kilt, he watched as she stared at the ceiling, her hands clenching the covers by her chin until her knuckles were white with the effort.

"May I?" he asked, just to be sure. He was getting mixed messages. The bed said she was waiting for him, while her reactions stated otherwise.

She nodded but didn't meet his eyes. He found that was common for her. She spared him quick glances but otherwise kept her gaze elsewhere.

"Did you have a pleasant day?" she asked as soon as he'd shifted into a comfortable position.

"Aye. It was good enough. Liam is coming along well with his blade. He'll make a fine warrior."

"I'm afraid I'm not familiar with their names. Which is Liam?"

"He's a tall, thin lad. Only ten and six, but filling out now since he's been working with us daily." He heard the pride in his own voice. "He might even make a good war chief someday."

"You would give up your duties?" his wife asked innocently.

She clearly wasn't familiar with this life. Even though she'd grown up in the Highlands, her father would most likely have protected her from the reality of battle between clans.

"I would not give them up. But if the worst happened..." He let his words sit there in the darkness. It was important that she understand the risks of his position. That she know what she had unintentionally signed up for.

"I see." Those two words spoken with a slight shudder told more than their weight. She had only known him a few days, and already she did not want him to leave her. Even if only because she needed his protection.

It was the thing he'd most worried about, remembering his mother and the way she fretted when his father went off to battle. How could Cam do that to a woman? How could he put her aside to jump on his horse when she wailed and begged him not to go?

This was exactly what he did not want in his life. Survival was at the top of his goals when fighting, but would his mind be distracted with thoughts of Mari worrying about him?

Maybe his warning would push her away. Now that she realized his life could be gone with the echo of a war cry, she would protect her heart.

And he would find a way to protect his.

"It's why I don't think it wise for a war chief to take a wife. The job leaves widows behind. I ken it well enough having lived so when my da went to fight and dinna come home."

"But you were promised to marry another," Marian pointed out. He was glad to change the subject. He didn't want to discuss such somber topics. He'd wanted her to know the truth, but knowing it and dwelling on it were two different things.

"I'd not say *promised*, but planned for certain. A McCurdy lass."

"You didn't find her to be…compatible?"

He heard what she was really asking and hid his smile. She wanted to know if he was interested in someone else. He thought of toying with her to see if she'd break out in jealousy but feared he might end up disappointed.

"I've never met her. In truth, none of us even knew the McCurdy had a daughter, so no one knows much about her." He shrugged. "It doesna matter now. I'm married to you." When she remained silent, he went on. "Besides, I have been telling Lach we don't need to marry into an alliance with the bloody McCurdys, whose word isn't worth a piss in the wind." He cleared his throat. "Pardon my language." The lass had been married to a bloody duke, and here he was speaking coarse in front of her.

She laughed and shook her head. "It's fine. It's been a while since I've heard such talk, but I assure you, I shall not swoon."

He smiled and went on.

"I'm training my men so we'll be ready to take over the McCurdy clan whenever an opportunity presents itself."

"A war?" she said with wide eyes.

"Aye. I think it's the only way to assure our access to the sea. I think the McCurdy will marry off his daughter to get what he wants from us—coin—and then he'll find some way to turn his back on the agreement. It's always been his way to cheat."

"But you said Lachlan doesn't agree?"

"Nay. He wants a peaceful agreement."

It was clear Marian agreed with the laird. Most women he'd met preferred peace to war. Even Kenna, who was generally bloodthirsty, didn't want to go that route.

"I'm not daft," Cam said. "I know we would lose men. But I think, if we're clever, we could bring down the McCurdy laird and his sons. Once they no longer hold power, I believe the rest of the clan will easily swear allegiance to Clan MacKinlay. It's a simple matter of which laird can keep their bellies full. McCurdy is notoriously miserly with his people."

"Still. It seems an extreme measure just to avoid a marriage you didn't want. Especially since you ended up shackled anyway." She frowned, and he reached out to squeeze her hand.

"Aye. We're in a marriage neither of us wanted, but that doesn't mean we canna use it to our advantage. You will keep me from having to marry someone who might expect more of me. And you have the protection of my clan."

"You're suggesting this is a good thing?"

"I'm suggesting it can be a good thing, so long as we both understand what can and canna be between us."

She pinched her bottom lip in an enticing way as she took a few moments to think it through. He was proud of her for deliberating her future so thoroughly.

"I think you're right," she finally said. "So long as we agree it will never be a real marriage, I don't see the harm in being legally bound to you."

"Good," he said, though something didn't sit quite right.

Wasn't this what he'd wanted? A way to stay clear of marriage to a woman who might make demands of love? Mari didn't want that any more than he did.

And that was a good thing.

A very good thing.

Chapter Nine

Marian spent the night tossing and turning. At the first hint of light, she was out of bed and off to find something to keep her mind busy.

The night before, she and Cameron had come to an agreement. A marriage in name only. Except, they were sharing a room, a bed, and a life.

While she agreed they couldn't expect love from their accidental marriage, she had to admit—to herself at least—that she was interested in what might eventually happen between them…physically.

And that shocked her to no end. After the physical nightmare she'd endured with the duke, how could she possibly be open to willingly share her body with a man? It made no sense, even to her.

And yet, she could not deny it—she'd felt something warm and pleasant flare within her when Cameron MacKinlay lay next her in the dark.

The idea of lying with him as a wife intrigued Marian in some deep, long-hidden part of her. But the risk remained too great. Her husband, as large and imposing as he was, could break her far more easily than Blackley ever had. Maybe violence didn't simmer on the surface with Cameron, but at some point she would displease him, and his patience would snap.

What then?

Slipping into the kitchen, she found the women busy with preparations for the morning meal. Kenna wasn't there. She must have given in to Lachlan's pleading that she rest until after the babe was born.

The other women—older than Marian and Kenna—offered her a smile as she hovered near the door, unsure of how to help. As a duchess, she'd never stepped foot in the kitchen, much less helped the staff.

Even as a girl she'd never been allowed to linger in the kitchens as Kenna had. Marian had been confined to her training and lessons, forgoing fun in order to secure a future with a nobleman.

She could only imagine what her father would say to find out she'd been handfasted to a Scot. And not even a laird. The thought gave her a flicker of happiness.

She was free to be who she wanted to be. No longer forced into the rules of being the laird's daughter or contorted into her role as duchess. She could simply be Marian.

Or Mari.

Cameron's simpler name for her made more sense in her new life. She had been reinvented, living a simpler, easier life.

From now on, she would be Mari.

"Would you be able to help crimp the tarts?" Espath—if she remembered correctly—asked as if knowing Marian—Mari—needed prompting.

"Of course." She offered them a smile and took her spot, eager to be of help.

This was her home now, and she longed to fit in. Her life

as Duchess of Endsmere had been lonely. Only Lucy had ever spoken to her like a real person. The other staff had kept their distance, either because they felt the duchess wouldn't embrace their relationship, or from fear of reprimand from the duke.

Mari let out a breath and took to her task. She was free. She was making friends. And she was safe.

As long as she did nothing to anger her new husband.

Though from the scowl on his face when he opened the door and ducked into the kitchen, she worried that might not be possible.

"Mari? Can I speak with ye outside?"

She glanced to the other women for help, but they offered nothing more than soft smiles. "Yes. Of course."

He stayed her with a hand and pointed. "You might bring a few of those with you?"

The women tittered, and Espath grabbed up four of the finished tarts and wrapped them in a cloth. Handing them over to her with a wink, she said, "Have a good morning."

Carrying the tarts, Mari followed her husband's wide back out of the kitchen and around to the stables. She wanted to ask where they were going but remembered how much the duke hated when she'd questioned him on anything.

A few times Cameron paused as if waiting for her to catch up to him, but she stayed behind him, as was proper. Maybe he didn't care about such things. Maybe he wanted her to walk next to him. Should she ask?

It was a strange situation. While she'd hated nearly every moment of her marriage to the duke, at least she'd known what was expected of her. Every word she uttered or move she made was watched and measured. If she said or did the wrong thing, she would be punished.

Inside the stables, she breathed in the sweet smell of hay and horses. Another place she'd not spent much time visiting in her past life. Though after fleeing London she'd sought them out as a quiet place of safety during her travels north.

As her eyes adjusted to the dim light, she saw two horses being readied. The ogre from yesterday cast her a baleful glare. He tended a giant beast of a horse. The second horse, looking smaller just for standing next to the other, whickered and tossed its head.

Cameron took her bundle and tucked it inside the bag on the larger horse, and dismissed the surly groom.

"It's a fine morning for a ride. I would like you to join me." It was made to sound like a request, but the firm tone revealed the command.

She blinked and looked down at her feet.

"I assumed you ride, since Kenna isn't happy unless her arse is in a saddle. If you do not, we could—"

"I do ride. Not as much as Kenna, but I can. I would like to go with you." She tried her best to mask the tremor in her voice. There seemed to be no way to keep from displeasing him. Staying behind would ruin his plans, but when he saw how ill-equipped she was on a horse he might well toss her off himself.

Her mind raced with all she knew of riding. It had been many years. Before she went to court. Hopefully she would remember and not embarrass herself.

"I wish to show you some of our lands," he explained.

It was clear he wanted to say something else, but he hesitated, his lips pressed into a firm line.

"Very well." She allowed him to help her onto her horse and followed behind him.

Knowing her way around the MacKinlay lands would make it easier for her to run if needed.

She stayed directly behind him, not catching up and not allowing too much space to fall between them. She thought it the perfect distance and worked hard to maintain it.

He occasionally turned in his saddle to see her, though she knew he could well hear she was still there. Each time he frowned, and she began to worry. He was clearly displeased.

Was it with her riding? She was glad it wasn't too difficult. The early lessons of her youth served her well.

He swiveled and cast another frown in her direction.

Fear tingled up her spine. Quickly she tried to remember the night before and the few hours this morning. What had she done to earn his ire? They'd done nothing more than sleep. She hadn't even seen him that morning.

Was that it? Was he angry with her for leaving his bed without his permission? Giving up, her mind went blank. She knew it didn't matter if she'd done anything offensive or not. The result would be the same. How many times had she been broken and bloodied for no crime or fault?

Her heart raced as she searched for ways to avoid his wrath. She knew reasoning didn't work. Begging only made it worse. Running wasn't an option—the punishment was far worse when she was caught.

Glancing over her shoulder, she could only see barest tips of the battlements over the trees. The castle was too far away. She'd never make it, especially after a beating. Her chest hurt from trying to catch her breath. She swayed in the saddle and closed her eyes.

"Mari? What is it?" Cameron's voice broke through her panic. Somehow he was standing next to her.

Her horse must have stopped. How long had she been sitting there before he'd come back to check on her?

"What is it? You're so pale." He reached for her, and she flinched. He paused a moment before placing his hands at her waist and removing her from her horse. "Are you hurt? Tell me what's wrong."

She could barely stand on her own feet, as lightheaded as she was. She couldn't pull in enough air to keep her upright.

Light flickered at the sides of her vision. She couldn't swoon here with him. She needed to stay alert. Be ready to protect herself if needed.

"You're shaking," he said, his eyes wide. He bent to look into her face. "Talk to me, woman. You're scaring me."

He was scared? This giant of a man was scared? Of her?

She blinked a few times and looked at him, seeing the truth. His golden eyes weren't scowling at her in anger or disgust. He looked upon her with concern and worry.

His hands on her shoulders didn't grip her too tightly but steadied her. Offering his support and his strength.

"Please, lass," he begged her.

She tried to slow her breathing by telling herself she was not in danger from this man, but it was too late. Her heart ran away all on its own. She pressed a palm to her chest, bidding it to stay there.

Before she could manage to speak, Cameron had scooped her up and carried her into the shade of a nearby tree. He pulled a flask from his side and held it to her lips. "Drink," he ordered. But the short command lacked anger or danger.

She took a sip and coughed at the burn of the whisky as it tore at her throat. Another sip, and then another. The warmth in her stomach spread out through her body to the very tips of her toes and fingers.

She managed to take in a deep breath and let it out slowly. Then another. Soon her heart slowed, and she sagged against him, exhausted from her ordeal.

"Do ye feel better?" he asked, his voice vibrating at her ear.

"I'm tired," she answered, not sounding like herself.

"Then rest. I'll watch over you," he promised.

She closed her eyes and drifted away, enjoying the comfort of his embrace.

・・・

Cam frowned down at his sleeping wife. She'd been curled up on his lap for most of the morning. He'd noticed the dark shadows under her eyes when he'd met her in the kitchen, and guessed she hadn't slept well the night before.

But that wasn't an explanation for what had happened here, when she'd gone pale and limp. When she'd been unable to speak for breathing too hard and her heart had nearly beaten out of her chest.

She'd worn herself out battling...nothing.

Nothing but fear.

"What had you so terrified?" he asked her sleeping form as he brushed her golden hair back from her face. Eventually she shifted, and her eyes fluttered open. She gazed up at him for a moment, then looked around as if confused as to where she was or how she got there.

"How do ye feel?" he asked, moving his stiff leg and flexing his numb fingers.

"I'm sorry," she said, her cheeks turning pink.

She had the loveliest blush. In another time he might say things that kept her blushing, just to see it. But a darkness lurked in her eyes, and he needed to focus on how to help her overcome it.

She kept her gaze away from his until he could stand it no longer. Moving slowly, he placed his fingers slightly on her chin and turned her face toward his so she had to look him in the eyes.

"What happened?"

She swallowed and would have looked away again if he hadn't kept a firm grasp on her.

"I'm fine." The lie came out in a soft voice.

"Are you with child?" he asked. He'd been thinking of how he might get the answer from her the whole time she'd been sleeping. He wasn't one for mincing words. Direct was best.

She blinked, and her mouth fell open in surprise.

"It's fine if you are. I'd understand. You were married directly prior to our...wedding." He swallowed and laid out his feelings so she wouldn't be afraid. "I'll be a father to your child, Mari. I'll raise and protect the babe as if it were my own blood. Give them my name."

"Why do you think I'm with child?"

"I've seen Kenna have dizzy spells when she was pregnant in the past. Though I never saw her lose her breath like you did. Mostly she just turns green and runs for the nearest door."

"I'm not." She shook her head. "I'm not with child. I was... I was afraid."

"Of what?" He looked around, genuinely puzzled. Then it dawned on him.

She glanced away, and he allowed her escape, fearing he didn't want to hear her answer.

"I thought perhaps you were angry with me and had brought me out here to punish me. You're so large, and a warrior. I don't think I'd survive it."

It took a few seconds for him to put her words together into some form of sense. Even then he was in shock at the absurdity.

"You think..." He paused to clear the anger from his voice. It wouldn't do to be mad at her while explaining how wrong she was about his being angry. "You think I would bring you out here and beat you?"

She bit her lip and shook her head.

Maybe he had misunderstood after all. He hoped so.

"You don't understand," she finally said.

"Please explain it to me so I can understand."

"I thought maybe you were upset. You looked upset when

you came for me in the kitchens."

He huffed out a breath and shook his head. "I dinna like seeing you working in the kitchens. You'd been a duchess before, and my station doesn't allow you many luxuries. I was upset with myself for not being able to give you a life fit for someone like you. I wasn't angry with you, I swear it."

She blinked at him. "I think I might have known that in my heart, but then my mind took the small thread of fear and added on to it, piecing together memories and other fears until it got so out of control I could no longer breathe. It's happened before. I can't seem to stop it when it starts. Even though I see now how unrealistic my thoughts were, at the time they seemed utterly possible and imminent."

He brushed her hair back and pulled her against him, thinking over what she'd shared. What terrible hell did she live in? And how could he help her out of it? Her demons weren't ones he could slay with his sword.

"Do you trust that I'm a man of my word, Mari?" he asked, pulling away so he could look at her.

She nodded and offered a soft "Yes."

"I'll not promise that I'll never be angry with ye. That seems the way of husbands and wives at times. But I can assure you, when I'm mad at you, you'll know it. I'm not the kind of man to let things dwell. I speak my mind right then. But it will only be speaking—occasionally, I may have cause to bluster a bit, but it will only be words. It will never be fists or anything physical."

She nodded again but didn't look convinced.

"By the saints, I swear I'll never lure you off to the woods to punish ye. We might go to our room to have words, but that would be the extent of it. Words. And I'll hear yours as well. I'm certain you'll have plenty to yell at me about. I'm not the most observant man and know little of women."

Again she nodded in agreement, even though it was clear

she didn't truly believe him.

He placed his forehead against hers, making a connection. "These are things you'll learn about me in time. I only ask that you don't make me out to be a monster until you have reason to. Is that fair?"

"Yes. I'll try to remember."

"That's something, I guess." He barely got the words out before a raindrop landed on her cheek. Another fell on his head and another on his arm. "It appears our adventure is over for the day. Let's get back to the castle before we're drenched."

He took her hand and they ran for the horses. He lifted her into the saddle and they made haste back to Dunardry. After they returned, they were each pulled into their own duties the rest of the day.

That evening at the meal they stole glances at each other. Each time he caught her looking at him he offered a smile, and she smiled back before looking away. At times he thought she was flirting with him, but then he remembered the events of the morning and held back on his plans to woo her.

She was afraid of him.

He'd have to be mindful of his next move so as not to scare her. He would give her space and time to settle with him. There would be time for more once she was comfortable.

He shifted as his cock hardened from looking upon her sweet lips. His body craved hers, but he would not claim her tonight. Or any other night.

Not until she wanted him.

He frowned at his food and wondered how he might speed the process along.

Chapter Ten

After the evening meal, Kenna asked Mari to assist her with finishing a gown in her solar. Since it was a gown meant for Mari, she couldn't very well refuse, though she had enjoyed the playful glances with her husband across the table and would have liked to spend time with him.

When Cameron smiled at her, it wasn't fear that made her stomach twist. It was something else. Something she hadn't felt for a very long time. Not since she'd flirted with the groom's son in her father's stables.

With distance between her and Cameron, and people all about, it was easier to feel safe with him. Easier to smile and tease him with coy looks. Especially when he offered her his own smiles and smoldering glances.

"What do you think?" Kenna asked, holding up the gown.

Mari smiled indulgently. "It's beautiful."

"You lie." Kenna sniffed. "Embroidery is still a skill I have yet to master."

"You have mastered many others. This one is of no

matter."

"Do you say that to challenge me? You ken I hate being bad at anything."

Mari shook her head. She found it ridiculous that Kenna worried over such things. Though she remembered how relentless their stepmother had been in pointing out Kenna's faults.

"You are an amazing woman, sister," Mari said with a grin. "And I daresay your husband doesn't give a fig about the lack of embroidery on his linens. It's clear he only cares that you're lying on them."

They giggled together as they had when they were girls.

Kenna shook her head. "It's strange that I still worry over it. I know how Lach feels about me. But I still try hard to make sure he has no regrets over our marriage."

"It's a waste of your energy. The man is beyond any thought of regret. It's quite obvious how much he loves you, and I've only been here a short time."

"We both know it's one thing to tell ourselves something, and another to know it in our hearts as truth."

Mari nodded sadly. She hadn't told Kenna about what happened earlier, when she'd lost herself in fear, but it seemed her sister understood.

"Try it on and see how it fits," Kenna demanded, changing the subject.

"Might I do it in the morning? I fear if I go to my room and take off my gown, I may collapse in my bed and not return for the entertainment."

"Very well." Kenna smiled. "Let's go join our husbands so they don't forget about us," she joked. Mari knew Kenna was anxious to get back to Lachlan.

When they returned to the hall, the music had started. Turning to join the crowd, she heard a giggle and looked around to see Roddy and Douglas laughing as they crawled over an imposing figure.

Cameron looked a sight with little boys climbing and hanging from his large limbs. In one hand he clasped a rag where a small dog growled in an effort to pull it from his grip.

"They love him. He is so patient with them. Even better, he tires them out so they sleep through the night." Kenna laughed.

Watching her husband playing with small children and a little dog brought shame to heat Mari's cheeks. Her earlier breakdown seemed so silly now. She'd seen the hurt on his face when she confirmed her fear of him. It wasn't right that he be blamed for the crimes of another man.

Unfortunately, she didn't have much say in the matter when her mind took over. Fear was fear, and she'd not yet found a way to conquer it.

She went with Kenna but spent the evening watching her husband with the boys. The way he laughed with them brought a smile to her lips. Even when he had to scold Douglas for tugging at the dog's ears, Cameron was gentle and offered the lad a hug afterward.

He was a good man. A tender, compassionate man. A safe man.

She would tell herself this over and over, until her mind and her heart accepted it as truth.

When the music was over, she headed for the stairs, glad the day was done. Cameron and the boys were gone, but she found them upstairs where he was tucking them into their bed. Brutus the dog made a circle and folded himself onto the rug at the foot of the bed.

"Are you going to bed?" he asked when he saw her watching.

"Yes. Unless you needed something."

"Nay. Go on. I'll see you soon."

Soon. She swallowed and wrestled with her feelings of

anticipation, excitement, and dread. Inside their room, she closed her eyes and let out a breath.

"It will be fine. Stop being a goose," she told herself.

She was still brushing out her hair when he came into their room. She hadn't had time to get into bed. Instead, she stood nervously before the fire in nothing but her shift. While she'd been waiting for him to arrive, in her mind she'd played through ways of enticing him to bed.

Unfortunately, what she knew of seduction wouldn't have filled the tip of a thimble. Now that he was here, those few ideas she'd been considering fled in a flood of anxiety. She wasn't brave enough to try tempting him, even if she knew how to do such a thing.

She crossed her arms to cover the peaks of her nipples, certain they showed through the thin fabric. Upon seeing him, her nipples had tightened all on their own.

He closed the chamber door and stood there gazing at her, his mouth slightly open. His hand hovered in midair as if he'd been frozen. Only his eyes moved, starting at her bare feet and rising slowly to her loose hair.

He swallowed and took a step closer, then another, until he was standing directly in front of her. His chest pressed up against her crossed arms. She had no choice but to drop her protective stance.

"I'm sorry I didn't knock. I interrupted you." He didn't look the least bit sorry as he studied her face, his gaze settling on her lips.

Her tongue darted out to moisten them, and his pupils flared.

"Are you?" she asked coyly, remembering her training on how to flirt. "Sorry?"

"No. Not even a wee bit," he admitted and shook his head. A slow, mischievous smile took over his handsome face. "In fact, I'm planning to be here earlier and earlier each night, to be sure to catch you just like this." He laughed, and she laughed with him.

"Soon we would be going to bed at noon," she suggested.

"I don't think I would mind that overmuch." His smile faded away again.

The heat sizzled between them, drawing her in.

He is kind. He is tender. He will not hurt me. She repeated the words like an oath, praying her body and mind would be at peace with what she both hoped and feared would happen next.

As he leaned down, she went up on her tiptoes to meet him. His lips touched hers with a tenderness she'd never known but somehow expected from this man. Everything about him—despite his hard muscles and intimidating size—was tenderness incarnate.

His large hand cradled the back of her head as he tilted her so he could deepen the kiss. His tongue danced with hers, and she reached out to steady herself. Her hands gripped his shirt. His other arm wrapped around her waist, offering support for her wobbly legs.

This was heaven. This was how it was supposed to be between a husband and a wife. Pleasure and softness. Hazy rapture and warm smiles.

When he pulled her up into his arms, she gasped with surprise and an unexpected flood of happiness. He set her on the bed and took a step back. Then he reached for the buckle of his weapons belt. She gasped again, though not with happiness. But innate fear.

A memory assaulted her of another man removing his belt with dreadful purpose.

Cameron stepped away and raised his hands. "It's fine, lass. I mean ye no harm."

She knew that, but she realized she'd instinctively pulled back and was crouched on the other side of the bed, ready to escape. All the glorious fogginess from a moment ago lifted, and they were just two people—no, two *strangers* in a room together.

"I'm sorry," she said and slipped under the blankets. Her heart and her breath were still heaving. *Please, not again.*

"Maybe I should stay on the floor tonight," he offered, and didn't give her a chance to argue before grabbing a blanket and doing just that.

She'd run him off with her fit. What must he think?

She touched her lips where they still sizzled from his kiss. She needed to get over this panic so she could be with Cameron properly.

Before he gave up on her completely.

• • •

Bloody hell, Cam thought as he tossed and turned for possibly the hundredth time that night. It wasn't just the discomfort of the hard floor that made him irritable. It was that he'd taken another step backward with Mari.

She'd recoiled in fear because he'd taken things too far. He'd told himself earlier to go slow. But then he'd seen her in her shift, the light behind her showcasing her shadowed perfection through the thin fabric.

There was no such thing as slow after that. He'd wanted her and had stupidly rushed to take what he'd wanted.

He'd asked her to trust him, but now he didn't think he could trust himself. What kind of message was he sending her? She'd enjoyed their kiss, he could tell that much. But he should have given her time to adjust to the idea before pressing for more.

It must have been two hours since he'd kissed her, yet he could still taste her on his tongue. That memory of her lips made him want another kiss. But she was across the room asleep.

Except…

He heard a small sound. A sniff. Then a whimper. Was she having a bad dream? Silently, as he was trained to move, he rose and went to the bed. She was lying on her side with her eyes closed and tears on her cheeks.

"Mari? Wake up, lass. It's another dream."

Her eyes opened immediately, unlike the last time when he'd had to force her awake. She sat up and wiped her eyes. It didn't seem she'd been asleep. Which meant he, not her dreams, had caused her tears.

"I apologize for my behavior earlier. When I reacted—" she started.

He didn't allow her to finish. "You have nothing to be sorry for, lass. You did nothing wrong. It was me. I need to be more patient. I'll not come to you again, not until you no longer fear my touch."

He felt the heat of shame on his cheeks and was glad for the darkness. She owed him nothing. He hated that she was crying because of something that had happened between them.

"It's not you or your touch I fear," she said softly. "It's just…certain things make me remember unpleasant incidents, and it taints what is happening between us."

Hadn't he just been berating himself for knowing one thing and doing another? He knew he needed to go slowly, and yet he'd practically launched himself at her for wanting her so badly.

"I understand. I sometimes have…bad memories too."

"You do?" she asked as he wiped away her tears. "How did you get over them?"

"Well, I can't say I've figured it out myself yet." He'd not share the example of his biggest failure tonight. Instead, he decided to tell her of another way his mind and body had not been aligned. "After a battle or raid, I think about it for a long time. Still react, sometimes. I know I'm not in danger anymore, but my body still has the need to protect and defend."

She nodded slowly. "Yes. That's it. I wonder how long it will be before I'm in control."

"I canna say for sure. But mayhap it will be easier if we try touching."

Her eyes went wide, and he shook his head at himself.

"Holding hands," he amended. "While we sleep. I think if we get over the shock of it, we'll get used to one another. Like when you first jump into the loch, it's terrible cold. But your skin becomes accustomed to it and then it's not so bad."

He should have left the fancy words to the poets. That was the most horrid thing he'd ever said to woo a lass.

"So, touching me is a bad thing for you?" Her brows pulled together, and he winced.

"No, not at all. Forget that part." The only thing jumping into a freezing loch had to do with moving slow with Mari was that both had his cods shriveled up. "Can I stay in bed with you?"

"Yes." She gave a nod that was more determination than enjoyment, but he'd take it if it meant sleeping in bed next to his wife rather than the floor.

He settled in next to her and reached for her hand. He gave it a squeeze and looked over at her even though he couldn't see in the dark room.

"That's not so bad, right?" he asked.

"No. It's not bad at all. It's nice."

"Good. See? It's the first step to feeling comfortable with one another."

He felt her nod and wondered in resigned frustration how many more steps lay before them.

Chapter Eleven

The next morning Cam woke to find Mari still in bed next to him. He'd never been a late sleeper, but she had been up and out of their room before he woke the day before.

Now with the sun coming in through the window, he was able to look his fill at his wife. She was a beauty. Long, dark-gold lashes rested on her cheek. Her brows curved in a way that made one think she was about to say something astute. And those lips...

He let out a sigh and got out of bed before he spent too much time gazing at her lips. His body was already hard from just the fact it was morning. Staring at her lips would not ease that ache, for certain.

He left their room as quietly as possible and headed downstairs. After saddling his horse, he left the castle to check in with the perimeter guards to the west. He was almost happy to find them sleeping so he had a reason to vent some of his frustration.

"And what if I'd been the McCurdys? The castle wouldn't have any warning of an attack."

One guard leaped to his feet, rubbing his eyes. "The McCurdys wouldn't attack us on one horse, but all the beasts they own. That many horses would have made the earth shake and we would have felt them coming."

That only provoked him more.

"You know how else you might know an enemy is coming on you?" Cam demanded, then paused to see if they'd dare answer. "You could keep your bloody eyes open and watch for them! Which is why you're out here in the first place."

"All's well, Cam. There's no reason to worry."

Cam could see as much, but he really wanted to yell at someone. Being stressed and frustrated with Mari would set them back even further in feeling comfortable with one another.

"Just stay awake," he ordered gruffly and headed back to the castle.

Mari was sitting in the back of the hall with one of the women from the kitchen. Rather than speak to her in his current foul mood, he went to the head table where Lach was eating with Bryce and Liam.

He flopped down on the bench beside the laird, still muttering his displeasure with the guards, the weather, and the world in general.

"How are things with you and Mari?" Lach asked, nodding toward where she was laughing with her friends. "She seems happy enough. Why do you look ready to bust through the castle walls?"

"Aye, she *seems* happy. But she's not. She's terrified."

"Of what?"

"Me."

"*You?*" Lach looked to Bryce and Liam, who also looked confused. Three sets of eyes glared at him. "What did ye do to her?"

"I didn't do anything to her, and you well know I never

would. Wipe that look from your faces right now or I'll help you do it."

"My mistake for thinking you rough." Lach rolled his eyes.

"I don't know what to do with her. She goes along with everything I say. She doesn't want to cause any trouble."

"My, that sounds wretched." Bryce smirked.

"It is. She's afraid of me. Her late husband was a right bugger the way he treated her. She flinches and cowers whenever I come near her. I can't stand it."

"You need to push her until she pushes back," Liam suggested. "Like a timid horse."

All three men looked at the boy and laughed loudly at his suggestion.

"Have ye even kissed a lass yet?" Bryce teased.

Liam's face and ears went red, and he scowled at them, then jumped up to go find another place to sit.

When their laughter faded, Cam rubbed his chin and shook his head. "It might not be a bad idea, at that."

"I was just thinking the same," Bryce agreed.

"If it works, I'll have to apologize to the lad," Cam admitted.

"If it works, I don't think you'll mind." Bryce gave him a wink.

Nay. Cam wouldn't mind at all.

...

"And he hasn't done more than kiss you?" Kenna asked as they sat in her solar later that morning.

Mari had seen Cameron at the morning meal, but he'd hardly looked at her, let alone come to speak to her. She didn't know what to do to set things right between them again, but she was certain Kenna could help her figure it out.

Mari tied off on a piece of embroidery while Kenna watched.

"No. He's been a proper gentleman. Which is quite infuriating." She'd liked kissing Cameron, and she wanted to experience what came next. The way he'd looked at her last night made her think he was ready to take that next step.

Until she'd frightened him off.

"He said we should take our time, to make sure we're comfortable with one another. We held hands."

Kenna smirked. "Held hands? You'll not get very far at that rate. *You* may need to kiss *him*."

"I couldn't." Mari shook her head quickly. It would be much too risky. What if he found such unladylike behavior forward and disgusting, like Endsmere? He was already annoyed with her for being such a coward and scooting away from him in terror.

No, she would have to wait for Cameron to make the first move.

She only hoped he would try again soon.

"Have you told him you want him to touch you?"

"No. Of course not. Proper ladies don't ask men to touch them."

Kenna nodded. "Mayhap that's why proper ladies don't get touched, whereas I get touched all the time."

"You ask your husband to touch you?" Mari asked, trying her best not to appear appalled.

"Ask? Nay. I walk up to him, grab him by the ears, and pull him down so I can kiss him. Then I reach under his kilt and grab him by—"

"You reach under his— *Kenna Elizabeth!*" So much for not being appalled. "You behave like a wanton!"

"I am wanton, I guess, since I'm wantin' my husband to touch me." She laughed with a wink.

Mari pressed her lips together, trying to hold in her own

mirth. "You are still the wild one, even though you're also beautiful."

"The English call us Scots savages for a reason. Mayhap it's time for you to put propriety aside and grab what you want." She chuckled. "By the ears, if need be. Or the—"

"Kenna!"

Mari was certain her younger sister enjoyed deviling her with bawdy talk. But when she was done laughing, she took the embroidery from Mari and set it aside to join hands.

"You have every reason to be afraid of a man's touch. So far, it's not been a pleasant experience for ye. But I promise, once you find your way into Cam's arms and his bed, you'll not be sorry."

Mari nodded and took a deep breath. "The truth is, I want his touch," she confessed. "I have even had thoughts of reaching up under his kilt, as you've said. It drives me mad thinking about it at times. But when he's there in front of me, I lose my nerve completely."

Kenna released her and got up. For a second, Mari thought she'd said too much and repulsed Kenna, but her sister was riffling through papers on a small desk.

"There's safety in distance," Kenna explained. "I wrote to Lachlan when he was fighting for the French. In a letter I could say things I would have been afraid to say in his presence. You should write to Cam. Tell him what you want, so there's no misunderstanding."

Mari regarded her sister with a blossoming smile. "That is a wonderful idea."

With newfound excitement, she sat down at the desk and studied the blank page before her. Dipping a quill in the ink, she poised it over the paper and…nothing.

"Perhaps if I leave you to it," Kenna suggested, and went for the door. "Take as long as you need."

It took Mari most of the day and a fair fortune in paper

and ink to get her feelings down in a way that sounded sincere and also alluring.

Later that evening, she paced in front of the fire in nothing but her thin shift. Her hair was down and brushed smooth. However, she was still pretending to brush it so she would be caught in the open when Cameron came up to bed.

She realized when she stood in front of the fire, the light shone through her shift, giving him a look at her curves without seeing her skin. It was the perfect way to tantalize her husband into kissing her again. And maybe more… The letter she'd worked so hard to finish sat on the stand. She'd unfolded and refolded it so many times, the creases were nearly worn through.

She would allow him to catch her getting ready for bed. Then she would give him the letter. From there, she didn't know what to expect. This was a whole different type of fear. One she was willing to embrace.

But it was already an hour past when he'd come to bed last night, and still he was not there. She sat down in the chair next to the fire to give her feet a rest, ready to jump up when he entered the room.

Her plan was flawless…except that she fell asleep in the chair.

When Cameron came stumbling into their chamber, she jerked awake at the sound of the door slamming closed. She stood quickly, giving him a chance to look, but he didn't look. He pulled off his belt and let his kilt fall to the floor. Still wearing his weapons belt, he stood on one leg to pull off his boot. He nearly lost his balance, but not before his shirt had come up enough for her to see one sculpted buttock.

She glanced away but returned her gaze immediately to get another look.

When he reached for her to steady himself, his hand grazed her breast. A pleasant feeling zinged through her body…but then she caught a whiff of him.

She stepped away, pressing her back against the wall.

He was heavy with drink from the smell of him and the way he laughed loudly. His unfocused gaze moved over her for a moment, then he flopped onto the bed.

She stayed in the corner, unmoving, until he began snoring. She edged closer and nudged his arm.

Nothing. He was dead asleep.

When the duke was in his cups he was even more violent than usual. However, Cameron seemed immobile and unthreatening with his heavy arms splayed across the bed, taking up her side as well as his own.

With a sigh she went over and picked up his leg to tug off the boot he hadn't managed to free. Then she undid the weapons belt at his waist and slid it off. Setting his sword and dirk on the table next to the bed, she worked out how she might cover him. He was lying atop the blankets.

After another moment of contemplation, she decided he was already more comfortable than he deserved, and went to the other side of the bed. With a huff, she pushed his arm aside before getting in and closing her eyes.

She crossed her arms, settling into her disappointment.

There would be no kissing tonight.

Chapter Twelve

It was all Cam could do to keep from pulling Mari into his arms when she removed his belt. He'd felt himself growing hard and forced himself to think of other things so as not to give away the fact he wasn't as drunk as he pretended.

He'd asked his friends what they did to make their wives angry. Coming home foxed was at the top of their lists. Yet instead of ranting at him, Mari had removed his boot and tried to make him comfortable.

However, before that she'd been terrified. Damn his eyes, he should have considered that her bastard of a husband may have beaten her when he'd been drinking.

Clearly, she wasn't the kind of woman who would kill a man unjustly. If she'd been pushed to the point of murder, it was certainly warranted. Cam hated that someone had hurt her so much she felt her only escape was to kill.

His plan would only work if she was mad enough to fight with him *and* she felt comfortable enough to give him a good blistering. Once she could yell at him without fear, it would mean she was no longer afraid of him. Or so he hoped.

Mari had been badly mistreated and did not trust his kindness. Gentleness alone wouldn't work with her. He had to earn her ire and argue loudly with her, in order to prove he would never resort to violence.

No matter how much it went against everything he'd ever done in the past when it came to women. His father had always told him women were to be honored and respected. He was never to lift his hand to a female or anyone smaller than he, except in battle for his clan.

"A large body doesn't mean you are a strong man if you use it to intimidate others. Being able to use your body to fight your enemies, while keeping your heart kind, is the truest meaning of strength."

Cam thought his father had the right of it. He would never raise a hand in anger to his wife. Or any other person. He just wished there was a way to convince her of that. Not touching his wife was taking more strength than he might possess.

At some point during the night she'd scooted closer, and he'd wrapped his arm around her to hold her. He wanted her badly, but he would wait until she felt safe.

Her whimpers and tossing woke him, and he pulled her from the depths of her bad dream. She cried and shook against him, and he held her as tight as he could without crushing her, hoping to help hold her together. He worried she'd shake apart into tiny pieces if he let go.

When she quieted, he stroked her hair. "Is it better now, Mari?"

"Can you hold me a little longer?"

"I'll hold you as long as you need, lass." *Forever.*

That thought made him shudder. She'd only been here a few days, and already he feared he was slipping into unwanted feelings.

He'd not wanted to marry, yet he was wed and at ease with it…because he thought it would be in name only. But now he was trying to earn her trust so they could share more intimate pursuits that had nothing to do with either of their names.

And tonight he found himself forgoing his interest in the flesh to simply hold her and offer comfort. Worse, he was content with the contact and didn't wish for more at the moment.

He was in dangerous territory. If he wasn't careful he could find himself feeling things he never intended, never wanted to feel.

...

At first light, Mari slid out from under Cameron's heavy arms and left for the kitchen. She didn't want to be around when he woke up in a foul mood with a headache and stomach issues. Although…he'd spoken to her in the middle of the night as if he was as sober as she. Maybe the whisky worked differently on a man of his size.

She liked helping in the kitchen. Her sister spent a lot of time there, though Kenna had promised her husband she wouldn't lift a finger while in her condition. The women told stories and shared tales. Occasionally they'd complain about their men or their bairns.

They never asked Mari probing questions or hinted that they knew why she was living there. She suspected if she told them, they would listen and keep it to themselves. She just hadn't grown accustomed to having friends yet.

Her maid, Lucy, had been her only true friend. There had been women from court, but she couldn't call them friends. They were catty women who had preyed on gossip and were just as happy to make something up if it was a dull day.

It was nice to be accepted as she was.

She was about to ask the women if Scottish men did not

wake up ill after drinking, when she remembered her sister's advice from the day before.

The letter.

Good lord. She'd forgotten all about it when Cameron stumbled in the night before. Even now, it was sitting in their room for him to find when he woke.

She jumped up. "Excuse me, I forgot something very important. I'll be right back."

She opened the door and only got a few steps from the kitchen when she encountered Cameron coming toward her. He was smiling, which was more than she'd expected in his state. He was also clean and bright-eyed, despite being up earlier than drunken men generally rose. He seemed to have suffered nothing for his indulgence the night before.

"May I speak with you, Mari?"

"Of course." Her voice cracked with nervousness.

Had he found the letter? Had he read it?

He didn't look angry…far from it.

He took her hand and gave it a squeeze. "I wondered if you might want to go for another ride with me this morning, since we didn't see much yesterday. We can take a meal with us and eat it by the river if you'd like."

After what had happened the day before, she hadn't expected him to want to try again. Too overcome with emotion to speak, she just nodded and hoped he could tell how pleased she was to be invited. Especially since he was in a good mood with no signs of overindulgence from the night before.

The morning sun exposed the hints of red in his brown hair as she followed him to the stables. The fear from the day before wouldn't return. She knew he wasn't taking her out of the castle to harm her where no one would hear. He merely wanted to show her their lands.

The pride on his face told her how happy he was to have

a place of power here.

Like the day before, she followed him out of the bailey. He paused until her horse came up next to his. When she fell behind again, he stopped. It took far too long for her to realize he wanted her to ride next to him. She made sure to keep up when he started off again.

"I don't know if ye remember, but that stand of woods over there is where you came running into my life." He smiled. "We canna see the field from here. It's on the other side."

She nodded.

"The river is just beyond this small hill. Be careful, though, it's misleading. There's a steep cliff on the other side. We'll skirt around to the right. There's a place where it levels out. It's a fine place to rest and eat."

She looked up at the blue sky of a perfect day, allowing herself to be happy. She was safe here. The woods, while dark and sinister when she'd been running through them for her life, were actually lovely in the way the sun filtered through the leaves, making everything below glow a brilliant green.

"Have you ever ridden bareback?" he asked out of the blue.

"Once or twice. Not since I grew up."

He nodded. "There's another reason I wanted you to become familiar with our lands. If ever there's a threat, if Ridley were to return to arrest you, I want you to be ready to run and hide. You may not have a chance to saddle a horse. If ever I give you the word, I want you to take a horse and come here, to this place. There are plenty of trees for cover. Then get in the river and walk as far as ye can downstream. That will throw the dogs off your scent."

She swallowed and looked around at her surroundings. The perfect day dimmed as the sun went behind a cloud. In the shadows of the forest she imagined faces watching her, ready to attack.

She shivered but nodded again as Cameron gave her more instructions for getting to safety.

Eventually, they reached the place he'd mentioned where they could eat.

He helped her down and took her arm to guide her to a flat area near the river. He spread out a plaid and dropped a tied linen of food in the middle. She settled on the blanket, still looking over her shoulder in case Ridley and the hounds were coming for her. While Cameron went to get them water, she opened the linen to prepare their meal.

"I need to apologize to you," he said as he sat across from her on the edge of the blanket.

She waited for him to say more, having no idea what he'd done or why he'd bother to apologize for it.

"For last night," he explained.

She raised her head to look at him. She wasn't sure if he was mocking her. His sincere eyes studied her face.

Her training kicked in automatically, and she took a cautious approach.

"It's your right to drink if you wish. I have no say in the matter." She knew better than to nag or pester her husband about anything. The duke had made it clear that a husband had the final word, and she had no right to speak her displeasure.

"I think you have a say. If ye do not like it, you should feel free to tell me so."

She looked away, and he reached for her. She winced and drew back involuntarily, making him frown. Moving slower, he reached out again and took her chin between his fingers so he could tilt her face up.

"You spend too much time looking down. I like to see your eyes." His grin made her grin back. He made her feel like a young girl again, flirting with the stable groom. Back when life had been simple and it was safe to make eye contact with men.

"You were not so in your cups you couldn't find your bed or get out of it the next morning," she pointed out.

"Still, if you feel the urge to share your displeasure, I'd certainly listen." He winked at her.

Was this some kind of trick? It was as if he was luring her into a disagreement. She had spent the last five years staying clear of such, knowing she'd never win, and losing was more than she was willing to risk.

"I have no complaints." Instinct had her looking away again, but he tugged her chin up once again. She watched his eyes, expecting anger, but instead she saw what looked like disappointment.

Surely he wasn't upset that she hadn't nagged him or started an argument. She needed to reassure him.

"In fact," she said, "I hope you had a pleasant evening with your men."

"Aye, it was...pleasant." He definitely seemed disappointed. He turned his attention to the food and looked out over the river.

"Have I done something to upset you?" she asked when she could stand the silence no more.

"Hell, no." His surprise startled her. He placed his hand on her knee, and a thrill shot through her. "You've done nothing." His voice was now calmer. "It's just that we are strangers, you and me. I'm not sure how to change that. All the women—that is to say—the few women I've known... um...intimately, were lasses I'd known my whole life."

She nodded. He couldn't have been more of a stranger when they'd wed, and she'd been certain he was far from chaste. She'd seen the way the serving girls smiled at him. He was a handsome man. She knew she wasn't the only one who'd noticed.

"Being strangers as we are, it is expected that we would have differences of opinions. Ours isn't a love match, but that doesn't mean we can't make the best of the marriage. This is your home now, and I want you to be comfortable here. Which means you'll have to tell me if you don't like something."

"Of course. I understand." She did understand—not that it mattered. She would never complain to or about the man who had saved her life. As he said, it wasn't a love match. He hadn't wanted to get married at all, yet he was being very kind to her. She would not be so ungrateful as to make him change his lifestyle for her.

Kenna might have words freely with Lachlan, but that was different. They were in love. Kenna knew well enough it was safe to pester him.

"Good. Feel free to give me a good blasting if I need it." He nodded, and she smiled in return.

But she knew that would never happen. Not in a thousand years.

Chapter Thirteen

Cam knew Mari was intelligent enough to understand what he was telling her. But he could tell by her easy smile that she had no intention of ever starting a fight with him.

A good argument with no harm to one another, where they could make up happily afterward, was the easiest way to prove to Mari that she was truly safe with him. That even if he was angry at her, he wouldn't touch her harshly.

But that seemed unlikely to happen anytime soon.

Meanwhile, her letter sat heavily in his sporran.

When he'd awoken to find her gone and a letter with his name waiting on the table, he'd had a moment of panic, thinking she'd left him.

But the words he'd found on the page had given him a very different type of panic.

He'd read the letter three or four times. Enough to burn the words into his memory.

Dear Cameron,

Please forgive my cowardice in writing when I should

be brave enough to stand before you and speak these words. I'm afraid, for now at least, it's the only way for me to communicate without fear.

While I don't know you well, I know already that you are nothing like the duke, and as such you wouldn't harm me. As I've said, I know it, yet my body is set to protect itself whether the danger is real or imagined. Please don't find offense when I flinch away from your touch.

In truth, I enjoy your touch very much. Especially that of your lips. And the way your tongue caressed mine was also quite enjoyable.

At the memory of her bold words, his cock throbbed excitedly, making his kilt move. As if the beast wished to throw his garment aside all on its own. He let out a groan.

"Are you well?" she asked.

"Aye, a bit of a cramp in my leg." He shifted his leg to hide the bulge. *A bit of a cramp* was close enough to accurate.

The rest of her letter had been mild enough. She mentioned her hope that she would one day be able to tell him her thoughts in person, and closed with her name.

He hoped for her to be able to speak to him as well. Letters were fine for a start, but eventually they'd need to talk face-to-face. It was the reason he'd invited her out with him this morning. To encourage her to yell at him for his actions the night before.

How would his plan work if she refused to cooperate?

He'd just have to try harder to vex her. It was his experience that he was a natural when it came to annoying women. Surely his wife would find that out soon enough.

That night when he came in to go to bed, he kicked off his boots in the middle of the room, then tossed his clothing around as well. Their chamber was quite a mess when he finally slid under the blanket next to her.

She made not a peep about it. She didn't even give him a dirty look or so much as frown at the mess. Maybe she was a messy person and it didn't bother her.

"Did you throw your clothes about when you lived in London?" he asked. "I guess it was nice having a servant to clean up after you."

She shook her head and looked away. "No. I had to be scrupulously neat. Plus, my maid was my only friend. It made no sense to cause her more work unnecessarily. I always cleaned up after myself."

Another attempt to anger her had failed. She must have the patience of a saint.

He thought of changing the topic to her letter, but the way she clenched the blanket proved she was nervous enough in his presence. She'd written to him precisely so she wouldn't have to speak the words. He'd not force her.

"Tell me about your friend," he asked instead, to get her talking about something easier. If she wasn't going to yell at him for his rudeness or ask him to kiss her, they could at least keep the conversation flowing about something neutral.

He'd wake early and tidy the room before she had the chance to clean up after him.

"My maid's name was Lucy, and she was always there for me when I—" She stopped talking abruptly and looked as if she didn't know what to say next.

"It's fine. You can tell me anything, and I'll not judge you for it. I promise."

"My apologies." She smiled the awkward moment away. "She was always there for me, no matter what I needed. Whether it be to mend a dress that had gotten torn or to sit with me when I had trouble sleeping."

Cam knew there was more to her words. He wanted to

ask how often her dresses were torn and why she had trouble sleeping, but to do so would mean pushing her into telling him something she obviously wasn't ready to tell.

Not that he was so sure he would be ready to hear. The more he heard, the more he hated her late husband and the terrible things he'd done to cause her to live in the shadows.

He pulled her close as she continued to tell him carefully selected stories of her maid. She didn't hesitate to come into his arms and even snuggled against his chest to get comfortable.

It was progress.

He'd never had such a difficult time speaking to another person, but he'd not give up. This was too important. He would one day claim victory over her demons. He would never be able to love her, but he'd damn well treat her better than the duke. Her dead husband would not win this battle.

...

Mari woke at the sound of someone passing by outside her door. For a moment in the darkness she'd forgotten where she was and thought it was the duke coming for her in a fit of anger.

But he was gone. He couldn't hurt her anymore.

The night before, she had started looking for the letter when she'd heard Cameron's footsteps approaching. Abandoning her search, she'd jumped into bed and waited for him to mention it.

Instead, he'd thrown his boots about and just held her.

Had he found and read her letter, or had it perhaps fallen behind the stand?

Thirsty, she slid out from bed to get a drink and to take another look for the letter. The moonlight came in through the window on that side of the room, so she hoped she might find it.

If she did, she would toss it into the fire. She was silly to write such things.

Quietly, she made it around the corner at the foot of the bed and then tripped over some large, heavy object on the floor. She went down so hard she didn't have time to stop her fall and landed on her chin and cheek. She tasted blood as it welled from the corner of her lip.

Her ankle throbbed from hitting the thing on the floor, which she realized was Cameron's carelessly discarded boot.

"Mari! Mari?" he called anxiously from the bed.

"Down here," she muttered as she pushed herself up to a seated position.

"What happened?" he asked as he came to crouch next to her.

"I tripped."

"Tripped?" He took the boot she handed him. "Bloody hell. I'm so sorry. Are you all right?"

"I'm fine." Except she wasn't fine. Her jaw and cheek were on fire with the burn of a blossoming bruise. Her lip was swelling, too.

"I shouldn't have left my boots like that. I'm not normally messy, I just—" He didn't finish the sentence. Instead, he ran his hand over his face. "What were ye doing up in the middle of the night?"

"I was thirsty." She hoped that wouldn't make him angrier. It was clear he was mad, he just hadn't directed it toward her. It seemed he was put out with himself instead.

Still, her hands shook in fear as he hurried toward her. She prepared for the pain in her arm, the burn in her shoulder from being yanked to her feet. Or maybe he would grab her up by her hair.

But he only leaned down with compassion in his eyes.

"Let me put you back in bed and I'll get you something

to drink." He picked her up as if she weighed nothing and settled her gently on her side of the bed. "Did you want water? I could get you tea, or maybe a whisky would be good."

"Water is fine. Thank you." Whisky would have taken the edge off the pain, but it would also burn the open wound on her lip.

"I'm sorry. This is all my fault. I'm such an oaf."

He lit a candle and carried it back with him, along with her glass of water. "Bloody hell," he blurted when the light revealed the extent of her injuries. "You're bleeding. I'll run down to the loch to get ice-cold water."

"There's no need. I'll be fine." This was nothing compared to what the duke had done when he'd found disfavor in her actions. "It's nothing."

"Nothing? Your face is a mess, and look at your ankle. It's swollen."

"I assure you, I've had worse injuries and healed just fine." She'd said it to put his mind at ease, but her words had the opposite effect.

She could feel the rage coming off him, yet he spoke quietly. "You've been injured worse than this, on purpose, at the hands of your duke."

It wasn't a question, but she nodded. She wanted to add that he hadn't been *her duke*, but kept quiet.

He stood and turned away. She thought he might leave, but he went to the pitcher and came back with a wet cloth to clean the blood from her lip. She hissed when he pressed it to the cut, and she saw him go pale in the low light.

"I'm making it worse. I'll go get someone to help. I can't stand to hurt you more than I already have."

"No. Please. Don't wake anyone. It's not so bad, really. I can do it myself." She reached for the cloth, and he handed it over. She dabbed at the cut and he brought her a new cloth. Eventually it stopped bleeding, and she reached for the glass to drink, careful not to reopen the wound.

Touching her ankle, she knew it would be stiff and hard to walk on the next day, but it wasn't broken. A mild sprain, she guessed. She'd had the opportunity to diagnose many of her own injuries over the years.

She lay back, and Cameron was right there to help her. "Mari, I'm such a clod. Can you forgive me?"

"Of course. It wasn't your fault. It's your room. You're free to put your boots wherever you wish."

"It's *our* room," he corrected as he gently put his arm around her. "And you have every right to be angry with me. In fact, I would very much like it if you yelled at me. Please just tell me what a bugger I am."

She laughed and shook her head. "It was an accident. I know you didn't leave them there on purpose to cause me harm. Let's go to sleep. I'll be fine in the morning."

It was an odd experience having a man care for her to the point of doting. She'd never imagined such a thing. Her father had been more interested in a strategic marriage for her than her happiness or well-being. And of course the duke… He definitely hadn't cared about her needs.

But Cameron was still fluttering about the room in a futile attempt to soothe her and ease her pain. Pain he hadn't even caused.

She would need to be more cautious in the future, since her husband wasn't a tidy person. Funny, he'd seemed quite orderly before. In fact, the first time she was in his room it had been extremely neat.

Perhaps he'd been expecting company that day. Then she'd barged into his life and forced him into a marriage he didn't want.

He eventually settled into bed beside her and blew out the candle. "I'm sorry, Mari. I'll not do anything so foolish again."

"As I said, it's your room. I'm naught but an unwanted guest forced upon you by circumstance."

The bed moved, and she heard a sound in the darkness that sounded like laughter.

"It's true I never wished to marry, but I'd hardly call ye an unwanted guest. I definitely *want you*."

She felt warmth against her palm as his fingers interlaced with hers in an intimate way. Her face felt hot for a different reason, and she was grateful for the cover of darkness.

Mixed in with the tangle of physical feelings she'd never experienced, she also felt safe. This large man, whose body was honed for violence, made her feel protected and cherished.

The night she'd left London fleeing for her life, she'd only wanted to be safe. But now she thought she might also have the chance to be happy as well.

She'd often wondered what she'd done to earn such a terrible punishment as being married to the devil himself. Perhaps it wasn't a punishment, but a payment of sorts, in advance.

And perhaps it was now time to reap her earned reward.

Chapter Fourteen

Despite Mari's promise the night before, she wasn't fine in the morning, and Cam felt wretched. His wife looked like she'd lost a battle with a rival clan. The left side of her face was bruised and swollen. Her eye was blackened, and a dark scab sealed the cut on her lip.

When she got out of bed on her own after refusing his assistance, she stumbled and sat back down. Her ankle wasn't up for holding her weight.

He moaned at seeing her in pain. Pain he'd caused with his stupid attempt to bait her into an argument. He'd only wanted her to get mad at him and let down her guard. Instead he'd hurt her.

He reached for her. "Please, let me help. I think I'll be ill if you don't."

She took his hand and leaned on him as she took the next step, and the next. His tiny wife didn't make a sound despite her discomfort. She didn't complain or demand to stay in bed. It was as much a testament to her strength as it was the bad things she'd lived through.

She acted as though this was nothing. And maybe in comparison to what her husband had done to her, it was nothing. Anger rippled through Cam's muscles. The urge to hunt down the bastard and make him pay dearly brought the taste of copper to his mouth. If he could focus his anger on someone else, it might ease his guilt.

But his rage went unsated. The man was dead. His tiny warrior queen had defended herself and stopped the devil from hurting her ever again.

"You're so strong, Mari," he said as he helped her down the stairs one at a time.

"I don't think so." She laughed. "After all, I was bested by an empty boot."

He grinned halfheartedly at her joke and kissed the top of her head. "I find you to be strong, and I'll not listen to an argument." He winked to soften his words.

"Can you help me to the kitchen? I'd rather take my meal there than in the hall with everyone staring at me."

How often had she been forced to hide away so no one would question her injuries? He'd not allow her to feel shame for damage he'd caused.

"You don't need to hide. I'll explain what happened. The shame lies with me, and I'll face it like a man who was wrong."

A frown pulled at her lip for just a second, but it must have hurt, and her lips went flat instead.

"This is my fault, and I'll damn well tell everyone so," he insisted.

She glanced up at him in surprise then peeked into the hall. "If it's all the same with you, I'd rather go to the kitchen with my sister."

"Of course," he said, pushing away undeserved jealousy because she wanted the comfort of her sister instead of him. Of course she wouldn't want to be with him. He'd caused her this pain. She didn't know he'd done it on purpose, but he'd have to explain that to her at some point. The guilt would eat at him if he didn't.

In any case, it was best he spent some time away from her. He cared about her far more than he'd planned to. Sure, he'd wanted to enjoy certain pleasures of marriage with his wife, and sharing a friendship with the woman would make the years before them more bearable. But he needed to stay a safe distance so she'd not become attached to him.

That was what he told himself...but the truth was, he needed to make sure he didn't become attached to her, either.

He picked her up and carried her the rest of the way to the kitchens. At the door, he kicked it with his foot until it was opened. As he set Mari on a stool, the women all gasped and turned to glare at him.

"I deserve your ire and more," he said. "I left my boots out on the floor and she tripped. Do you have some of that nasty tea that lessens the pain?" He was fine with their disregard, but he wanted them to help Mari if they could.

"We do," Kenna said, her lips pressed together as she turned Mari's face one way and the other to appraise the damage.

"Her ankle is swollen as well. I'm such a fool. Can ye help her, please?"

"Yes." Kenna waved him to the door. "Go have your morning meal. We'll take care of her."

He waited there by the door despite his desire to flee their narrowed glares. "I want to help if I can." There was no way he'd be able to eat anything with blame tearing up his belly.

"You can't help, so just go away." Kenna patted his shoulder and smiled.

"It's fine. Go and have your meal," Mari said, and he realized she was trying to hide her pain for his benefit. She was sparing him more distress by pretending she wasn't hurting.

He blew out a breath. "I'll be back to take you where you need to go. I don't think you should walk with your ankle puffed up like that."

She nodded, and he turned to the door.

"Promise you'll wait for me to come back before you go anywhere."

"I promise," she said easily.

In the hall, he sat down, and a serving girl came rushing over with his meal. He waved her away. He was afraid to eat for fear it would come back up. The knots in his stomach only twisted tighter. He was supposed to be working with his men today, but at this rate he'd not be able to focus on his sword and would be sliced in two.

Nay. He'd not be good for anything until he confessed his sin.

• • •

"I truly did fall. Cameron didn't do this on purpose," Mari repeated. Again. She'd told the women the story as soon as her husband left.

They all looked at one another and nodded.

"Of course we know Cam didn't do this," Kenna said while stirring the foul-smelling brew. "He would never hurt a woman. He's a wreck because you're hurt and feels responsible, which he should—how careless to leave his boots lying about!—but he's a man who would sooner die than cause his woman harm."

Mari knew this in her heart, but the duke had also seemed peaceable in public though truly was not. Sometimes people acted one way when around others and another in private.

She'd only been in the kitchen a little while when Cameron stuck his head in again. "Are you well?"

"Yes. I feel better now that Kenna forced this sorry excuse

for tea down my throat." She and Kenna shared a smile.

"You're not in pain."

"Not much." She thought her answer would appease him, but he frowned and rubbed his forehead. "Really, not at all," she amended, hoping it would soothe the sorrowful look from his face. When it didn't help, she gave him a smile.

From the strained look on his face, her smile must not have been all that reassuring. When she felt the trickle of blood from the opened wound, she understood. She was a mess.

"It's not your fault," she offered.

Espath harrumphed. "Mayhap next time you won't leave your boots lying about so someone might fall over them," she scolded him.

With a groan and another apology, he backed away and left the kitchen.

"I don't know what he's about. Normally he's a very tidy man." Kenna shook her head and went back to her ministrations with Mari's ankle.

"You shouldn't be working," Mari said, watching the door. There would be trouble if Lachlan came in and saw Kenna bending over her ankle.

"You do remember I have two wee boys already who keep me moving all day? I'm glad for this small rest. I love them dearly, but all their energy… They get it by draining other people, I think."

They laughed together.

"Try walking on it now," Kenna ordered.

Mari took a step and then another. She nodded. "I wouldn't want to walk for miles, but it's not so bad now. Thank you."

Kenna gave a pleased smile. "Good."

"I'll try my best not to limp in front of Cameron. I don't want to pile more guilt upon him."

Kenna's eyes went wide. "Are ye mad? You're in the perfect position to get whatever your heart desires. He's so guilt-ridden he'd likely do anything for you."

"Anything?" Mari wondered with a raised brow…though more to herself.

"Well, perhaps not that. Men have a funny idea that they will hurt you worse if they give in to their randy ways. They think us fragile and breakable."

"Anyway, I wouldn't want him to do…that…simply because he felt guilty."

Kenna chuckled. "I'm sure it would be no hardship for him. You should give it a try."

For the rest of the day, it seemed Cameron avoided her. Twice she'd seen him come into the hall, and both times as soon as he saw her he turned and left again.

Was he repulsed by her injuries? A shiver of fear went down her spine at the memory of her late husband looking on her with disgust. She swallowed down her unease.

Cameron was nothing like Endsmere. He was kind and gentle.

Thanks to Kenna's suggestion, Mari had been thinking of the things she might ask for, now that Cameron was pliable to her wishes.

Things like kisses and touches. And other things that made her face heat.

Despite coming up with a number of good fantasies, she knew she'd be too frightened to ask Cameron for what she wanted. Though it wouldn't make a difference if he stayed away from her until she healed.

She almost hoped he had gotten her letter. She thought about the words she'd written. How she'd told him she liked his kiss.

She was sitting in the corner of the hall working on her sister's embroidery with her foot propped up per Kenna's instructions when the young man, Liam, came in and handed her a letter.

"The war chief asked me to deliver this to you."

"Thank you," she said with a puzzled nod.

"Yes, madam."

As soon as he was gone she opened the letter and found a page full of Cameron's large script. He seemed to have no regard for the size of the paper. It reminded her of how he took up the majority of their bed. She smiled until her lip pinched.

Dearest wife,

I canna tell ye how truly sorry I am for causing you this pain. I ken you're quick to forgive me, and I'll not play the coward and confess my sins in a letter. Just know that I'll stand before ye soon and state my wrongdoings. I can only hope you'll forgive me.

I must also apologize for not acknowledging your letter yesterday. I'm not one for correspondence, and I was impatient to move forward. But I now see the allure of the written word. And how easy it is to pour your soul onto a page.

Please know you are not alone in wanting physical pleasure between us. I think of ye in that way most of my waking hours, and many of my sleeping hours as well.

I fear I've ruined any chance for further kissing in the near future, but know I will take advantage of the opportunity if you feel me worthy of such affections.

Your repentant husband,
Cam

Another smile split her lip open again, but she didn't mind. She was too overcome with joy. He'd written to her. He said he wanted to kiss her and thought about it often. He also thought she wouldn't want him to. She went to Kenna's solar to retrieve a paper and quill.

She'd just have to tell him how wrong he was.

Chapter Fifteen

"I'm going to bloody kill you." Cam grabbed Bryce up by his shirt, lifting the man off the ground.

"What did I do?"

"You suggested I should be messy and toss my things about." Cam waved a hand in the air as he dropped Bryce back to his feet. "Did you see my wife? She's hurt, and it's all because I listened to your stupid talk. God bless Maggie for dealing with the likes of you for the too-few years she was here with us."

"Do not speak of Maggie." Bryce's dark eyes flashed in warning.

Cam had overstepped, but he wanted someone else to blame for Mari's pain, and Bryce was somewhat responsible. Even if he hadn't been the one to throw his boot in the path of Cam's poor wife. *Bloody hell.*

"I'm sorry." He ran his hands through his hair. "How do people stand this? She's so little and delicate. I don't want to hurt her."

Leaving his boots out where she might trip was bad

enough, but if she consented to lie with him, what then? How would he make love to her without injury?

"Even the dainty ones are stronger than you think. They birth babes, Cam. They're not weak. You or I wouldn't stand it."

"Christ. What if I get a babe on her? I should keep my bloody hands to myself. I'm going to go stay in the woods until we're old and gray. Then I'll be too feeble to cause her harm."

"You're talking nonsense. You wouldn't make it two days knowing food and a warm woman await you here."

Cam wanted to argue, but Bryce was right. And it wasn't the food that was the biggest lure.

"I need to talk to her."

He'd kept his distance the entire day. Using her method of communicating by letter was a bit easier than speaking to her directly. He hadn't been strong enough to face her most of the day. Seeing her limping, with her beautiful face bruised, made his chest hurt as if he'd been stabbed through.

But it was time to confess. Time to face it straight on like the warrior he was. If she hated him, it would make things easier for both of them. He'd find a place to sleep in the hall, and they'd not need to speak again.

He should want that. It would give him a perfect excuse if Lach complained of the arrangement.

But he hoped for something else.

He stood at their chamber door and rested his head against the wood. He was out of ideas and ways to make his wife comfortable with him. Rather than come up with another bungled plan, he decided to be honest and hope for the best.

He entered to find her already in bed with the covers pulled up like a shield, as on the other nights she'd been in bed when he arrived. He closed and barred the door and went to sit next to her by the bed. As usual, she flinched when he moved too quickly.

He let out a breath. "You remember the talk we had down by the river? When I told you to tell me if you dinna like something I did or didna do?"

"Yes. I remember."

"But you've not said anything. Not when I flirted with the serving girl right in front of you the other evening. Not about my clothes scattered about the room. Not even about my boots in the middle of the floor causing you to trip and injure yourself. Nothing. Not so much as a peep to show your displeasure."

She hesitated, then said, "It almost sounds as if you did those things on purpose to earn my ire."

"That would be bloody foolish." His gaze glanced away from hers. "But it's also true." He winced. *Christ almighty.* "I'm sorry."

"You *wanted* me to be angry with you?" She looked confused, and rightfully so, but still not angry.

"Yes—no. I wanted you to feel comfortable enough to argue with me. I thought if we had a disagreement and you and I scrapped a bit, when it was over you would see I hadn't hurt ye, and you would no longer be afraid of me."

Damn Liam for suggesting such a plan. And damn Bryce and Lach for agreeing with such a farce. But mostly, damn himself for thinking this was the way to go about making someone feel safe. What an arse he was.

She shifted slightly. "I appreciate your efforts—I guess—but I'm not afraid of you, Cameron."

"Nay?" He reached for her, his heart filled with hope, but she instantly pulled away, her eyes wide with the same fear he saw each time he moved too quickly.

He let out a breath. "Aye, I can see that. Never mind. I'll bed down in the hall. You can sleep here in peace." He stood to leave again.

"No. Wait." She slid from the bed and hobbled over to him.

He grimaced, hating that she was obviously still in pain.

"As I said in my letter…it's not you that I fear. I know violence is not your way. But my body remembers the past and reacts without my consent. Just by instinct. I can't help it."

He shook his head. "It's not just your body. You're a timid little mouse around me, and I can't take it. If I do something wrong, you should feel free to let me have it. I know he hurt you, but I'm not the duke. Never would I hurt you."

Cam turned for the door but stopped when she placed her hand on his arm.

She stepped closer, still touching him. She swallowed and looked him in the eye. "You take all the covers and leave me none."

One foot moved back and her hand dropped, but she stayed before him. He could see the strength it took for her to stand there and not retreat.

Come on, Mari. You can do this. If she was ready to do battle, he would help her along.

He crossed his arms in his most imposing stance. "I'm bigger than you. I deserve more of the blankets, don't you think?"

She pressed her slightly trembling lips together. "Maybe. But I should get some. It's only fair."

"It's my bed," he pointed out and leaned over her.

She winced away, but after a few seconds she straightened and leaned toward him. "It's *our* bed. We're married," she snapped. Then looked surprised and rather proud of herself.

He refrained from smiling, though his heart was flying with joy. His wife was scrapping with him. She felt safe enough to argue. He'd make sure not to take it too far, but at the moment he was enjoying her spark.

Slowly, he raised his hands to her shoulders. He squeezed gently in encouragement. "You snore," he accused, and reveled in the way her eyes went wide with outrage.

"I do *not* snore." Her voice rose into a disgruntled squeak.

"Aye. I dream I'm lying with a sow from the barns and wake to find ye beside me."

When it was clear she was so angry she couldn't find words, he bent and kissed her. Careful of her wounds, he pulled her into his arms in a silent promise never to let go. And kissed her again.

...

One moment Mari was pulling in breath to scream at her husband, and the next her body was crushed to his. His lips crashed down on hers and his large arms wrapped around her, pulling her close.

She was startled and alarmed at first, but he softened the kiss. When she realized what he'd done she relaxed against him.

He released her just enough to free his hands to roam down her back. A sound escaped her lips that she'd never made before in her life. A pleasure-filled moan. He answered with an enticing groan of his own.

His tongue tickled her lips, and she opened enough for him to enter and tease her. His heat surrounded her, and she shivered with nervous excitement.

"You don't really snore," he said as his lips found her neck.

"I don't mind that you take the blankets," she confessed. "It means I get to snuggle against you while you sleep."

He raised his head to look at her with a sly grin. "I steal the blankets so you have no choice but to sleep closer against me."

"You naughty—" She didn't have a chance to finish the sentence because he was kissing her again. Gentle kisses intentionally kept away from the side of her mouth that was cut.

She hadn't noticed he'd moved her backward until the backs of her thighs touched the edge of the bed.

The bed.

She knew what would happen next. Or what should.

When she tensed, he backed away, giving her room. "What is it? Did I hurt ye?"

She almost cried at the difference between the two men she'd married. One constantly worried he'd hurt her when he had not, while the first had hurt her deliberately over and over with no regret.

However, that was not what worried her at the moment. She had braved an argument with Cameron only to end up faced with the next problem.

The marital bed.

It had always been the source of her late husband's anger, but she didn't want to risk turning Cameron away. He'd told her she could tell him anything and he wouldn't be angry. But certainly he had expectations now. She did not want to disappoint him.

There was no time to write it in a letter. She'd have to figure out a way to communicate her concerns.

Instead of speaking, she reached for him and drew him down to kiss her again. Because of his response to her, she felt more powerful than she ever had before. She had initiated this kiss and it was wonderful.

They got caught up again in their kiss. Her earlier worries faded slightly as passion took over.

"I want you," he whispered. "Can I remove your shift?"

The fact that he asked meant the world to her. She

nodded, even as her heart sank. Things between them would change as soon as he saw her body.

She expected him to reach for her immediately, but instead he removed his own shirt, freeing it from his waistband and pulling it over his head in one fluid movement. He smiled and stepped closer. She looked up from the sight of his sculpted chest into his happy, golden eyes. Slowly he reached for her.

It felt so good when her body didn't automatically flinch away. If he took it slowly enough, perhaps she could control those negative reactions after all.

He tugged up her gown and pulled it over her head. She couldn't help but cover her chest with her arms, yet another thing her body did without her permission.

Gently he took her wrists in his hands and drew them aside so he could look at her. His head tilted to the side, and his eyes narrowed on her breasts.

Oh, God. Here it comes—the disgust, the revulsion.

She tried desperately to cover herself, but he didn't release her hands.

A familiar panic began to rise at being held. Her heart pounded, and she had to take a deep breath to remain calm. This was Cameron. He would release her. She only needed to ask.

She didn't.

"Do they hurt you still?" His voice cracked as his gaze lingered on the scars across her breasts.

"No. They are years old," she said, her face flaming.

"I wish the bastard wasna already dead so I could have the pleasure of killing him myself."

The vehemence of Cameron's vengeance didn't scare her. He was a war chief, a fierce warrior who had killed men. Yet, she was not afraid of him. At least not at the moment.

"He was my enemy," she said quietly, as she'd told Kenna.

"Aye. I hope someday you will stop having to fight him in

your dreams."

He spoke of her nightmares and the fear that still lived in her mind and in the way her body responded.

"I do not fear you, Cameron MacKinlay." She lifted her chin to show her courage. It was the truth, she wasn't afraid of physical harm.

However, she was worried about what would happen next.

He kissed her as his fingers loosened her braid and tangled in her hair. She reached up, placing her hands on his broad shoulders, his neck and shoulder muscles moving under her palms as he bent to kiss her. Such power harnessed by such a kind heart.

She gasped in surprise when he touched her breasts, lifting them into his hands and kneading them tenderly. It was...pleasant, but she felt acutely self-conscious about all the scars.

Then he went to his knees before her and kissed her stomach, her abdomen, and breasts, and her thoughts scattered in a flood of pleasure. He paid special attention to her left breast, where the nipple was twisted and puckered.

She'd expected him to be disgusted when he saw her naked, but his groan of need told her otherwise. He truly didn't mind the scars. He stood, and the hardness of his arousal pushed against her through his kilt.

She didn't want the barrier of fabric between them any longer. Reaching for his belt, her fingers trembled as she made short work of the buckle. His kilt dropped to the floor with a *thump*. She was both too afraid to look and too excited not to.

She glanced down and wished she hadn't. She swallowed in alarm, but he just chuckled with a smug grin.

"Not only was he an evil bastard, but he was lacking as well, aye?" He shook his head. "Nay, I'm sorry. I don't want thoughts of him between us. I'll take care of you, Mari. I promise, we will get on well together, and it will be better than it ever was."

She nodded in firm agreement. He didn't know how right he was.

Now was the time to tell him the truth.

Chapter Sixteen

Cam was still berating himself for his smugness. But when he saw the surprise on Mari's face when she looked upon him naked, he hadn't been able to help himself.

He'd heard English men were hung like twigs, and her shock proved it must be so.

She pulled back to look down at him again and swallowed. He waited for her to speak. It was clear she wanted to say something.

Whatever it was, he would soothe her concerns so he could make her his wife in every way. He would care for her and see to her pleasure. Something it was clear her prig of a husband hadn't done.

The scars on her breasts were made with a savage blade by someone with a callous heart. She'd covered her breasts again, and he thought maybe she was still self-conscious of her marks.

With his kilt already on the floor thanks to his wife, he tugged off his boots. He moved the candle closer, setting it on the stand beside the bed so the light splashed across his chest, enhancing his own scars.

"I am marked by battle as well. Our scars are proof we have faced horrible things and lived." He took her hands and gently pulled them away to place them on his chest. Her cool skin caused a shiver against his heated flesh. "Don't ever be ashamed. You are beautiful."

She smiled briefly before focusing intently on him. Her fingers traced over his many scars. Some were no more than nicks and scratches along the surface of his skin. Some were deeper wounds he'd thought might end him.

"You are beautiful as well, husband." She frowned. "I hope you are not offended. I guess that was not an appropriate compliment for a man." She licked her lips nervously. Not in the seductive way some of the lasses in the village did it.

He knew she was no longer afraid of him in the physical sense. But he could see she was uneasy about the act they were moving toward.

"I am not offended," he reassured her as he took her trembling hand and held it tight against his heart. "If ye don't want to do this, we won't. We have plenty of time to make sure you're comfortable."

She winced and glanced away. "That's just it. I don't think it's possible for me ever to be *comfortable*."

"Did he hurt you in that way as well?" Cam asked.

He'd not considered that possibility. Probably because the thought of anyone forcing her repulsed him. He stepped back. He'd not add to her pain. His needs were nothing when compared to her anxiety.

She shook her head. "No, that's the thing. He never touched me in that way. I am still a— I'm a virgin."

• • •

Cameron stepped away from Mari so fast one might think

she was infested with fleas. Her heart hurt at his reaction, but his shock quickly changed to confusion.

"But... You were married for years."

"Yes. And throughout all the horrific days of our life together, he never consummated our marriage."

Cameron looked skeptical. She didn't blame him; it did seem impossible. That someone so horrid had not taken liberties was one of the few things she had to be thankful for in the years of her marriage.

"I may not know exactly what goes on between a man and wife, but I know enough that I'm quite sure it never happened. Especially since my late husband never spent a moment in my bed."

Cam nodded and looked at her breasts again. This time she didn't attempt to shield herself from his gaze. He'd told her not to be ashamed. She wasn't.

He walked around her, and she trembled under his gaze.

"You're perfect, Mari. I've never seen anyone more beautiful in my life."

He made his way around to her front. He didn't flinch or skim over looking at her chest; instead, his eyes paused in their movement and he reached out to caress the side of her breast.

"I'm far from perfect." She'd hardly seen herself in years, always looking away whenever she was naked in front of a looking glass.

"I know ye may hate what the scars mean to you, but they don't detract from your beauty. Instead, I see strength and courage. I'm so glad you didn't let him win. I would have missed out on knowing you."

A tear slipped down her cheek when she thought of how close a thing it had been.

Cameron kissed the tear away and kissed her lips briefly. He stepped even closer and wrapped his arms loosely around her waist.

Leaning down, he pressed his forehead against hers. "I do not wish to speak of him again tonight, unless you need to tell me something. I feel we have been given a great gift. This first time for you will belong only to us. That is, if you wish to continue."

"I do," she said shyly.

He raised his head and smiled down at her. "My brave lass."

He brushed her long hair back and rested his hands upon her shoulders. "We'll ease our way through this together. I'll trust you to tell me if I do something you like or don't like. That way, we can slowly learn one another and build upon the enjoyment."

She nodded. Impatient to get underway, she stood on tiptoe so she could reach his lips.

His tongue reached into her mouth, stroking hers, and she moaned at the contact. She might not be skilled, but she knew this was what it was supposed to feel like in a husband's embrace.

Exciting, yet safe.

He laid her on the bed, and she scooted backward to make room for him. But he didn't lie next to her, he crawled over her, not letting his weight rest on her but caging her in with his arms. Her heart raced for a fleeting moment, but when his lips touched her throat, her collarbone, her breasts, she let out the breath she'd been holding.

He didn't stop at her chest. He continued down her body, stopping here and there to place kisses. Her ribs were ticklish. His touch caused her to jump and laugh. So different from before, when her body had reacted in fear.

She felt his lips pull up in a smile against her skin as he placed his next kiss on her hip bone. She assumed he would circle back up, but he continued down her leg. The kisses above her knee and along her ankle sent a jolt of yearning to her core. The man must know some dark craft to send such intense sensations from one part of her body to another. Finally, after placing a kiss on the arch of her foot, he began kissing his way back up her body, stopping in different places as he made his way up her other leg. This time, instead of moving along her hip, he turned inward.

His large hand gently pushed her legs apart. She hesitated for a second before aiding the movement. He'd already seen her breasts; she didn't mind that he saw the rest of her.

He was her husband, and it was normal for a man to want a woman.

When his lips touched her heat, she jumped again, this time in surprise. She hadn't known he would kiss her there. She wished she had asked Kenna and the other women for more details, but sharing her inadequacies meant admitting she'd never been a true wife.

Another moan escaped her as he stroked his tongue over her. Slowly, he slid one thick finger inside her, and she shifted closer, needing something she had no words for.

As when she was afraid, her body moved without her telling it to. She writhed and tensed as he continued touching her, building her up for…something.

"Let go, Mari. It's fine. It's good, I promise ye."

She couldn't catch her breath or quiet her sounds. When he curved his finger just the slightest bit, he touched a place that shattered her. She cried out and gripped the blanket under her as her body throbbed and convulsed in the most blissful way.

He didn't stop his touches, so the pulses continued on and on until she was limp and wrecked. She hadn't even noticed when he'd moved over her until she opened her eyes to see him smiling above her.

"Did you like that?" he asked.

Right. She was supposed to tell him if she liked something.

She nodded in wonder. "Yes. I— I did. Most definitely. Very much."

He laughed, but she wasn't bothered. He seemed so happy, she didn't mind.

"I'll give you a moment to catch your breath before we continue."

Continue? She could barely move. Though she did feel better when he slid to his side and began trailing his fingers over her sensitized body. She loved his touch.

Then she realized he was the one doing all the touching. Surely she should be touching him back? She shifted to her side, as well, and reached out, placing her hand against his chest. The heat of his skin warmed her palm as she stroked down and across his stomach, following the path of hair that started at his navel and moved toward the thicket between his legs. At first she avoided his cock, not sure what to do with it. As if it had a mind of its own, it lurched out, touching her hand.

She laughed and looked up at him. "Did you do that on purpose?"

"Nay. The wee beast does tricks to gain attention."

She shook her head. "I'd certainly not call him *wee*." She bit her lip, wondering how this would possibly fit inside her. "He's terribly imposing."

She wrapped her fingers around him and frowned at the width. Her fingers barely touched around it.

Just as she was about to tell him it wouldn't work, he groaned and placed his hand over hers, guiding her in the way he liked to be touched. Once she'd gotten the way of it, he released her to her own rhythm.

A powerful force came over her as she controlled his pleasure. Seeing him close his eyes and toss his head in the same sweet sensations she'd felt caused her body to rouse again.

Perhaps men were not so different from women when it came to pleasure. Following that logic, she bent to kiss his nipple, flicking her tongue as he'd done to her.

"Christ." He pulled her hand away and she jumped back.

"I'm sorry!" She was quick to apologize out of habit.

He kept his eyes closed and shook his head. "Don't apologize, lass. You did nothing wrong. It just feels so damn good. I don't want it to be over too soon. There's more I wish to show you."

She wanted to tell him it was fine. What she'd had already was enough, but touching him made her yearn for the more he spoke of.

She pressed closer to kiss him.

With his hands around her waist, he lifted her on top of him so her legs straddled his sides. His manhood rested in the cleft between her legs, and she couldn't stop herself from pressing against it.

The moisture from her body covered his as she slid against him.

"God, Mari," he groaned. "I need to be inside ye."

She agreed but didn't know how to go about such a thing. She'd always been told she would be on her back and her husband would lie atop her. This arrangement, with her on top, was not expected.

She moved to one side, but he stayed her with his hands on her hips.

"Nay. We'll do it like this the first time. That way you can control it. You've not had near enough control over what happens to your body in the past. Tonight will be different."

When he looked at her, she nearly broke into tears at the compassion in his warm whisky eyes.

"You'll help me do it right?" she asked.

"Aye, but you're a clever lass and will do just fine. Let

your body guide you."

Using his hand, he grasped his cock and held it up as if in invitation. If she understood correctly, she should just slide down and allow her body to envelop his.

He rubbed the end of his member against her, and she moaned at the pleasure. He stopped at her entrance. She moved down slightly, and his hands gripped her waist. Not pulling her down, just holding on to her as if he needed her to help him.

She slid down a bit farther and encountered a tight pinch. Sucking in a quick breath, she retreated slightly, back to where it felt good. She'd known for most of her life that losing her maidenhead would be painful. How painful, she wasn't quite sure. She'd been told by her stepmother's maid it was a terrible thing. But then Kenna had said it was quick and well worth the small discomfort because what came afterward was so magnificent.

Mari imagined the truth lay somewhere in between.

"If you're not ready…" Cam said, his voice tight with need.

She bent to kiss him. He was tense with desperation, yet he was willing to stop if she wished it.

She shook her head. "No. I'm fine."

Determined to be Cameron's wife in every sense, she pushed down until her husband filled her completely.

Body and soul.

Chapter Seventeen

Cam gasped when Mari took him in one quick clench of heat. He wasn't expecting the assault to be so complete and winced at the pull of his body to press up from the bed to fill her deeper.

He stayed still, wanting to give her time to get accustomed to his size.

After a few moments he stroked her back and bottom. "Whenever you're ready, the next step is just to move up and down at whatever pace feels good to you."

She sat up, and he gasped again at the friction. She was so tight even the smallest movement clenched him in a wave of heat. He needed to make this good for her, yet his instincts called for him to push up into her immediately and spill his seed deep in her body.

She moved the slightest bit, and he remained still. She moved a little more as she gradually rose upward. When she was almost free of him she started to descend again. Mercilessly slow, killing him by inches.

"Hmm," she said.

"What's *hmm* mean?" he asked, opening his eyes to see her hair falling around them.

She smiled. "It doesn't hurt anymore."

"That's good." It was the other reason he'd positioned her on top. He didn't think he'd have the courage to push his way into her, knowing it would cause her pain. He'd made her a promise, and even though it was for a good reason, he didn't feel comfortable breaking his word.

She began to pick up speed, and he watched her as she found her way. Placing her hands on his chest, then his stomach, she sat up and rode him like a skilled lover.

Her head fell back, and a whimper of pleasure left her lips. Watching her had his body ready to spend. He reached toward where they were joined and used the pressure of his thumb against her as she rocked her body onto his.

The whimper grew into a moan, then she called out as her body grasped his in waves of delight. His name filled the room as she reached her release. Unable to hold back, he thrust up into her the few times needed to finish him. She had already collapsed on his chest as he grunted with the force of his own climax.

The moments after were lost to him. When he regained enough of himself to move, he kissed her hair and her forehead. She raised her head to look at him, and he kissed her lips.

"Are you well?" he asked when she said nothing. Worry creased his brow.

"I'm so well, I don't think I'll ever be anything else but well for as long as I live."

He smiled and guided her to his side so he could cover them with the blanket. "Rest now. The night is young. We'll need our strength."

"You mean we'll do it again? Tonight?"

"If you're hurting we can wait—"

"No," she said so fast he smiled. "I'm fine."

"Now that I've gotten a taste of you, wife, I'll want another and another. You'll have to chase me away from ye with a sharp stick."

She laughed as he snuggled against her and kissed her neck. "I'll be sure to get a very sharp one, then. In the morning."

He backed away to catch her gaze, serious now. "If you're not feeling up to it, you must say so. You may be sore this first time, and I don't want you to have any regrets from our first night together."

She smiled. "I'll tell you, I promise."

He kissed her again and closed his eyes. Not only had they taken a big step together, but she felt comfortable enough to tell him if she couldn't abide him. He was so happy he could have gone out to the battlements and shouted for all the world to hear. Except he was much too exhausted for so much activity.

It wasn't but maybe an hour later when she stirred in his arms enough to waken him. They were still naked, and her round arse was wedged up nicely against his cock.

It was an easy thing to position himself to slide into her. It felt as though he'd come home. When she ground her body back to meet his, he grunted and held her still. "I'll not last long if you keep that up. Now settle and let me tend to you."

She laughed at his scold and clenched around him, causing him to hiss with pleasure.

"You transformed from a meek maiden into a lustful minx right before my eyes. I don't know how to handle ye."

"Perhaps I simply want to help you along," she said with another breathy laugh. She was teasing him.

He'd need to be careful, or sharing pleasure with each other could shift into something he had vowed to avoid since swearing his oath as war chief.

Tonight had been wonderful. But he told himself once again, love was not for them.

...

Mari pushed back and gasped as she stretched in the most wonderful way at her husband's invasion. In this position it felt different. The familiar pleasure she'd experienced twice already began to stir deep in her belly.

She'd always expected the act to be disgusting. Something to be done with as quickly as possible. But with Cameron, she found herself wishing it could go on forever.

The deep thrusts of his cock were exquisite, but there were other things that added to the experience. His touch on her breasts, his breath on her neck. The sounds he made, and the way he said her name in a tone that spoke of desperation and pleasure, as though she was the only person on earth who could satisfy his needs.

She knew, of course, that wasn't true. One body was as good as the next for such things, she imagined. But she had to think there was something special between them for it to be so unbelievably good.

Her pleasure continued to build, and she panted his name.

"That's it, lass, take your pleasure."

Like the other times, her body clenched around his in rhythmic spasms of intense delight. She cried out, still shocked by the force of the convulsions.

Cameron tensed and let out a groan as his heat filled her. He didn't move away. Still inside her, he pulled her tighter against him.

"You're lovely," he whispered, then his breath evened out in slumber.

Smiling into the darkness, she caressed the large arm

wrapped around her.

"You're rather lovely yourself."

She knew it would be an easy thing to let her heart follow her body into the pleasure of this new marriage. But her smile faltered as worry trickled in to disturb her happiness. If she allowed herself to fall in love, it might be impossible to leave him if ever it became necessary.

The next morning, with the light shining in his chamber, everything looked different. Brighter somehow. Full of hope and promise. Her body zinged with pleasure and a bit of soreness.

Cameron was still sleeping against her back, though he'd slipped out of her while they'd slept.

"Are you awake finally?" he asked, causing her to jump.

"I thought you were still sleeping."

"Nay. I've been awake for an hour. Just lying here watching the sun change the color of your hair as it came up."

"That sounds horribly boring. You shouldn't have let me keep you."

He laughed. "It wasn't boring at all. And I've no place to be but here."

Except that wasn't really true. He normally would have gathered his men to practice their drills. So they would be ready if ever Lachlan gave approval for a takeover of the McCurdy clan.

While she'd understood his impatience, a larger part of her was glad her new brother-in-law resisted. Staying at Dunardry meant there was less risk of danger.

She turned to see him propped up on his elbow. He was still very naked, and she felt the heat on her cheeks when her gaze drifted low enough to see his manhood resting against his thigh.

He reached out to caress her cheek, and she only twitched the slightest bit. She knew he noticed, but didn't say anything or remove his hand.

"I wonder if you'll ever lose that maidenly blush," he mused with a smile on his beautiful lips. Lips that had touched her body in so many places the night before.

Another wave of heat washed over her face. And below.

"Don't fash. It suits you."

When she looked up into his honey eyes, she saw curiosity. His lips opened to speak, but he said nothing. Clearly he wanted to say something but hesitated.

"You told me we should feel safe to tell each other anything. Did I misunderstand?" she asked when he looked away from her.

She didn't want that distance from before to return.

He chuckled and shook his head. "No. You didn't misunderstand. And I will talk to you about this. It's just that I don't want to ruin this moment."

She had an idea what it was he wanted to discuss.

Sliding closer to him, she kissed his cheek. "Go ahead. He cannot hurt me anymore. I'll not give him the power to ruin anything in my life ever again."

"Don't get me wrong, I'm beyond pleased to be the first to lie with you. It's just I'm not sure how you remained a virgin. Men have urges, and I expected a violent man like the duke would see to them whether ye wanted him to or not."

She glanced away in embarrassment.

"This is nothing you should feel shamed about. I'm glad you were spared that, at least. But I can't understand why he'd never touch you. I wanted you in my bed the minute you climbed down from my shoulders."

She smiled at her husband's honesty. It was nice to be wanted, treasured.

"I think he wasn't able to—" Her lips pressed together. She didn't want to have to tell this kind man who had admitted he'd desired her that her last husband had been repulsed. But they were not keeping secrets from one another...

"He beat you because you didn't provide him with an heir, but he never bedded you so you could give him one." Cameron shook his head and let out a breath. "The bastard."

"I thought it was me. I thought I wasn't appealing. Or that I hadn't done something right."

"You're the most appealing woman I've ever laid eyes on. I want ye so bad I ache with the need to touch you. Believe me. It wasn't you, Mari."

She nodded. "Last night when you looked at me—even with my scars—and weren't disgusted, I knew I must have been wrong about his reasons."

"You were very wrong." Cameron winked and traced a finger across her bare stomach. "You're stunning."

Her lips pulled up slightly so he would know his words pleased her. What woman didn't want to feel attractive?

Leaning over, he kissed her, and she responded by melting against him. Her soft curves matched perfectly against his hard muscles. She gasped when his male hardness jabbed her in the side.

"As you can see, I don't have any problems responding to you. It wasn't you. Don't think it for a minute." He kissed along her jaw and down her neck.

Her soft moan of arousal spurred him to move lower. He bent so he could draw in one of her nipples.

"I had planned to be the courteous lover who gave you peace today, but I must beg ye to forgive my eagerness to call upon you again. I can't seem to help myself."

"I am just as eager to receive you." She laughed at the way they made it sound like a visit.

When he pulled her under him, her laughter drifted off into a different form of bliss.

Chapter Eighteen

Mari rested her hand on Cam's arm and allowed him to escort her down for a rather late morning meal. He noticed the slowness of her gait and frowned.

He'd hurt her despite his promise. Damn it!

When they'd finally left their bed, he aided in washing her body, and she helped him with his. Then he helped her dress for the day, putting an extra knot in her corset as a reminder he needed to let her recover from the enthusiasm of his ardor.

She nearly fell on the last step, and he supported her, turning her to face him.

"God, I'm sorry, Mari. I was too rough with you."

"No." She smiled. "It's my ankle that still bothers me."

He blinked, having forgotten about the earlier injury he'd caused. "I can't ever seem to do right by ye."

"Oh, I wouldn't say that. I feel very right this morning." She gave him a saucy wink that might have made him grab her up and carry her back to their room if not for knowing of that blasted knot in her strings.

"Shall I carry you to the table?" he offered. "I wouldn't

mind having a reason to press your body against mine. And not just because it would disguise my obvious discomfort." He glanced down at the place where his kilt tented out and wondered if he'd ever grow tired of making love to her.

...

The answer turned out to be no. At least not in the three weeks since Cam first had Mari naked in his bed. Each night since, he had followed her to their chamber.

His men had mocked him in the mornings, calling him a needy pup, but he didn't care. He simply smiled wide and pushed them harder during their drills as punishment.

If it had been just him, he might have found a way to rein in his urges, but Mari wanted him just as often, and he'd not let her go unsatisfied. It wouldn't be the husbandly thing to do. Instead, he serviced her as often as she liked, and made sure to keep his heart secure. It was getting more and more difficult as she became familiar enough with him to be playful and happy. He still never got her to scrapping with him, but he knew it wasn't from fear. They got on well, especially since he'd stopped doing things on purpose to anger her.

They fell into an easy routine. She would go to the kitchen in the morning with the other ladies, and he would push his men most of the day in drills. Later, he would make his rounds of the border.

Occasionally Mari would ride with him. Even more frequently, they would find a quiet place hidden in the trees to satisfy their needs when the time before retiring for the evening seemed too far away.

"I'd like to ride the borders with you today," Lach told Cam as he headed for the stables.

But Cam had already made plans with Mari. He'd even shared his plans for what he wanted to do with her when they were alone.

"Aye?" Cam said.

"Och, it's the first time I've seen you without a smile on your face in weeks. I'm sorry to interrupt your afternoon interlude with your wife. If you don't think you'll make it the rest of the day without having your hands on her, by all means let me know, and I'll stay behind." Lach's grin pulled up on one side.

"Bloody arse."

Lach laughed at his displeasure.

"The least you can do is hurry along." Cam sent Liam to inform Mari of the change in plans. He might have gone himself, but he didn't know if he'd be able to leave her again if he saw her.

Lach was still snickering as they rode through the gates.

"I remember a time not so long ago when you and Kenna went to your chamber soon after the noon meal was served. I ken she's too large to service ye at the moment, but I don't have such problems."

The other man laughed even louder. "You think we canna manage it in her condition?"

Cam's brows creased in confusion. "Truly?"

"Aye. Some women have a mighty appetite when they're increasing." Lach winked at him. "Not just for food. You ken?"

With wide eyes, Cam stared at the man. "I don't know how I'd survive a mightier appetite than Mari already has."

"I'm sure you'll try your best when the time comes. Make sure to eat when you have the chance. You must keep your strength up. Be ready for anything at any time."

Cam shook his head. "It's not something I plan to have to worry about."

"Nay? You don't want children?"

"How can you ask me such a question when you know I

dinna even want a wife?"

"I thought things had changed."

Things had changed. Cam cared for his wife and enjoyed her company in and out of bed, but his vow had not wavered. He would not fall in love, and he would not allow Mari to feel love for him.

"I like bairns well enough, but I don't want any of my own. It would not be fair to Mari or the children."

"You mean if you don't come home to them, like your da?"

"Aye."

"You'll give up the gifts life has to offer on the off chance you could have it happen the same as before? It seems a lot to give up for something that may not happen."

"Nay, it's a lot of grief to give up. Bedding her is one thing; it's pleasant and we have become friends. But I'll not let us risk our hearts. Not when I could end up breaking hers."

"I wish you could find happiness together."

"Happiness is enough. Mari and I have that already. If ye mean love, I'd ask you not to curse us with such a wish." Cam shook his head.

"I wouldn't be able to live with Kenna and not love her. I didn't have a choice. It just happened."

"Love is not for everyone. Even if the laird wishes it so."

Lach nodded and gave up, but Cam found himself thinking of Mari often during their ride. He wanted to brush it off as lust, but it wasn't just her naked body that filled his thoughts.

He envisioned her smile and her laugh, and the honesty in her eyes when she leaned up to place a kiss on his chin. He would need to keep watch over himself, lest he became smitten with his new wife.

For both their sakes, he needed to avoid her.

And for the sake of the clan, he needed to eliminate any

chance of losing the upcoming battle.

...

Mari became worried when Lachlan sat at the table for the evening meal, but Cameron hadn't returned.

"Did my husband come back with you?" she asked after giving Lachlan and Kenna a moment to reunite properly. She looked away as he placed a kiss on Kenna's cheek, but she didn't miss seeing him press another kiss to his palm and place it tenderly on her round belly. It was an intimate moment between them she shouldn't have seen. It made her feel things that weren't to be.

"He'll be along shortly. He went for a walk down by the loch."

Mari relaxed and finished her meal, all the while keeping an eye on the entrance to the hall. When she was done and Cameron still wasn't back, she went looking for him.

She loved the MacKinlay lands, the rolling hills and sharp peaks under a wide sky. Freedom. She could breathe here like she'd never been able to before.

As she walked the familiar trail, she thought of how nice it would be if she came across him bathing. The thought of seeing his wet skin against the setting sun caused her feet to move faster. She was only slightly disappointed to find him fully clothed and sitting on a rock. He was tossing small stones into the water, causing the ripples to span out from his perch.

As she stood there, she felt as though she'd encroached on a private moment. Similar to the way she'd intruded earlier on Kenna and Lachlan's moment. As much as she loved it here, she knew she didn't truly belong. She needed to keep everyone at a distance so she would be able to leave them at any moment if it became necessary.

It was odd to see Cameron so still other than in sleep. Before she had the chance to leave him to his thoughts, he turned and spied her. Instead of the normal smile he offered upon seeing her, he turned back and looked out over the water again.

"Is everything well?" she asked, her body stiffening. Was he angry that she'd tracked him down? Had he wanted to be alone? Had he planned to meet someone else there? Instinct caused her to take a step back.

His single laugh was harsh, and her hands shook as she looked over her shoulder, ready to make a quick escape. He shook his head and tossed out another stone. "My health is good, but I'm not well. I think I'm going mad."

"What's happened?" Despite her fear, she stepped closer, only to find the ground leveled off so she wasn't able to reach him on the rock where he sat. She wanted to touch him. To make sure he was well.

The man sneering out at the loch was not her husband. Perhaps he was going mad...

"We had an agreement. This marriage was to our mutual benefit, but it's not to be anything more. Safety, freedom, and pleasure. *Those* were things we agreed upon."

She swallowed and once again instinctively stepped out of range. He was angry. Though, she was sure he wouldn't hurt her. Mostly.

"And what makes you think that has changed?" she asked.

He turned to look at her, his eyes dark in the waning sun. They weren't the soft honey that made her melt. They were hardened amber. Her feet moved another two steps back all on their own.

"Tell me you don't want more from me." His voice was low and challenging.

She took another step back as he turned on the rock to

face her. His legs were dangling over the edge, so it would be an easy thing for him to slide off and land right in front of her. Grab her. Shake her...

"I don't," she barely whispered, and hoped it was true.

She felt something for him. She obviously cared about him enough to check on him when he didn't return. Was that bad? Many marriages started out of convenience and became more over time. Things changed between people. Especially when they got to know each other the way she was getting to know Cameron.

Perhaps she had gotten to know him too well. It was clear he was not pleased to think she cared for him.

"I suppose I've come to care for you as my husband. But I don't have any expectations for more," she amended, as much for herself as for him. She needed to be reminded that her time at Dunardry was temporary.

At some point Ridley would return, and she would need to escape. She knew Cameron would protect her. He'd most likely send Ridley on a wild goose chase to buy her time to get farther away. But she had no doubts when she left her new home, she would be leaving alone.

"I told you I didn't want you to care about me," he said harshly. "What will happen when I'm called off to battle? Will you be standing by my horse wailing for me not to leave you? And if I don't return? What then? I warned ye it wasn't safe. I told you—" He winced in anger and let his head fall. "This isn't what I wanted. I was verra clear."

"If you think I will not worry about you when you're in battle, that's ridiculous. You are my husband. We may not be bound by emotions, but I do not wish anything to happen to you. You're a good man. I would hate to see any good man taken in battle."

He let out a sigh. "We should be apart for a while. Let things settle a bit between us."

"Whatever you think is best." She nodded and stared at the ground. He was right to worry. She'd begun to crave his kisses. Hadn't she even hoped to see him naked as she'd come to the loch? A little distance would do them good.

"I'm going scouting. I'll be away for a few days. We'll talk when I return."

She nodded again and left before she did something foolish.

Like ask him to stay…

Chapter Nineteen

Once in the protection of the dense forest, Mari let her tears flow and her quiet sobs echo through the trees as she ran through the brush. She'd been a fool to come looking for Cameron. She'd acted like a moon-eyed bride who missed her husband.

And she only realized now that she truly had missed him. He was kind and funny, and always ready to share a good story. Normally he made her feel safe and protected...but tonight had been different. And yet, under the circumstances it was silly to be upset that he wouldn't even consider the notion of feeling something for her. Did she want him to mourn when she was forced to leave?

He'd told her many times he'd never wanted to marry. Why would she ever think she could change his mind?

Why would she even want to?

The more distance between them, the better. She would already be heartsick to leave Kenna and the boys. Even Lachlan had grown on her. It was better that she didn't form any attachment to Cameron, nor him to her, in order to spare them both pain when she needed to leave. Which she would, for there was no doubt Ridley would come for her eventually.

Night had fallen soft and warm around her, as if trying to comfort her. But she wouldn't be comforted. She continued to scold herself for coming to the loch.

When she finally realized she should have reached the clearing leading up to the castle by now, she stopped to look around. The trees cast dark, eerie shadows, and the wind rustled the leaves, mimicking the sound of footsteps.

Her heart pounded in her ears, and she did her best to slow her breathing.

She was safe. She was on MacKinlay lands. She was somewhere between the loch and the castle. She couldn't be far lost. She could call out for Cameron, but then he would see her tears and he might think they were out of worry over him instead of frustration with herself.

Turning in the direction she'd come from in the hope of finding where she'd gone wrong, it yielded no clear direction. The trees were too tall for her even to see the moon for guidance.

Deciding to head in one direction, she started off, the brush stinging her cheeks as she rushed by in a hurry to get home.

When she heard voices, she let out a breath of relief and headed toward the sound. A light above directed her, and she was actually smiling with the joy of freedom when she stepped through the last ring of bushes into a small clearing filled with light.

She blinked at the sight before her. Five large men sitting around a fire stared back at her. One by one she studied them, looking for some sign of recognition. She'd only been to the village a few times, but she didn't know these men.

The one closest to her smiled in an unnerving way.

"Look, lads, my prayers have been answered. A lovely

lass for my own. No more sharing for me."

The other men grumbled.

A whimper caused her to turn her head. She saw a woman—a girl, really—dirty and bedraggled, tied to a tree with a cloth in her mouth.

Lord in heaven.

The man's words clicked into place, and fear swarmed around her to the point she could taste it. She thought she might faint, but if she did, she would be at their mercy. She drew in a deep breath, reaching for calm and control despite the terror that caused her to shake.

"Stand down," she said when the man rose. Her voice sounded surprisingly firm. "I'm the wife of the war chief of Clan MacKinlay. Touch me and he'll kill you all."

"Och, an English lass, we have." The man laughed, clearly not taking her warning seriously.

There was no time to reason with them as another man stepped out behind her, cutting off escape. She screamed with all her might, but a second later the man clasped his meaty hand over her mouth.

• • •

When throwing small stones into the loch did nothing to temper his mood, Cam changed over to hauling large rocks to the edge and tossing them in. The large splash and gulp as the boulder was pulled to the bottom was only somewhat satisfying.

He'd made a mess of things with Mari. He'd accused her of breaking their arrangement, but he had to admit, he'd also come to care for her more than he'd intended.

He planned to leave on a scouting trip, hoping distance would ease the feelings between them before they had the chance to grow even deeper. But he already missed her like mad.

Another plunk of a large rock in the water, and he dropped to the boulder beneath him.

He must go talk to her and tell her she wasn't alone. Despite what they'd planned for their marriage, things had changed. It had been inevitable, he supposed. Life was like that. Repeating itself over and over. Winter to spring, spring to summer, summer to fall, and fall to winter. But he had a will of his own, and he'd be damned if he repeated his previous mistakes.

His mother and father had fallen madly in love and were broken because of it. He would do whatever necessary to ensure he and Mari didn't fall victim to the same fate. Even if it meant staying away for months at a time.

Just as he slid down from his perch, the calm night air was rent with a blood-curdling scream. It was cut off abruptly, but he'd heard enough to know it had come from his wife.

He took off in the direction of the sound, drawing his sword. Thankfully, she wasn't far off. He'd be to her soon. When his nose caught a whiff of smoke, he slowed and approached more cautiously.

In the light of a campfire, he saw five men surrounding his thrashing wife. There were hands all over her body. Holding her arms, her shoulders, her mouth. One set of hands was pushing up her dress as another hand yanked at her ankle.

What happened next was lost to time. Cam heard a battle cry leave his throat, louder than he'd ever sounded in his life.

Moments later, five men lay dead at his feet, their blood dripping from his sword and hands.

Mari threw herself at him, and he dropped his sword so he could hold her.

"Did they—" He could barely choke out those two words. He couldn't bring the rest of the sentence to his lips.

"No. They didn't have the chance, thanks to you."

"Thanks to me?" He laughed bitterly. "Thanks to *me*? I left you to walk back to the castle by yourself. This is *my* fault. What kind of husband sets his wife off in the dark alone, knowing she's upset?"

He'd thought the death of his parents was the deepest pain imaginable, but this...

The weight of his guilt was staggering. He dropped to his knees, clinging to Mari's waist, begging for forgiveness.

...

Mari swayed into Cameron's grasping arms and held him as best she could. In the dying firelight, she could see the wetness of blood in his hair. His face and skin were covered.

It was no surprise; she'd seen the vehemence of his attack. Like an avenging angel he'd rushed to her aid, slaying the demons who'd planned her harm. They hadn't so much as pulled a dirk in defense of his wrath. She shivered as she glanced down at them. Sightless eyes stared at her, reminding her of the night she'd killed the duke—the blood on her hands. The blood everywhere.

She crumbled into Cameron's strong arms. When her eyes fluttered open a few moments later, she was looking up. Cameron hovered above her, and stars filled in behind him.

He dropped a tender kiss on her lips. "Are ye all right?"

She nodded, feeling the heat of embarrassment on her cheeks. She'd fainted after the danger was past. He must think her weak.

She tried to get up, but he stayed her for a moment.

"I'm sorry about before. It wasna you I was angry with, but myself. Can ye forgive me, Mari?"

"You're forgiven." In her eyes, there was nothing to forgive. He had been trying to protect them from themselves.

"I'm so glad they weren't able to hurt you." He pulled

her close and held her for what felt like an hour. His strength made her feel safe, but this wasn't the place to tarry.

The coppery smell of blood filled the area, and she recoiled again. "The blood," she whispered.

He nodded in understanding. "Let's wash in the creek."

When he helped her to her feet, she kept her gaze away from the bodies and parts of bodies that littered the ground. She noticed the place at the edge of the light that was now empty.

"The girl." She pointed to the spot where she'd been lying bound and gagged.

"What girl?" he asked, looking around in a circle.

Mari forced herself to inspect the bodies, expecting to see the girl among the wreckage of her husband's fury. But she wasn't there.

Placing his finger to his lips, Cam bade her be quiet. They stood still, but the only sound was the sizzle and pops of the dwindling fire.

Then they heard it at the same time—something moving in the bushes. Drawing his dirk, Cam moved slowly toward the dark edge of the circle.

Mari lit a branch and followed him. There, only a few feet from where she'd been, the girl rolled and twisted in an effort to get away from them.

The girl—she looked no older than sixteen—had dark eyes which seemed black as they widened in alarm.

Mari quickly soothed away her fears. "It's all right. We won't hurt you. Please let us help."

Cam sheathed his weapon and reached for her. The girl's mumbled scream tore at Mari's heart. He ignored her struggling and pulled her to her feet. He steadied her when she leaped away and stumbled.

Mari came closer and removed the cloth from her mouth. "What's your name?" she asked as she took Cam's dirk to remove the bindings around the girl's wrists. The ugly marks beneath the cloth spoke of the length of time they'd been there.

"Evelyn," the girl answered in a cracking voice.

"What clan are you from?" Cam asked. His tone, though calm, caused Evelyn to flinch.

She didn't answer. Tears welled in her eyes, and she began to sob against Mari. The girl was filthy...and so was Mari, for that matter. But it wasn't the dirt that bothered her most. It was the scent of the men that lingered on her from their touch.

She smelled it on the girl, as well.

"Let us wash in the creek. Let's wash them away," she suggested softly.

Evelyn's eyes snapped toward Cameron.

"Go on," he said. "I'll stand guard to make sure you're safe."

At the creek, Mari tugged off her gown and shift. Stains and filth covered the girl's only garment. She had no gown, and her shift was ripped and thin, barely covering her. She drew off the rag and settled in the cool water, dunking her head to wet her hair.

Mari did the same, wanting to cleanse away the bad memories. "My name is Mari MacKinlay. The man who saved us is my husband, Cameron."

"Saved" might not have been the most accurate word. It was clear vengeance had been the only thing on his mind when he'd rushed the men. The result, however, had been their safety.

"He'll not harm you," she added. "He's not like those other men."

Evelyn said nothing but seemed to relax.

They spent more time in the water than was necessary for bathing. They were both chilled and shivering when they finally emerged. When Evelyn picked up the rag she'd been wearing, Mari couldn't bear to see her in it another minute.

"Hear, take my shift. We shall burn yours. It's filthy."

Evelyn made no argument as she slid Mari's shift over her thin body. Mari put on her gown, and they went to find Cameron.

He was also clean and dripping water. His shirt was bunched in his hand, and he offered it to Evelyn. "It's not exactly clean, but it will cover you."

She nodded and took it, quickly scooting out of reach to don the large shirt. Once she was covered, she picked up her old shift, took it to the fire, and tossed it in.

With a nod of approval, Cam gestured in the direction of the castle. "Come. Let's go home."

Chapter Twenty

Cam, Mari, and Evelyn had just made it inside the hall when Kenna saw them and came running.

"What's happened? Are you injured?" she asked Cam when she saw the blood staining his kilt.

Lach was right behind her. Cam met his eyes, silently communicating that he was whole.

"It's not our blood," Mari explained. "It's a rather long story, and we're exhausted. Can we tell it in the morning?"

Cam wanted nothing more than to spirit Mari off to their room so he could check her over thoroughly and hold her close. But there was the matter of their visitor.

"This is Evelyn," he told Kenna. "She was being held against her will. She hasn't given us the name of her clan yet. Mayhap in the morning. For now, can ye fetch her some food and drink and find her a safe place to sleep?"

"Aye," Kenna said, and called over a serving girl to request food be brought to her solar. "I'll put you in my solar. It's next to my room, so I know you'll not be disturbed there."

"Thank ye," the girl croaked, still trembling.

Kenna frowned and wrapped an arm around her. "You're safe here. We'll take care of you."

With the girl tended to, Cam took Mari's hand and led her to their own chamber. They said nothing as they disrobed, tossing their ruined clothes in a heap on the floor.

Mari moved for their bed, but he stayed her by taking her wrist and gently tugging her to him.

"Are you well?"

"If you're asking if you'll be awakened by my nightmares, I can't say you won't." She offered him a strained smile, and he admired her all the more for the strength it took to keep it there.

"I'll hold you extra tight tonight to protect you from your bad dreams."

They settled into bed, her chilled skin against his heated flesh.

"Rest now, wife. Know that ye are safe. I'll postpone my scouting trip."

"I'm sorry you won't be able to go," Mari said quietly.

"Are you sorry?" he asked, moving away so he could look down into her face.

"Nay, not even a little bit," she said.

He kissed her and reveled in the feel of her heart thumping against his chest and her breath on his neck.

He could have lost her tonight. The thought of it caused a twinge in his chest. Only his hand on her warm skin chased off the fear of what could have happened. The heat of her skin was proof she was alive.

...

Despite her predictions of nightmares, Mari woke fully rested. She hadn't even moved away from Cameron, she'd slept so soundly.

Cam was awake, his eyes focused on the ceiling above them. When she kissed his chest, he turned to look at her.

"What is it?" she asked, noticing the shadows in his eyes.

"Those men never should have been on our lands. I need to take my guard to task for it this morning. It's my duty to punish them for putting the clan at risk, but I fear I may not be able to be fair, as angry as I am."

"Then you should ask Lachlan to do it for you. Or wait until you are calmer."

He nodded, and she wasn't sure which of those options he was agreeing to. She respected him all the more for seeing he was not able to maintain control of his rage and spare his men.

"I'd like to go see to our guest," she said, eager to help the girl in some way. Mari had seen the terror in Evelyn's eyes and knew what that felt like.

Another nod, and Cam rolled out of bed. Before he stood, she shifted behind him, wrapping her arms around him and kissing his shoulder, then his neck. "Please tell me you don't still feel guilty about what happened."

"I canna tell you that, for I promised I'd not lie to you."

She twisted until she was sitting on his lap. "If you'd walked me back to the castle last night, those men wouldn't have been found, and Evelyn would still be with them. For whatever momentary discomfort and panic I felt, I'm glad for it so we were able to save her from what I assume was a horrendous ordeal."

He gave a nod and pulled her close. "You are a good woman."

She smiled at his praise, happy to have him here instead of leaving for a scouting trip.

Outside their room, Cam kissed her again. "I'm going to deal with my men. See if you can get the lass to give you her clan's name so we can deliver her home, if that's where she wishes to go."

Mari nodded and went to join Evelyn and Kenna in the solar. As expected, the mistress of the castle was fussing over the poor girl. A new gown had been brought in, and two maids were tending to the girl's hair. It was clear Evelyn wanted no part of it.

"Kenna? A word, please?"

Kenna waddled out to the hall and closed the door. "The poor dear. You found her with nothing to wear?"

"No. She was wearing but a shift when we met. She was in the company of five beastly men who tried to attack me. It was clear she had been at their mercy for some time."

Kenna pressed her lips together. "She's but a lass." Tears shimmered in her sister's eyes.

"I know, but no longer an innocent one, judging by the vile behavior of her captors."

"The men…?"

"Cam dealt with them." Mari refrained from saying how quickly he'd dealt with them or how savagely. It only mattered that they were gone and would never bother anyone again.

Kenna nodded and took a deep breath. "We must make her feel as comfortable and safe as possible. Shall we?"

When they reentered the room, Kenna sent the maids away and settled the girl in a chair by the fire. She and Mari sat across from Evelyn and offered soothing smiles.

"I know you probably don't wish to discuss what happened," Mari began. "I was only with them a few minutes, and I find it difficult to talk about them myself. But there are some things we need to know, only so we can help you."

Evelyn said nothing. She sat up straighter with her hands in her lap like a proper lady.

"Were those men from your clan?"

Evelyn shook her head slowly.

"Do you wish to return to your clan?"

Mari expected a clear answer to this question, but the expression on the girl's face was torn. Hope warred with dismay.

"The men weren't from your clan, but did someone from your clan give you to them?" Kenna guessed the next logical conclusion. Something Mari hadn't thought of.

Evelyn shook her head again.

Kenna—not known for her patience—let out a quick breath and leaned as close as her belly allowed, taking the girl's hand in hers. "We are friends. You can tell us anything, and I truly hope you'll confide in us. We'll not judge you, of that you can be certain. I wear men's breeches when I'm not with child, and Mari here killed a duke."

Both Mari and Evelyn gasped at the bald announcement.

"I hardly think that was necessary." Mari frowned at her sister, then turned to Evelyn. "It was self-defense. I was married to the brute, and I thought he was going to kill me, so I…" Mari shrugged and let the explanation drift off. It wasn't important.

Their honesty relaxed Evelyn enough to speak.

"I am a Stewart," she said, her voice still rough. "The laird's daughter."

"I was a daughter of a laird, as well," Kenna said, patting the girl's hand. "Mari is the elder daughter. We're sisters."

"Do you wish to go home?" Mari asked, trying to recall how far away the Stewart lands were from Dunardry.

"I do…but they may not want me back." Evelyn's voice was barely a breath. Her fair skin turned blotchy with shame she shouldn't have to bear.

"Why would you think such a thing?" Kenna asked, her voice soft and encouraging.

"I ran off. I was upset about something trivial and decided to show my displeasure by running away." Evelyn swiped at a tear. "I hadn't really planned to be gone long. In honesty, I was only looking for attention."

"I'm sure they miss you dearly and want you back," Kenna said, clearly thinking like a mother. It was easy now for her to think the best of a parent, even after their own father and stepmother had married them both off for the most strategic alliances, without a care to their well-being.

"How can I go back now? I'm… I've been…"

Mari knew what the girl was trying to say, and pulled her into a hug to spare her having to put it into words. "I know what it is like to live through something horrible. To think that is all you are. But you survived. You will heal. Every day, the truth of what happened to me in London is one day further in the past. And as I create wonderful new memories with my family here, the bad old memories are harder to recall."

"I'm a mother, and I can tell you, a parent's love is a fierce thing. No doubt yours will be so happy to have you back they will only want to help you heal," Kenna said.

Evelyn hung her head. "I was so foolish to leave on my own."

"Foolishness is a part of youth. You can't make it to adulthood without a bit of it. What ye did was certainly not worth the punishment you've paid for it."

The girl started crying in earnest, and Kenna and Mari took turns comforting her. They didn't try to stanch her tears, for they both knew how important it was to get them out.

Later, a tray of food was brought in, and they all ate in silence.

When they were done, Evelyn let out a breath and raised her head. "I would like to go home. I'll just hope they accept me."

"If they don't, lass, you get right back on the horse and come straight to Dunardry and join our clan. You will always have a home here, if ever you find yourself in need of one."

Mari knew how important having a home was for making

someone feel safe.

But that worked both ways.

There wasn't a day that went by that she didn't worry she was putting her new home and the people she loved at risk.

Chapter Twenty-One

Cam put Liam in charge of escorting Evelyn Stewart back to her clan lands. After a few days of rest, it was clear the lass was eager to get home. With Liam's selected entourage and a letter from Lachlan, the group left at first light after hugs and well wishes.

Cam felt his cheeks flush with embarrassment when the girl hugged him and claimed him her hero. He didn't feel like such.

When the group was on their way, he stayed Mari with his arm around her waist. "Will you go for a ride with me on this beautiful day?"

"Don't you have drills?"

"Aye. I've put my men to their tasks. I can spare an hour." He kissed her. "Or two."

"I should get back to the kitchen to help."

"The kitchen ran fine before you arrived. They'll do so today."

He waited for her next excuse, waiting to put it down with the others. His wife had been frightened, and since they'd returned that horrible night, she hadn't stepped a foot outside the walls. He knew how easily fear could breed when it went unchecked. A warrior who was left to stew in the terror of battle quickly became lost to it. He didn't want that for Mari.

He wanted her to feel safe on their lands. Ensuring her happiness was the reason he pushed when he saw her discomfort. It was not an easy thing to watch, but she needed him to be strong.

She grasped at another excuse. "It looks like it could rain."

"There's not a cloud in the blue sky. Now, either come with me to the stables or tell me the truth of why ye do not wish to take me up on my offer," he challenged.

"I think it's clear why I wouldn't want to go out. I'm wanted by the crown for murder."

At least that was a valid concern. Though easily dealt with.

"We've been out dozens of times since you arrived, without issue. We'll be fine today as well. I've vowed to protect you. Unless you don't find me up to the task...?"

She bit her bottom lip and looked toward the gate. "I'm scared," she finally admitted.

"Aye. I don't doubt it. But you're also strong. You don't back down from fear, you face it. I've seen you do it time and time again. Why is this different?"

"Because you were put in danger because of me," she snapped, as if it had been on the tip of her tongue, eager to come out of her mouth for days.

He shrugged and winced up at the sun. "We could go round and round over who put who in danger, lass. But it would be a waste of a fine day."

She let out a breath and nodded. "Very well. I'll go with you."

He bent to kiss her hard, then stepped away just as she

melted into the kiss. With a wink he took her hand to lead her out to the stables. There would be plenty of time later to make sure they didn't get too close. For now, he was going to enjoy the advantages of being married. Even if it was just for convenience. There was no reason they couldn't make the best of the situation.

As soon as they left the protection of the curtain walls, Mari tensed. Her eyes shifted constantly, and he was sure she was watching for danger. She'd fallen behind his horse instead of riding next to him.

It was difficult to see her so nervous. "I can assure you the guards will not let anyone wander onto our lands again. They've been dealt with." Not as severely as Cam had wanted, but he trusted Lach's decision to be sound instead of the punishment of a man who'd nearly lost something precious because of their incompetence.

Cam led Mari in the opposite direction from the loch. He would take her back there at some point, but it didn't need to be today. They would work through this slowly so as not to cause her more distress than necessary.

Stopping his horse, he waited for her to come up beside him, then leaned closer in his saddle.

"When I'm in battle, I always have a man riding beside me," he explained. "The two of us side by side are safer because it means we only have to protect one side. Each is guarded at all times by the other warrior."

She bit her lip, thinking over his words. "I'm not a warrior. I can't protect your side."

"And I can't protect you at all if you're behind me where I canna see."

"Very well. I'll stay at your side. At least I can call out so you're prepared if we are ambushed."

He smiled. "Aye. That would be a great help." He kept her talking, sharing other tricks to defend oneself in battle.

Slowly she relaxed and stopped looking over her shoulder constantly.

He took her to a cliff that looked out over a valley. It was one of his favorite spots, for he could see in every direction. They got down from their horses to take in the view.

"This is the safest place on MacKinlay lands, save for behind the walls of Dunardry," he pointed out as she spun in a circle.

"No one can sneak up on you here," she observed.

"That's right. And if armed with a bow, you can easily pick off anyone who might try to advance on you."

"We don't have a bow."

"No. Someday, I'll show you how to shoot one. Or mayhap Kenna will do it when she's not bulging with child." He winked. "For today, you'll have this." He reached for the sheath at his waist and pulled out a jeweled dagger.

She gasped and covered her mouth rather than take it from him.

"Go on. It's for ye. A gift."

"It's beautiful."

"Aye. It belonged to my mother. My father didn't like leaving her behind unarmed, so he had this made. I guess he thought if it was made fancy as a piece of jewelry, she would want to keep it with her."

"And did she?"

"Aye. Always."

Mari took it from him, holding it up to the sun and turning it so the light glinted off the colorful stones. "I'm afraid it would only be something for me to carry. I wouldn't know how to use it as a weapon."

"That's the other reason I brought you out here with me today. Your days of using anything handy to defend yourself are over. There won't always be a fire poker within reach. It's time you learn the proper way. You're a tiny thing, but not helpless."

She nodded and squared her shoulders. "I never thought I was capable of killing anyone. But that night, I didn't need to think about it. It was the natural thing to do. When those men attacked me, I fought, but all the while I was looking for something I could use to protect myself. It was no use."

"Against five full-grown men, you would exhaust yourself trying." He hated the memory of seeing her under them. Their dirty hands pinning her to the ground. The thought of what could have happened… "Let's get started, shall we?" he suggested so he could stop his thoughts before they brought on a panic.

"What should I do?" she asked, seeming eager for her lesson.

"Surprise is a smaller person's best defense." He went on to show her where and how to attack. They practiced for hours. Occasionally when they tumbled into each other, he would steady her and steal a kiss.

"This is so much more useful than how to flirt with noblemen and how to speak properly."

He chuckled and kissed her on the nose. "I wouldn't say the lessons on flirting were a complete waste of time." He wrapped his arms around her waist and pulled her closer. "I like it fine when you practice your skills on me to get your way."

A saucy half smile tugged on her lips. "Is that so?"

"Aye. It's so."

"Perhaps there's another advantage to being on higher ground," she hinted.

"And what might that be?" he asked, knowing where the conversation was going as he bent to kiss her neck. Rather than risk scaring her with an encounter similar to that night, he spread out a blanket and lay upon it so she could be in control of the situation.

It was a beautiful fall day. The leaves had changed, and there was a crispness to the air, but the sun was bright and warm. Perfect for his plans.

He was careful not to hold her too tightly or grasp her quickly. He made sure she was free the entire time. He hadn't brought her out here to move to this step. He'd simply wanted her to feel safe outside the walls again. But the chance to make love to his wife was an unexpected gift.

He trusted her to know what she wanted, and didn't thwart her suggestion when she offered it. His wife had spent most of her life being told what to do and how to do it. She'd been a prisoner all her life, both in her father's home and the duke's.

He wanted nothing more than for her to be free.

· · ·

Mari stayed next to Cam as they entered through the gates of Dunardry after dark. She'd learned so much that day. Not only how to defend herself, but how to let go of the fear that weighed her down.

Cameron had been careful to explain that she was not invincible just because she carried a wee dirk on her waist. But if she was prepared, she'd have a chance to protect herself if the opportunity arose. She understood what he was saying. No one was safe against an enemy. Not even a war chief with a large sword and a broad back. She shook that thought away to concentrate on the other thing she'd learned.

That she was able to move on to a physical relationship with her husband without being haunted by what happened. She'd not waste a moment thinking of them again. Not when she had a hearty husband to hold her.

The way he touched her was so different from any other man, she couldn't mistake him for an attacker. There was nothing similar that called up the terror of that night, or her horrible marriage. He claimed her, but only because she allowed it. Those other men were nothing but brutes. Not worth a thought. She'd not let them take anything from her. Especially not her peace of mind.

When she and Cam got back to the castle, everyone was bustling around and chattering despite the late hour. Something important had happened.

It was then that Mari heard a loud scream and realized the important thing was *still* happening.

"Kenna!" she shouted and shot off toward the stairs, followed closely by Cam.

She found Lachlan pacing outside their room, his face pale and his hair mussed from tugging it. The little dog, Brutus, kept up at his side despite his short legs.

"I thought it would be easier this time," he said, his expression stricken. "I know what to expect—the screaming and yelling. But it's surely no easier this time than it was with the twins." His eyes went wide and he stopped in his tracks. "Dear God. What if it's twins again?"

"Let's get ye some whisky," Cam suggested as he rested an arm on Lachlan's shoulder.

"Nay. I can't leave. I must stay in case she needs me."

"I'll go check on her and let you know how she fares," Mari offered, and slid through the door into the chaos.

Kenna's hair was damp, and sweat ran down her face as she sucked in quick breaths.

"Mari, thank God." Kenna winced but reached for her to come closer.

Mari took her hand and gasped from the intensity with which her younger sister squeezed her fingers. She decided not to complain since it seemed petty in light of what Kenna was enduring.

Had Mari really thought she wanted this? Pain had been

such a constant part of her life for so long—something to be avoided. But this was different. This was pain and joy mixed in a way that gave Kenna the strength of a warrior.

"You're doing so well," Mari assured, though her face must have betrayed her concern because Kenna gave a strained bark of laughter.

"How many women have you seen birth a babe, sister?"

"Admittedly none, but I have to say you're doing it wonderfully because that's how you do everything."

Another laugh.

At least Mari was keeping her sister entertained in her time of what was clearly excruciating pain. Mari couldn't believe her sister was even capable of laughter.

But then Mari remembered the sheer insanity that took over a person when pain reached that unbearable state. When one became lost to it and couldn't care or focus on anything.

Kenna screamed through another pain, then slumped against the bed. "Poor Lachlan. I know he hates to hear my cries, but it's beyond me to hold them in."

"He looked rather pale when I arrived," Mari admitted. She thought of what Cam had told her about being at his side. How it made them both stronger. "I wonder that it wouldn't be better for him to be in here with you offering his strength. Surely he would feel relieved to know what is happening. From out there, he's sure to think the worst."

Kenna blew out a sound of agreement. "The man is banished for some reason that makes no sense to me. I surely didn't get this way on my own. Why should I have to bear it by myself?"

Mari stood and went to the door. She wasn't able to help her sister with her pain, but she could do something about this nonsense at least.

As soon as she opened the chamber door, four men spun to face her expectantly.

"Is the babe here? I didn't hear crying. What's wrong?" It seemed Lachlan's legs wouldn't hold him.

"No. The child hasn't been born yet, but you have bigger hands than I do, and you can allow Kenna to squeeze them without damage. Come in."

Lachlan blinked twice in surprise before rushing into the room.

"What are you doing?" Abagail scolded. "You can't allow a man in the birthing room."

"He's not a man, he's the father. Besides, it's his room. It's his wife. It's his child. Why can't he be here? He's seen men mangled on the battlefield. This can't be nearly as bad as that."

Lachlan gave her a grave stare. "It's far worse, I assure you."

Mari swallowed and nodded. She understood. It was different because this was the person he loved above all others, and Kenna was in a dangerous position while he could do nothing to assist except hold her hand.

"Still," Mari pressed on. "I believe your place is here beside your wife, to encourage her. It has to be better than waiting out there."

"Kenna, do you want me to go?" he asked, because the decision was hers.

She shook her head, her wet hair curling up at her temple. "Stay, please."

"Of course. I just wish I could do something," he said, kissing her head. "I'm in awe of you, wife."

Mari went to get a fresh cloth and gave it to Lachlan, instructing him to use it to wipe Kenna's brow.

Kenna spared a small smile and then groaned with pain. Lachlan's face went even paler—if that were possible. Perhaps that was the true reason men weren't permitted into the birthing room. For all their physical fortitude, muscles didn't make them strong enough for such things as birthing babes.

Mari pushed him onto a stool facing the head of the bed and Kenna, so he wouldn't see what was happening below. Mari had gotten a peek of that and didn't think she'd ever recover. No good would come of shocking Lachlan. He was distraught enough.

His hand surrounded Kenna's, only her white knuckles were visible between his strong fingers. He whispered encouragements as Kenna panted through the next pain.

"Do ye hate me?" he asked Kenna when it had subsided.

She shook her head. "Not as much anymore— Oh!"

Another pain came on quickly, and Abagail—still frowning at having a man in her domain—nodded. "It's time."

Kenna let her head fall back and nodded as if understanding the vague instructions from the healer. This time she pushed, and Lachlan moved to her side, supporting her and talking her through it with soft words only for her. Mari felt a twinge of jealousy at the intimacy of the moment.

When she looked down to see a dark head protruding, the moment of jealousy subsided.

"Again," Abagail demanded.

Mari lost track of time, and the number of times Kenna pushed, but eventually the child—another boy—was free from his mother and wailing up a storm.

Abagail wiped him briefly and wrapped the babe in a linen as if she'd done such a thing hundreds of times. Then she dropped the child in Mari's arms while she attended to Kenna.

"Hello, nephew. What a weighty lad you are," Mari cooed while carefully taking him to his waiting parents. "A big, beautiful boy."

Kenna nodded that Lachlan should take him. Mari saw him brush a large hand over both cheeks before reaching out to take his son. He smiled and laughed and cried a bit more as he looked at him.

"He's a strapping lad, love. You did so well." He brought the child close. "This is your mother. You've worn her out, so go easy on your fussing."

The babe stopped crying as if obeying his father's command.

Lachlan glanced over at Abagail. "'Tis just the one, aye?"

"Look at the size of him! Surely there's no more room," Kenna said with an indulgent smile. "He needs a name."

"Aye. A big boy will likely be a big man someday. Like Cam, I hope he also has a big heart. What do you say to naming him Cameron?"

Kenna smiled and nodded. "Yes, that is a fine name. Don't you think so, sister?"

"Yes. It's lovely, indeed." Happiness filled her heart, but a small shadow cast darkness across the moment. This new child was yet another tie to this place.

Someone else she'd have to leave if—when—danger followed her to her new home.

Chapter Twenty-Two

"Just because the father is no longer out here doesn't mean they can just forget about us," Bryce complained as Cam made another path across the stones. He could almost feel the floor wearing away beneath his feet. Even the dog had given up and lay in the corner fast asleep.

"Aye," Cam agreed, knowing the parents were busy with more important things than informing the men left out in the corridor what was going on.

Just then the door opened, and Mari stepped out carrying a bundle. Her eyes were wet with tears, but a smile stretched her beautiful face. "All is well. It's a boy. Cameron Lachlan MacKinlay."

She gazed down at the child adoringly as Cam came closer to see him.

"Cameron? They named the babe after *me*?" He couldn't describe the pride and surprise at this news.

"Yes. You see, he's rather large." She shifted the babe's weight and held him out so Cam could hold him. The child was large, but in his arms the bairn felt tiny.

He laughed. "It's a pleasure to meet you, wee Cameron." The babe made a sound, not an unhappy one at first, but soon the lad was voicing his displeasure in a loud cry.

"Let's get you back to your mother and father." Mari took the babe and slipped back into the room. She was back a few moments later, and they shared a smile.

Cam reached for her. "What ye did for Lach was appreciated. How did he fare?"

"Very well. No swooning. Though for a moment it was a near thing."

"Let's get you something to eat before you swoon," he said, leading her toward the stairs.

"I don't even know what time it is."

"Late afternoon," he answered, just as her stomach growled. She hadn't eaten since the day before. "Once you're fed, we'll lie down for a bit. You must be exhausted."

She nodded. "I am tired. The excitement kept me from realizing it. But now…" She yawned.

He understood. Being in battle was similar. The rush of action kept him from realizing how tired his body was. Once the danger abated, though, fatigue set in.

His fearless warrior had stood by her sister all night, and now it was his turn to care for her.

"You did well. Now you need your rest."

They had a quick meal of bannocks and ale, then he led her upstairs, steadying her on the steps when she stumbled. He helped her disrobe and did the same before tucking them both into bed for a few hours of much-needed sleep.

"It was an amazing thing to be part of," she said quietly.

"I find it terrifying," he said, causing her to laugh. The smile fell from his lips as he looked past that initial feeling. It was true he didn't want to be the one waiting outside the door listening to Mari scream as she brought their child into the world.

But it was the thought of their child that made the fear seem almost acceptable.

He'd never considered wanting children. In fact, he'd made it his goal not to become a father. It wasn't fair. He'd grown up without his parents, and he didn't want to leave a child without a father. Still, a selfish part of him wanted to hold his own babe in his arms and rock him or her to sleep. A hefty lad, or an angel of a lass who looked like her mother.

"But I do hope our union is blessed with a child," he confessed, unable to keep the thought to himself. He wanted to see her expression and hoped she would want it as much as he, even though they'd not spoken of children before.

She turned to face him, and his heart dropped. She twisted her fingers nervously in the blanket. Of course she'd be worried.

After witnessing the birth of wee Cameron, it was no wonder she'd not want to consider such a thing right now. Especially not with a man of his size, who was more likely to sire large bairns.

When she finally spoke, he realized she had a different fear.

"You don't worry having a family would make things more difficult if Ridley returns?"

"I'm not worried about Ridley. He'll never take ye from me." He pulled her into his arms to comfort her. Or possibly himself.

She nodded unconvincingly against his shoulder and closed her eyes.

It was clear she didn't believe him. The thought that Ridley might come to MacKinlay lands demanding she be returned for trial was a distinct possibility, but he'd not let her face execution in a city he'd never been to by people that weren't their kin.

She hadn't voiced her fears in some time. He should have

known she'd not forgotten or dismissed the danger lurking from her past. But it had been far easier to be happy and ignore it for as long as they could.

"We have time. It's not something we need to decide today," he said.

He'd promised to keep her safe, and he would die upholding that vow. But waiting around for the English to come back was a mistake. He needed to do something now to protect her.

He would speak to Lach about finding a way to clear her name. Cam knew the laws would not be in her favor, but surely there was someone smarter than he who could find a way. Then they would be free to look forward to a future, possibly with children of their own.

Cam drifted off, thinking of such things, and woke still thinking about them.

It was dark. Letting Mari sleep, he slipped out of her warm embrace and dressed. In the hall he found Lach in a chair holding a sleeping twin in each arm. He'd heard the new babe crying and assumed Lach had brought the boys down so they wouldn't be disturbed by their new brother.

"Can I unburden half your load?" Cam offered, and Lach passed over one of the lads. "Roddy?"

Lach nodded. "You're getting better at telling them apart."

"It's more difficult when they're asleep."

"Aye. When they're awake, their personalities tell you which is which. But in sleep their features even out, and I canna see how they think about things."

Cam nodded in agreement and studied the sleeping boy on his lap. "Roddy is a bit thinner for he runs around more than his brother, who is more cautious."

Lach smiled. "Aye."

"Thank you for the honor of naming the new child after

me."

Lachlan placed a kiss on Douglas's head. "I hope he grows to be a strong man like you, with a good heart." He let out a sigh and rested his head back on the chair. "A man who can help me puzzle out how to salvage an alliance with the McCurdy now that I have no chief able to marry his daughter."

"You haven't given up on the alliance?"

"Nay. Having another son makes me even more determined. Our clan is growing. I need to find ways to provide for them. Access to the sea opens up a variety of ways to earn a better living."

"I hate to earn your ire again, but I'll remind you, you had no chief willing to marry the McCurdy lass in the first place, so as I see it, you're no worse off today than you were before."

"And you think I would have allowed ye to shirk your duty had you shown up that day with your cart full of rocks? Penance paid, all forgotten and forgiven? Nay."

"Can we not find another warrior to marry the lass?" Cam suggested.

Lach looked at him and tilted his head. "You know who would be next in line. Do you think he'd be more willing than you were?"

Lachlan spoke of their other cousin, Bryce. They both knew he would do far more than dig up rocks to get out of marrying again. Years ago he'd been wed, then he and his Maggie had a daughter. But both lasses had died of illness when Bryce was away on a raid. Bryce had lost his heart and since then had refused to wed again. He rarely spoke of bedding another lass, and Cam had never seen him with anyone. It was something he didn't speak of. Ever.

Once again, Cam was reminded of what he had to lose.

"I'll make sure the men are ready. Whenever you give

the word, we'll take their clan by force and you'll have your access to the sea."

"We have time," Lach said, resisting the need for war as always.

Cam knew well enough the laird wasn't a coward. He'd gone off to fight for the French for years. Lach's blade had certainly drawn more blood than Cam's. But he didn't want to take the clan from the McCurdy laird, despite the man running it into the dirt with lack of food and funds.

"Why do you not consider it?" Cam asked.

Lach looked up and blinked. "I have considered it. Many times. It's simply too great a risk." He brushed a lock of hair from his son's forehead and smiled sadly.

Cam frowned. It wasn't an issue of respect, but of caution.

"You may be war chief," Lach said, seeing his reaction, "but you're not the only one in danger of not returning if an attempt to bring down the McCurdy fails. When I was in France, I didn't think too often of my death, but I find that now I want to be here to see these boys grow into good men. I want to love my wife until her hair turns white. I want those things more than fulfilling my father's legacy. And I have to think if my da was here, he would want them more as well."

Cam nodded. It was easy to understand, even if he didn't agree. "As ye said, we have time."

Though he wasn't sure if his words were true. Not for Mari, at any rate. Even now, Ridley could be heading for Dunardry.

Cam had never wanted to take a wife or have a family for fear he'd leave them early if he was struck down in battle. In all that time, he'd not considered the opposite could be the case—that his wife could be taken from him.

He'd be alone again, but with a broken heart...just like Bryce.

He couldn't ever let that happen.

Chapter Twenty-Three

Mari came down to the hall in the morning to find four men asleep in chairs by the hearth. Well, two of them were not men yet, but they were on their way. Cam and Lachlan dozed, each with a twin sleeping in his arms.

Seeing Cam with Lachlan's boy brought back the concerns and wishes she'd been feeling the night before. How she longed to see Cameron holding their own child while they slept peacefully.

But Mari didn't think it could ever happen. She could be carrying his child this very moment, so that part of the dream was possible. What she doubted was her ability to give her family any kind of peace.

Safety and tranquility were the things she'd longed for over the years. But in securing her safety, she'd sentenced herself to being hunted down and put to death. Which in turn put her entire family in danger.

It seemed the worst kind of irony.

Cam's eyes opened, and he smiled, scattering her worries for the time being. When he looked at her like that, she couldn't think. Could barely breathe.

"Good morning, wife," he said quietly, holding out a hand toward her. The other hand held the sleeping twin.

He pulled her closer, and she sat on his free knee.

"One can almost think them angels while they sleep," he teased.

"They *are* angels." She picked up the boy's hand as Cam made a sound of disagreement. She laughed and relented. "Which means they are normal, active little boys."

"Demons, in other words." Cam brushed the black hair away from the child's forehead and placed a kiss there. "I would give my life for them without a thought, and they are not even mine. I canna imagine what it would feel like, the bond with a child of our own."

"I imagine it would be much the same. Maybe more intense. You would protect them body and soul from anything that threatened."

Mari couldn't help but think her presence was the biggest threat to these boys, her husband, and her clan. How much time did she have before she'd need to make a fateful decision?

Years? Days? Mere hours? Before a messenger delivered the grim news that Sir Ridley was there with orders from King Charles to take her back to England…

"You were smiling, and now it's gone. What's amiss?" Cam asked.

She shook her head and let out a breath. "Nothing. Nothing to worry about now."

It was true they didn't need to find a solution that instant. They could enjoy a quiet moment with their nephews.

Someday soon, however, they would need to make a plan. To prepare for the worst.

For now, she was content to take some breakfast to her sister and help with the new babe. She gave her husband a kiss and rose.

From the window in her sister's room an hour later, she watched him running drills below with his men. A smile full of pride pulled at her lips. He moved so gracefully, and yet she knew well the man was lethal. Like the flames of a fire that could draw you in by their mesmerizing colors but burn you with that same beauty.

"You may want to wipe the drool from your chin before you get a spot on your dress," Kenna said from her place on the bed.

Mari didn't pretend she wasn't in danger of such a thing. But fortunately not at the moment. She went to sit on the edge of the bed while her sister nursed wee Cameron.

Kenna wiped away wetness from her cheeks, but Mari knew they were happy tears. She'd come to recognize them in the past month.

"I couldn't ask for anything more than I have on this day. Did you ever think we'd be so happy?" Kenna asked, her eyes brimming over with it.

"Our father didn't give us a great example of happiness. But I remember Mama. She was happy despite being married to Papa. Perhaps Father was happy with her and I don't recall. Still, our home was nothing like here." Mari fell quiet as she remembered the worries that were never far from her thoughts.

"What is it?" Kenna asked.

But Mari refused to ruin the perfect moment. She pasted a fierce smile on her face and said, "Nothing is wrong. How could it be when we are celebrating this precious new life?"

Her enthusiasm must have shown false, for Kenna reached out to touch her hand. "You are safe here. No one can take you from us."

Mari wanted to believe her fervent words, but the truth of the matter was that the king of England did have that power.

And no one could refuse the king.

• • •

Cam knew something was amiss with his wife. She'd been tired after staying up with Kenna, but three days later, Mari still wasn't herself.

When he asked, she assured him she was fine with a brittle smile he thought might crack into pieces before him. He'd hoped it was fatigue. But he could guess the true cause of her distress.

She was worrying.

He understood. He was worried, too. It was only natural. With each day they grew closer, but there was a good chance that everything they'd built together could come to a sudden stop and be ripped away.

Lach had reached out to a few people to see if something could be done legally to protect Mari. In the meantime, Cam had plotted out three possible escape routes from the MacKinlay lands. In the next few weeks, he rode them at night to make sure he knew the way in the cover of darkness. He rode during the day, as well, looking for places to hide along the way so as not to be discovered.

His planning missions kept him away from their bed until well after Mari was asleep. He missed her. He missed her genuine smile. She was lovely when she smiled. But her smiles had been all but absent lately.

He hoped someday he'd be able to give her a reason to smile again, and this time for good.

• • •

When Mari woke one morning, she found Cam sitting on the edge of the bed gazing down at her. In the past weeks he'd been gone when she woke, off on some secret mission outside the castle. He hadn't invited her to ride with him, and he'd been gone well into the night.

He hadn't made love to her, either, and a small, silly part of her worried he'd found company in the bed of another woman. But in truth, she knew him better than that. He was an honorable man. Far more honorable than the supposed proper gentleman she'd been married to before.

She took a good look at her husband sitting there in his best shirt and plaid, with an unreadable look about him. His hair was combed back neatly instead of in the wavy locks he normally wore.

"What is it?" she asked, sitting up.

"Will you come for a ride with me this morning?" he asked, not meeting her eyes.

In the past, his expression might have made her nervous. But she had come to know this man and knew she was safe with him. He'd sooner cut off his own arm with a dull blade than cause her a moment of pain.

Cam was safe for her body, but not necessarily for her heart. In truth, her heart was engaged in a full-scale battle. On the one hand, she was trying her best to keep her distance from him, to be ready to run at the first sign of trouble. On the other, she yearned for the closeness they had briefly shared when they became lovers.

There hadn't been any sign of Ridley, but she remained vigilant.

For this day, though, she wanted to spend it with her husband, being happy while she still could.

"Of course," she said with a real smile.

She got dressed quickly, the sooner to be on their way in the sunshine. When she was ready, she looped her arm through his, and he led them straight to the stables in silence.

That made her uneasy. Her husband was many things, but silent wasn't usually one of them. Any time they walked together, he was quick to tell her a story of the place they visited. Something that had happened there when he was a boy, a person or animal he'd encountered.

But now he was uncommonly quiet.

It was a puzzle and was made more so when they headed directly for the forest. After several minutes, he stopped and slid down from his horse, then helped her down. There was a blanket tied to his saddle, but he made no move to get it.

Glancing around, she recognized the same woods she'd been in when the dogs had come after her. Her heart pounded at the memory.

That day she'd run for her life through these trees and bushes, not sure where to go to escape. When she broke free of the forest and saw Cam in the field, she'd run toward him, desperate for help. She hadn't even considered he might turn her over to the men chasing her. She hadn't thought for a moment that he would not protect her.

She'd instinctively known him on that day.

And she still knew him today. He was her faithful protector.

Without preamble, he showed her where to hide if she needed to, how to cross from the field without being detected, and where he'd hidden supplies in case she wasn't able to take anything with her if she had to flee.

"If we're not together, you'll need to go alone. The rise there"—he pointed—"that's where we'll meet up. Wait for me and I'll join you as soon as possible."

Mari nodded, but she knew when the time came she wouldn't wait for Cam to meet her. She wouldn't put him in danger by helping her.

He'd done enough for her already.

Chapter Twenty-Four

With his sword raised and sweat on his brow, Cam smiled, ready to beat Lach. They were only sparring, but Cam never missed an opportunity to let his cousin know he was the weaker MacKinlay. Victory was interrupted by a lad tearing into the bailey with a message.

"McCurdys are raiding our cattle along the west border," the boy cried out, breathless.

Lach lowered his sword and headed for the keep. "Let's go."

The call went out, and everyone at the castle was prompted into action. This was not new. It was the normal way his people reacted when intruders invaded their lands with the intention of stealing from their clan.

But this was the first time while collecting his armor he was met by his wife.

"How can I help?" she asked, standing back out of the way as he filled his strap with daggers and grabbed up his ax.

"Can you get my extra flask?" He nodded to where it hung and she hurried to collect it as he affixed the rest of his weapons.

"I'll see you out," she offered when he hesitated by the door. She stayed right behind him as he rushed to the stables to mount up. "Cam?" Her voice was quiet in the hustle and clanking of men getting suited up to leave.

He turned and saw the worry and fear in her eyes. He knew what she would say next, before her mouth opened.

"Promise you'll come back."

It was unfair for him to make such a promise. These things were out of his control. But it was also unfair of her to ask him to make it, so he nodded and kissed her hard and quick before pulling himself up on his horse.

"I'll see ye soon, wife." With that he tore out of the gate to catch up with his men.

He moved to the head of the line with Lach at his side as they strategized and planned for a successful stop to the raid. A ridge on the east side of the field would give them the advantage of sight, but the McCurdys would see them coming before they could do any damage. And if they'd already fled with the cattle, his men would need to give chase. Who knew how far they may have gotten.

There was always a risk, but Cam knew the McCurdys were short on coin so they couldn't pay for weapons. And their warriors had been reduced in previous battles. This incursion would be an excellent opportunity to eliminate even more of their army. If the MacKinlays made a good showing today, they would be better positioned to take over Baehaven Castle and the whole McCurdy clan.

Cam held his reins tighter in anticipation. He was always the first into a skirmish. It was his duty as war chief. But this time he was also a husband. He'd never had to be both.

Going with his warrior instincts, he did his best to forget about what awaited him at home for the time being. It was not good to be distracted when facing the enemy.

He let out the war cry and descended on the McCurdys spread below them on the field. For a moment he hoped they'd retreat so he'd not need to fight at all. And not risk breaking his promise to Mari.

But the damned McCurdys stood their ground to fight.

And they fought hard.

Cam had taken down six on his own when he saw Liam struggling with two warriors. The boy had only returned the day before from his task of taking the Stewart lass back to her home. He was a good fighter, but his age didn't give him the strength needed to fight off two grown men, and he was most likely still tired from his travels.

Hurrying to offer the support of his blade, Cam slid from his horse and spotted an older man to his left. Cam raised his sword to take him down and was struck hard from behind. The shock of the blow stilled the force of his movement.

The old man gave him a toothless grin as his blade arched across Cam's chest. Vengeance fueled a burst of energy, and he thrust his sword forward to impale the man and wipe the ugly smile from his face. Cam didn't want that to be the last thing he saw in life.

Closing his eyes, he pictured his wife. The kind smile she offered when she noticed him across the bailey or the hall. The trusting look she gave him when she was close to finding her pleasure in their bed.

He dropped to the soil, glad that he'd die on his own clan's lands.

He'd leave Mari a widow, just as he'd expected.

As darkness came for him, he truly wished he'd been wrong about that.

...

Mari stood at the battlements next to Kenna as the men

approached. At first they were too far away to distinguish individuals, but as they came into sight, Mari checked the men, knowing Cam would be the tallest of them. He sat his horse nearly a head taller than the other men.

She didn't see him.

Scanning the line again, she waited. There were still more warriors cresting the hill, and while Cam's place as war chief was at the front, leading his men, it was possible he'd trailed behind to speak to someone.

That excuse was quickly brushed aside as they approached the gate. There was no way a war chief wouldn't enter the castle with his flags flying, if he were able.

"Cam," she whispered fearfully. "Oh, God."

Kenna said something, but Mari was already running for the stairs and down to the bailey. She'd just cleared the gates when the first men rode in looking battle-weary but happy.

The crowd that had gathered for their return cheered as Lachlan made the announcement of their victory. That was all well and good, but she still hadn't set eyes on her husband.

"Brother?" she called to get Lachlan's attention.

He frowned and slid down from his horse, patting a few backs as he fought his way through the growing crowd to get to her.

"Where is he?" she asked, her voice sounding so small she wondered how he'd heard her with all the noise around them.

"He's sure to be fine. He's coming along in the wagon now. He was injured. It's made him cranky, but he'll be all right. We'll have Kenna and Abagail take a look at him as soon as he's brought in."

Mari twisted her fingers together as she nervously waited for the wagon to drive into the bailey. She didn't even wait for it to stop before she climbed up into the back. There were two men bouncing along. One man was staring up at the sky in death.

The other, thank God, was her husband.

"Help me get him inside," she ordered as if she were still a duchess at Blackley House in London. Here at Dunardry she had no authority, but the men listened anyway. They hurried to take Cam into the keep and straight up to their room.

He still hadn't spoken or so much as moaned. His eyes were closed, and the gray color of his skin startled her.

"Cam?" She settled by his side and placed her hand on his cool cheek. "Husband?"

Then she moved his ratty plaid away and saw blood covering his chest. His shirt was soaked with it.

"Kenna!" she screamed, earning a slight wince from Cam. "Cam? Please hang on. Kenna will help." Leaving him alone in their room and sprinting to the door, she nearly ran into Kenna and Abagail. "Help him, please."

"Light the fire and get a pot of water to boil," Abagail ordered.

Mari was grateful to have something useful to do and turned to her task.

"Cam, can you hear me?" Kenna said, and Mari paused to see if her husband responded. A slight grunt from the bed nearly made her drop the pot. She let out a breath in relief.

She knew he was far from fine, but he had responded. There was hope.

Abagail cut off Cam's shirt in one quick move and hummed in disapproval, only glancing at the gash before looking away.

Mari's hands trembled as she bent to start a fire. It took a few tries, but soon there was a blaze glowing in the fireplace, and she placed the pot over it to boil. She left the room briefly to gather linens, then started ripping them into strips for bandages.

When she returned, she stayed off in a corner, out of the

way. She told herself she kept back so the others could help him, but in truth she was afraid to get too close. Afraid he wouldn't make it. She couldn't stand to see him like this, for she was too much a coward. She'd come to need this man for much more than his protection.

Using her arm she wiped a tear from her cheek and focused on the small part she could do to help the man she loved.

Lachlan came into the room with a scowl. "How is he?" He directed his question to Kenna, who was handling the situation like a warrior.

"The cut on his chest needs to be stitched. He's lost a fair amount of blood."

"Check him over well. I saw him lying in the field, and before I could get to him I saw a horse run past. It may have stepped on him. I wasn't close enough to know for sure."

At that, Mari gasped and came back to Cam's side. She took his hand, hoping he wasn't bleeding internally. Many times when a horse stepped on someone, the injury was not easily seen.

Abagail added her own assessment. "A few ribs are broken. Nothing too bad. You stitch him, Kenna. You've a fine hand."

Mari turned away so as not to tell them to hurry. It didn't matter how the stitches looked—the man was already covered with scars. They needed to stop the bleeding quickly. They needed to save him.

How had she become so reliant on this man in such a short time? She'd not wanted to marry, yet now she couldn't imagine the pain of losing her husband. So much had changed.

"Mari, open the window so we can get fresh air," Abagail said.

She did as she was asked, feeling helpless. She wished she could take her husband's care into her own hands. She knew a bit about healing, but unfortunately she'd been on the wrong end of it to do any good now. The few times the duke had allowed a doctor to be called, she'd been in too much pain to pay close attention to the practice.

"Mari," Cam whispered so low she thought she might have imagined it.

When the other women looked at her expectantly, she hurried to his side. "I'm here."

"Sorry…promise…"

It only took her a second to realize he was speaking of the promise she'd forced from him before he left.

"Shh. Don't worry. I knew what could happen. I made you say those words so I would feel better. It was wrong for me to ask it of you. Besides, you promised to come back, and you did come back."

He winked at her.

"Save your strength."

"Stay," he said, squeezing her hand.

"Of course. I'm not going anywhere. I'll stay as long as you need me."

"Always."

She smiled and kissed the back of his hand. "If that's what you want, then fine. I shall stay forever."

His lips moved in the slightest hint of a smile.

Moments later, guilt tugged at her heart as she recalled her words. She'd asked him to promise something out of his control, and now she'd just made the same kind of promise. She could be gone by morning if Sir Ridley returned with an order from the king.

She shivered and squeezed Cam's hand tighter.

He asked about Liam, and Lachlan assured him the lad was fine. He seemed to relax…or maybe he'd lost consciousness for a moment.

She squeezed his hand, and he squeezed back. "Did you

at least take down the arse who did this to you?"

That got a little more of a smile. "Aye," he managed, then hissed when Kenna pushed her needle into his skin.

"Hold tight, Cam. Let's think of other things. Something nice, like..." She tried to think of something she could say in front of the others, but all their best memories were of the naughty variety.

"Trees," he whispered.

Yes. They'd made love in the cover of the trees. She glanced over her shoulder to see a knowing grin on Kenna's face and a raised brow from Abagail.

"What about the first time we went for a ride by the river?" she said to him. "You told me I could tell you anything."

A grunt indicated either he remembered how she'd passed on his offer at first, or Kenna's needle was not so gentle. Mari wasn't sure which.

"I'm glad you were the one standing in the field that day," she whispered by his ear so only he could hear. "Please don't leave me."

He opened his eyes to slits and then winked at her again. "Not today."

Those two words caused the breath she'd been holding to gust out of her in relief. After that, she kept him busy rambling about silly topics. She told him about London. About the strange animals she'd seen on display. He reached out and touched her cheek, and she was surprised to see he'd brushed a tear away. She wasn't aware she'd been crying.

She smiled. "They're happy tears. I'm so glad you'll be all right."

"There we go," Kenna said when she'd finished and cleaned the wound with some foul salve.

Mari briefly wondered if it were possible to make something that healed a person smell or taste better.

"Aside from the gash, you have a few broken ribs,"

Abagail told him. "Your shoulder is inflamed. And you have a nasty lump on your head. We'll check it tomorrow after you've rested. You'll have a devil of a headache, I wager. I made you some tea for it, but I doubt you'll drink it, stubborn as you are," Abagail complained. Clearly, she'd mended him more than just this once.

"He'll drink it. Won't you, Cam?" Mari said. "Please?"

He let out a breath and gave a slight nod.

"Good for you," Abagail said with a kind smile as she handed over the cup.

Mari coaxed the tea down Cam's throat and sighed in relief when he drifted to sleep.

"While he rests, you should get your own sleep so you'll be rested and able to help when he awakes and needs you," Abagail instructed.

Mari looked toward the window to find it was already dark. The day had rushed by while she cared for Cam. With a nod, she climbed into the bed next to him, careful not to get too close and hurt him.

Kenna smiled and closed the chamber door.

"I'll be fine," he said when they were alone.

"I know. I feel like this was my fault. I shouldn't have made you promise. It put an unfair burden on you. It won't happen again."

He let out a breath. "Just know I'll always do my best to come back to you, with or without a promise in place. Always."

"I do know. And I'll trust in that."

She felt his lips on her forehead as a tear rolled down her cheek into her hair.

All their promises were nothing but empty words. Wishes cast into the wind. Neither of them had any control over what their future held. They only had here and now.

And time, at least for her, was running out.

Chapter Twenty-Five

Cam woke with his wife's hand on his chest. He winced and moved it lower so it wasn't resting on his freshly stitched wound. He knew she would feel awful to find it there when she awoke. The last thing he wanted to do was make her feel worse. She was already dealing with unnecessary guilt over the promise she'd forced from him.

He'd worried about exactly such a thing. Just as he'd worried that having a wife or a family would cause him to be too cautious. But that hadn't happened. In the heat of battle, he'd felt the same as he had in the past. His training had kicked in, and he'd moved from enemy to enemy, taking them down. It had been Liam's predicament that caused his distraction. Not the promise he'd made to Mari.

He reached out to brush a strand of hair from her face and felt a burn in his shoulder from the action. While certain uninjured parts of his anatomy wanted nothing more than to wake her with kisses and make love to her, the rest of his body gave a hearty *nay* to his plans.

It was for the best. She was sleeping and needed her rest.

She'd worried herself into exhaustion.

He had to admit, it wasn't as awful as he'd thought to have someone care that he came home alive and mostly in one piece.

...

Two weeks later, Mari ducked into Kenna's solar and found her sitting in the sun with a book. "Please tell me you need help with the children," Mari whispered frantically.

Eyeing her skeptically, Kenna nodded. "All right. Will you please help me with my bairns, who are all sleeping peacefully?"

Leave it to her sister to understand what was required without explanation.

"Splendid. I'd be happy to help." Mari made her rounds of the room, finding exactly what Kenna foretold. Wee Douglas was sleeping on the end of the settee, while Roddy had nearly scooted himself under the same piece of furniture. Baby Cameron was in his cradle, his lips moving as if dreaming of being nursed.

Mari wasn't actually needed, so she sat next to her sister and let out a breath.

Since the day after the battle when Cam awoke and was told he needed to stay in bed, it had been clear the man was not one for sitting about doing nothing. He was miserable, and misery bred frustration…as well as out-and-out defiance. He'd grumbled and complained to the point she'd taken advantage of a lull to escape.

"Cam's not enjoying being waited on while he convalesces?" Kenna's mouth pulled up in a mischievous smile.

"No. He's the worst patient. He told me to go on with my life and let him rot."

Kenna's brows rose and she laughed. "So here you sit."

Mari couldn't help but laugh as well. "Under normal circumstances I wouldn't mind spending time with him in bed, but this has been beyond trying. I hope Abagail agrees to let him up and about when she comes to check on him. I'll not survive another day of his restlessness."

Kenna frowned. "Oh, dear. I'm afraid Abagail was called away to the village. Thomas Hardy broke his arm."

Mari covered her face with her hands and bent over, muttering a prayer for sanity mingled with a few curses.

"I'll call the nurse to watch the boys, and I'll tend to him myself," Kenna offered.

"I hate to take you away from your rest. You get so little time to yourself."

"I'll be fine. Especially since you'll owe me." With a wink, Kenna left the room, and Mari followed after.

When they entered Cam's chamber, they found him sneaking back into bed.

"What is this?" Mari scolded. "You're supposed to be abed."

"Marian, I swear, if you don't let me up, I'll draw my sword and finish the job the damned McCurdy muddled."

She knew he was serious when he used her given name rather than his shorter version.

"Kenna is here to take a look." Mari pulled back the bandage so her sister could see how much he'd healed. The wound was clean and dry. No swelling or inflammation.

Kenna nodded. "These stitches can be removed. But you'll still need to mind your ribs. Don't do too much."

"I won't."

Mari refrained from rolling her eyes. The man would agree to anything just to be freed from his prison.

To her surprise, he didn't go running from the room as soon as Kenna finished and left them to get back to her children. Instead, he carefully washed himself with Mari's help, then reached for her.

"I'm sorry I've been so irritable. It's just that I've wanted ye and could do nothing about it."

"I understand. It's no fun being injured." There had been many times she'd been unable to get out of bed after the duke showed his displeasure.

Cam's hands rested on her waist as he bent slightly and kissed her, once, twice, then deepened it into a real kiss. She felt the tug on her dress as he fumbled around to unfasten her gown.

"What are you doing?" she asked in alarm. He didn't answer, instead making his intentions clear with a kiss on her neck. "Kenna *just* said you weren't to do too much."

"Aye, and I agreed. I'm not planning to do too much." He smiled devilishly, and she placed her hands on his bare chest high enough not to touch his wound or his still-healing ribs. "I plan to do just enough," he assured her as he took her mouth in a deep kiss.

. . .

Cam had been miserable all the days he was confined to bed. He knew his wife wouldn't lie with him until he was all better. Her nursing, touching, and leaning over him had driven him wild with unrelenting lust. Now that he was able to move a bit without the tug of the stitches, he was ready to make up for the days they'd lost.

"You can't possibly think to—"

"Och, I'm thinking it. I've been thinking it for the past week or more." He rested a palm on her breast, feeling her nipple harden and her breath catch. "I'm done thinking, Mari. I plan to do something about it."

She didn't bark at him to be cautious of his wounds.

Instead, she stood on tiptoe and nipped at his jaw when he was out of reach. The quickness with which she'd changed tactics made him smile. His wife had missed his touch as well.

"You promise we'll stop if you have any pain," she said, relenting.

"The only thing causing me pain at the moment is my cock, the way it aches for wanting ye." He hadn't redressed from his wash, so his cock lurched against her, proving his words true.

"I did vow to nurse you back to health," she teased, taking him in hand.

"Aye. You did."

"I know you are in a hurry to get out of bed, but do you think I could coax you back into it?"

He nodded and sat on the edge of the bed as she knelt before him. He hadn't planned on this, but when her warm mouth took him in, he groaned and let her go about it.

He leaned back but readjusted when his shoulder protested at supporting his weight. He repositioned himself and watched her as she took to her task heartily. He didn't want to spend so quickly, so he looked away from the sight of her mouth on him. He might not be back to fighting form, but he was a prideful husband who wanted to see to his wife's pleasure.

"Stop," he ordered, and she did so quickly, a look of concern on her pretty face.

"Don't worry. I'm not harmed." He was quick to allay her worries. "I want to see ye take your desire. Sit on me so I can watch you."

He inched back onto the bed until he was lying across it. He stroked himself as he watched her disrobe and crawl atop him. She was a glorious sight.

"Go slow," he said when she was fully seated. "I don't want it to be over too soon. I've waited so long for this."

With his good arm, he kneaded her breasts and tugged her nipples until she was gasping and rocking against him faster than he wished. He could tell she was close, so instead of bidding her to slow, he used his thumb to hasten her release, then followed her with his own, pushing up into her, not minding the slight burn in his chest from the action.

The pain was easily forgotten as his release poured out of him.

His wife slumped beside him, and he pulled her close, kissing her hair and her lips.

"That was what I wanted," he said contentedly, not able to move.

"So, all I had to do to get you to stay in bed was ride you a bit?" she asked in a naughty tone.

"Aye. You've found my weakness, lass, but I can't be sorry for it. Any time you want me to stay in bed, you know your power."

"Shall we stay here awhile, then?"

"I just need a quick rest, then I plan to show you how well I've recovered, thanks to your caring touch."

They chose to take their meal in their room so he could continue to show her how fully his health had improved.

There would be time enough to leave his bed tomorrow.

Chapter Twenty-Six

After two days of staying in bed with Cam as he proved his stamina, Mari walked to the village with Abagail to check in on a woman who'd given birth the night before.

Abagail was kind not to mention the slowness of Mari's steps, which was the opposite of her husband's smug smile. He had offered to carry her down to the morning meal, but she'd declined with a light slap to his arm and a reluctant smile. He was barbaric, but she enjoyed his wickedness. Even as she'd left him at the table with Lachlan, she'd returned his naughty grin. There would be time enough for that when she returned home.

Meanwhile, she'd made a decision.

After the helplessness she'd felt when Cam was injured, she'd asked Kenna and Abagail to teach her to be a healer. Today was to be her first lesson.

She smiled up at the morning sky as the sun touched her face. She loved coming to the village. The pleasant cottages and happy families made her feel as if she belonged.

It took a moment for her eyes to adjust to the dim light of

the cottage after being out in the sun, but once she was able to see, she offered a smile to the small family inside. Abagail instructed her to check the mother for fever, and how to check over the new bairn.

"He has a mighty grip. A strong lad," Mari said when the baby had fisted his wee hand around her smallest finger.

"Aye. He'll grow up big and strong like his da. He'll make a fine warrior," the mother said.

"Your husband is a warrior?" Mari asked, wondering if she'd ever met him while watching Cam with his men.

"Aye. But my man grew up in the village and wanted his family to live in the village rather than the castle," she explained.

Mari nodded. "How do you manage when he goes off to battle? I fear I did not handle it well the first time as a wife."

The woman patted Mari's hand. "It's one of the hardest things a wife has to bear—watching her man go off, not sure if he'll return. But everyone finds a way to handle it. Some find distraction in other activities. Some pray. Some—like me—hold our children tight and send our love and strength to our husbands. It gets easier."

Mari wasn't sure how that was possible. Cam had been injured this last time, and she feared for when he'd be called out again, now that he was back in good health. The fear had only grown, not gotten easier. But she'd promised Cam she would not put undue stress on their partings in the future. If he was too distracted, he might fall to an enemy's blade, and she would feel responsible.

When Abagail finished showing her other things to look for that would indicate a complication from birth, they gathered their things to leave.

"I'm glad they're both happy and healthy," Mari said to the healer. "'Tis a great blessing, to be sure."

"Aye. Are ye hoping for a similar blessing between you

and Cam?"

Mari looked away. The truth would count her as selfish. She did want a bairn with Cam. But she lived in the constant dark shadow of an uncertain future. She didn't know if she was safe here. Any day could be the day the English showed up to take her back to London to face punishment for her crimes.

It wouldn't be fair to a child.

"My future is unknown," Mari said vaguely.

The other woman didn't respond with words, just a sound of agreement.

They cut between two cottages and headed toward the castle. Suddenly, she heard a noise and turned back to see Abagail had slumped to the ground, the contents of her basket scattered in the mud.

Before she made it to the woman to offer aid, Mari was lifted from her feet. A smelly hand was placed over her mouth, muffling her cry for help. Kicking, she connected with her captor's shin. He dropped her to the ground, only to snatch her up roughly by the arm and give her a good smack on the head.

Stars swarmed her vision, but she didn't lose consciousness, even when she was tossed into the back of a cart and a tarp was thrown over her.

"Make haste, before she wakes up and calls for help." Odd, but the man next to her sounded more like a boy.

Her thoughts went to that night in the clearing when she'd been unable to free herself. All the hands grabbing at her, holding her. She kicked and slapped harder in an effort to fend them off.

"Tie 'er so she don't escape. I don't want to lose the reward because you let her get away."

Mari's mind cleared at his words. These men were planning to claim a reward by turning her over to the English.

Her hands were bound, and she couldn't see or move. Her previously injured ankle ached as it bounced along the edge of the cart, her feet sticking over the edge. An idea came to her moments later, and she began wiggling the toes of one foot to tug the boot off the other. If she could get it loose, maybe she could drop it as a clue for Cam to follow.

She only had the two shoes, so she'd need to be careful as to when she dropped them. Maybe she'd be able to loosen her stockings and use those as well. That would take a bit more effort.

When the sound of the wheels softened from hard-packed mud to grass, she knew they'd gone off the path and into a field. It was not a smart plan. The wheels would make marks in the grass that could easily be followed. She realized her captors were not the smartest lads, and hoped that would work in her favor.

She shook the boot loose from her foot and started working on the other. Once again, she listened for a shift in the sounds of the wheels. This time the crunching of leaves indicated they'd entered the woods.

She wiggled the other foot, allowing the second boot to drop. Plucking at the strings of her garters through her skirt, she felt one stocking come loose on her thigh and inched it down slowly. Hindered by the fabric and the numbness in her hands because of the ropes, it seemed to take forever until she was able to take over with her other foot, pulling and tugging until the stocking was dangling from her bare toes.

When the echo of trees faded she knew they had exited the woods, and she dropped the stocking. Tears welled in her eyes as she fussed with the stubborn tie of the other stocking. Her hands were like lumps of wood at the ends of her arms. She squeezed them, causing sharp tingles of pain to shoot down her fingertips. Still, she managed to work the tie loose. Her breathing picked up with her struggles to free the stocking.

She only realized the sound of the wheels on hard dirt when she'd gotten the other stocking in position. How long had they been on a road? She wiggled her toes to free the last clue available to her, and then she rested.

If her clues were not found, she would need her strength to fight these men and win her freedom.

Would others come in their place? How long did she have?

Even if she escaped today, what was in store for her tomorrow?

If there was a reward on her head, she would forever be looking over her shoulder.

...

Cam was grateful for Abagail's interruption as she entered the bailey, calling his name. He'd wanted to get back to drills, but now his shoulder and chest protested at the weight of his sword.

He'd let the healer squawk at him a bit, then retire to his room to rest with his wife.

His wife, who had been with Abagail earlier but wasn't with her now. He hushed his men so he could hear the healer tell him a horrid tale. No matter how many questions he asked, she could only tell him she'd been hit from behind, and when she woke, Mari was gone.

"Bryce, Liam, you're with me. The rest of you spread out through the village until you've found my wife."

He and his men led Abagail back to where she'd been attacked, and they followed a trail of wagon tracks.

They'd already found Mari's shoes, but Cam had to swallow back a flood of fear when her first stocking was found at the edge of the woods. The bastards were removing her clothing.

What were they doing to his wife? He would find them and sever their heads from their bodies for hurting her.

"This way," he ordered Liam and Bryce, who were

already on the trail.

"Shouldn't we have more men?" Bryce asked.

"Nay, it's but one cart. It can't be more than a few men. It's clear from the footprints there were at least two. Not very big men, from the size of their feet."

"What if they're meeting up with the English?" Liam asked, sitting taller in his saddle. "Not that I wouldn't slay them all."

"Relax, lad. If there's a line of redcoats at the end of the trail, we'll send you back for the rest of our army."

A lift of Bryce's eyebrow told Cam the army might not come. All the more reason to get her back before she was turned over to them.

He spurred his horse, and the others followed behind him. He saw another stocking lying in their path, but he didn't stop. He could already see the cart rumbling along the road ahead of them and sent his horse after it at a gallop. Bryce let out a war cry and drew his sword, causing the driver to leap from the cart and run for the trees.

"Get him. Bring him to me," Cam called to Bryce as another lad jumped from the back of the cart and ran in the other direction, leaving the cart to continue down the path with no driver...and presumably with Mari in the back.

"I'll get that one so ye can see to Lady Mari," Liam yelled, and tore off after the other lumbering fool.

Cam chased down the cart, which had slowed with no driver and tired horses. He snagged the reins and pulled it to a stop.

"Mari," he called as he slid down from his horse. He pulled the tarp from the back and found his wife gagged and blinking in the sunlight, her hands tied in front of her. "Are you hurt?" He removed the gag and pulled his dirk to free her hands as she started to weep.

"No. I'm fine."

"Did they touch you?" he asked when she was sitting up rubbing her hands. He looked into her eyes, silently waiting for a reply that would send him into a rage that would end with blood on his hands.

She shook her head. "No. They spoke of a reward for turning me in."

"But I found a stocking..." He let his tone ask the question again. Being a Highland lass, she would know what would happen to the men if they'd dishonored her with their foul touch.

She wiped her tears. "I removed them myself, to make a trail for you."

Finally he relaxed the tension in his spine and pulled her close.

"You are a clever lass. You led us right to you." He kissed her and smiled when she blushed at his compliment. Ever the lady.

Liam was the first to return with his captive. The boy was big for his age, but probably no more than fifteen. He had a time of it, keeping up behind Liam's mount, to which he was tied with a rope.

Bryce returned moments later with his quarry thrown over the back of his horse. He tossed the scrawny lad to the ground, who scampered up to his feet to face his punishment.

"Why did ye take my wife against her will?" Cam demanded.

"The tinker had a sheet with her likeness on it. There's a reward for her return to the English. One hundred pounds."

Mari sniffed, and Cam didn't know if she found the sum to be insulting or impressive. He didn't care, since no one would ever collect it. He'd keep her safe.

"You'd turn over one of your clanswomen for coin?" Cam growled.

"She's no MacKinlay. She's sucked English cock. We'd be

glad to have her off—"

The crude comment earned the boy a hard crack across the face that put him out cold. Cam stretched his fist, feeling the blood trickle down his knuckles. His ribs protested as he turned to the larger of the two lads, but he was easily able to put the pain out of his mind. Anger kept him focused.

The other boy proved to be smarter than he looked. He bowed to Cam. "I do not share the same sentiment as my companion, I assure you. I was only out to make things easier for my ma and sisters after my da died. I dinna know who she is, nor much care, as long as I'm able to put food on the table for my family."

"And if your mother or one of your sisters was pictured on that sheet, would you have turned her over to the English to make things easier for the rest under your roof?" Cam asked heatedly.

The boy swallowed, and a tear cleared a path of grime from his cheek. "Nay. I see now what I've done, and I'm sorry for it."

Cam was still too angry to deal justly with the lad. "Bring them to the castle so the laird can mete out their punishments. I can't look at them. I may kill them just for breathing."

He set Mari upon his horse and mounted behind her. "Are you sure you're well, lass?" he asked when she slumped back against him.

"Yes. I am for now." Her voice hinted at her doubts regarding the future.

They'd been wrong not to talk about what could happen. They should have planned for something such as this. They needed to be ready. He'd trained his men for any potential threat and planned an escape route for his wife, but it had been a while since they'd practiced. He'd become lax.

He hadn't wanted the possibility of this situation to darken their happiness. But to ignore the problem wouldn't ensure it stayed away. Problems were like that. Persistent.

"You'll stay in the keep from now on and only go out with me or one of my men with ye, do you understand?"

She nodded, but it wasn't good enough. He knew how women could twist things at a whim.

"Say it aloud, that you promise."

She glanced back at him. "I thought we weren't asking each other for promises any longer."

"Aye, but I'll have this one from you."

She let out a sigh. "Very well. I promise I'll not leave the keep unless escorted by a MacKinlay warrior."

"Thank you. It's not that I wish to restrict your freedom. I trust ye completely. It's for your own protection. I can't lose you, wife. I could hardly breathe when I found that first shoe lying in the mud. I was terrified I'd never see you alive again."

She squeezed his hand, which he'd wrapped around her waist.

"I'll be careful," she said before twisting around to kiss him.

He was grateful for her quick compliance on the matter, but it didn't ease his concerns. They had spoken of her running away and meeting him on the rise, but beyond that, they had no plan. Where would they go from there? How would they live?

Starting tomorrow, he would double the daily drills and work his men into deadly weapons who could protect his wife adequately. He'd enlist more men from the village to learn to fight. The more men the better.

What men weren't at drills should be at the smithy helping to make more weapons. As the war chief, it was his duty to protect his people. This new plan would ensure that every MacKinlay was safe on clan lands, not just his wife.

But if the English decided to come for Mari, they would get a war.

Chapter Twenty-Seven

When the group made it back to Dunardry, Cam took Mari's arm, led her straight up to their chambers, and barred the door.

"What are you doing?" she asked. It was almost time for the evening meal. Much too early to go to bed without starting talk.

Her husband didn't seem to care. He turned her around and plucked at her laces until her gown fell down around her feet. Then he turned her so she faced him, and kissed her with a passion that bordered on desperation. Instantly, she was caught up in it. Soon she was pulling his shirt from his waistband and loosening his belt.

"I know you're too bruised from your ordeal for me to take ye, but I need to feel you alive against me, skin to skin."

"I'm not too sore," she said honestly. Her leg muscles were still a bit shaky, but the rest of her was fine.

He groaned at her consent and asked her again. "I don't know if I'll be able to stop. I want to hear your sounds and slip into your heat. It's battle lust. Something men go through when they've been scared out of their wits."

"I'm well," she repeated, needing to feel him for much the same reasons. She'd known what would have happened if those boys had turned her over to the English. Worse, Cam would have hunted them down and tried to get her back. It wouldn't have mattered how many there were, or how outarmed and outmanned he was. He would have attacked in an effort to save her.

She gasped as he plunged into her. She felt his need in each firm stroke and matched his urgency, crying out when she peaked. He didn't last much longer, and soon they had collapsed together onto the bed. His heart pounded against her ear.

She remembered the injuries to his chest and ribs and moved to give him room, but he stayed her with a gentle hand on her back. Slowly, like a snake, his arm coiled around her, pulling her tight to his body.

"I'll never let anyone take you. Never."

She heard the truth in his promise and made her own. Though silently spoken, it was just as true.

She vowed she would protect him with her life.

・・・

When Cam was rested from both rescuing and making love to his wife, he made his way to the bailey. Some of his men had remained to practice, while others had dispersed.

He couldn't give up what was left of the day. There was no time to spare. After sending the men off to fetch the others, he picked up his sword and swung it with a frown. In the weeks he'd spent abed, he'd grown weaker. He'd have to push himself to make up the time lost.

When the men had all gathered, he broke them into two groups. Half were sent out to find ways to leave the castle without using the front gate. The more escape routes, the better.

The rest of his men were put through their paces until the late meal was served. He told them to be there before dawn the next morning, and when they complained, he told them they would stay past dark.

He heard a few of the men grumble as they left, saying they didn't need extra training to take Baehaven Castle. Cam decided to let them go on thinking that was the cause for the extra effort. The other men didn't know the reason Mari had been kidnapped, and he wanted to keep it that way.

He trusted his men, but a hundred pounds for a half-English lass—his wife or no—might be more temptation than a poor warrior could pass up. He'd rather not put his wife or his men through that.

He shared the news with Lach and swore Bryce and Liam to silence on the matter.

"Are you planning to run?" Lach asked when they were alone at the table.

"I want to be prepared for that possibility. If I can take her away until the danger is past, we could come back when they've gone."

"Have you ever seen an English search?" Lach asked with a frown. "They leave no stone unturned. You would need to leave the lands for a long time."

"Your wife has never needed to live rough on the land for verra long," Bryce commented.

"I ken it well enough, but she's a strong woman. She'll do what needs done." She'd managed to get from London to the wilds of northern Scotland all on her own. He frowned, thinking of the state she'd been in that day. Thin, dirty, and dressed in ratty clothing.

He liked to imagine Mari as a duchess, sitting in a parlor in pretty dresses with maids to do her bidding. Being married to Cam was not elegant or luxurious. Though he'd never once heard her complain.

"It will not be the only time," Lach said. "They'll come back over and over again to check to see if she is here."

"Then each time they return, we'll not be here."

Cam would do whatever it took to protect his wife.

...

While Cam worked every waking hour with his men, Mari spent the days gathering and making spare clothing she could hide beyond the castle in case she needed to flee. Since the incident with the adolescent bounty hunters she had remained in the keep, guarded by one of her husband's men when he was unavailable.

"You've received a letter," Kenna said, handing her a thin envelope.

Mari used to love to get mail, though she rarely did, thanks to the duke. But now, here at Dunardry, mail addressed to her could only mean trouble.

"Who knows I'm here?" she asked as she took it. They had agreed not even to tell their brothers she was here. If anyone mentioned it to any of the many English soldiers who patrolled the lands, she would be found.

"Read it."

The missive had been addressed to Kenna, and the seal was broken.

Mari shook her head and unfolded the letter. Peering at the parchment, she squinted to make out the poor scratching on the page. It was from Lucy, her maid.

Your Grace,

I hope this letter finds you well. Or for that matter finds you at all. I remembered you once said you had a sister in Scotland who'd married a laird. I looked through your things and found a letter from her. Don't worry, I burned the letter after I copied the address. I'm doing everything in my power to make sure the crown's tracker doesn't find you, but he is relentless. He's questioned everyone in the house many times and has made threats that if we servants didn't confirm that you ran to Scotland, we would be put out without a reference.

He's a beast with a juicy bone and won't give it up.

He says as soon as one of us verifies you went to Scotland, he will have enough evidence to go and fetch you home for trial.

Be vigilant, Your Grace. It won't be long before one of the staff corroborates his claim just to be done with him. And when that happens, he will be heading for you.

Stay safe, Your Grace.

Your faithful servant,
Lucy

Mari had been a fool to hope she'd been forgotten. She'd prayed that enough time had passed and that she was free to live her new, happy life with a man who treated her kindly.

It was so easy to pretend things were fine, being so far north. Away from London. Away from her past.

But Sir Ridley, the tracker, hadn't given up. She was not safe here. Nor would she ever be. Eventually the tenacious man would be granted his warrant, and he would show up at the castle gate to collect her.

What would happen when he did?

Visions of Cam being hauled away or killed for trying to protect her haunted her mind. He'd vowed to protect her with his life, and she didn't want him to be forced to honor his promise. Especially when there was no chance of saving her.

Even if he gave his life to keep her safe, she would still be taken to stand trial for a murder. And since she was in fact guilty, she would surely be hanged.

There was no reason for Cam to be harmed. Her plight was hopeless, but his need not be. She would do whatever she had to in order to keep him safe.

"We must not speak of this letter to Cam. I will not ask you to keep a secret from your husband, but please tell him not to mention it to mine. I don't want him to be upset or worried over this."

"*Worried?*" Kenna's eyes went wide. "Worried isn't even half of what the man will feel when he finds out."

"Even more reason to keep him from finding out. I can't have him sitting on the south wall day and night, waiting for the English to arrive."

"What will you do?"

"Let me think on it. I'll come up with a plan."

Kenna patted her hand, anxiety clear in her eyes. "I will wait to mention it to Lach until we've come up with a plan. I canna lose you, Mari. I just got you back."

Mari's sister wasn't one for dramatics, but being a mother brought on strong emotions, and they were getting the best of Kenna as her eyes brimmed over with tears. "All my bairns love ye, sister. You're their only auntie."

Mari took Kenna into her arms, and they swayed together. "Things will be fine. You'll see," Mari promised, though at the moment she had no idea how things could ever be fine again.

• • •

Mari was quiet at the evening meal, and quieter still when they walked to their chamber that night. Cam had seen her angry, but that wasn't the case now. She wasn't mad as much as distracted.

"Is everything well with you, wife?" he asked when they were in the privacy of their room.

"Yes." She smiled, but it wasn't her normal smile. It was the fake duchess smile she forced to her lips when she was being pleasant and didn't want to be.

That was no kind of smile for him. He wanted her real smile, or he wanted to know why he wasn't worthy of it.

"Now I know for sure something is the matter. Your lips are pressed into the false smile of a duchess."

"I was a duchess, if you recall." She looked away.

He crossed his arms, trying to read her, but she would not meet his gaze.

"I recall what you were. But I thought the days of seeing that forced expression were over. What has ye unhappy, lass?"

"I believe I answered your question already. Do you plan to interrogate me until I invent something merely to satisfy you?"

Who was this woman in his wife's skin? His Mari's fiery green eyes stared back at him for a few seconds before skittering away once more.

"A dog growls so he doesn't have to bite," he said, waiting her out.

She scowled at him. "Are you calling me a dog?"

"Nay, and you're doing it again."

"What are you accusing me of, exactly? I can't be sure with all the talk of biting and growling."

"I'm accusing you of starting an argument with me so you don't have to speak the truth. You're hiding something. Why not just tell me what it is so we can deal with it together?"

"Can we not just go to bed? I'm much too tired to puzzle

out what you want from me." With that, she dropped her gown on a chair and crawled into bed in her shift.

As was his habit, he watched the way the thin fabric caressed her skin. His cock stirred, but he frowned, knowing he wouldn't approach her tonight. It was clear she didn't want his conversation or his touch.

Very well. He would give her space. She'd lived with her first husband's demands for many years. It might take as many years for her to realize she was free to be upset with him or simply in need of solitude.

He slid into bed next to her and kissed her shoulder since she was facing away from him. "If I've done something to upset you, know I'm sorry for it."

"You've done nothing wrong." Her voice was thick with tears.

"Why do you weep? Will you at least let me hold you and offer comfort if you don't want to discuss it?"

She turned toward him and nuzzled against his chest so close they all but shared the same skin. She kissed him and ran her hand lower along his stomach.

"Make love to me, husband," she whispered.

"I'm always happy to oblige." He rolled her onto her back and kissed her everywhere. "I'll pleasure ye until a real smile is back on your face," he promised.

He knew her interest in being with him was genuine, but still, it was clearly another distraction.

He brought her pleasure, but the smile he longed to see didn't return.

Over the next few days she stopped snapping at him, but she kept him at a distance. He was certain he hadn't done anything specifically to cause the change. But no matter how many times he asked, she wouldn't share her burden with him.

He thought of it often as he trained with his men. Pushing

them into the night so they'd be ready for whatever happened to break the unrelenting tension.

Each night when he went to his bed, she made love to him with the eagerness of a condemned woman in her final hours on earth.

Chapter Twenty-Eight

Mari turned for another pass along the battlements, feeling trapped despite the miles of rolling land spread out before her. A calm breeze tangled strands of escaped hair, but she still had trouble breathing. A raven circled high above the castle, and she wished she were as free as that.

Cam stepped into her path. "What the bloody hell are you doing up here?" he asked. "I've been looking everywhere for you."

"I needed some air, and since I'm forbidden to leave the keep without one of your men, and you have them all training every second of every day, I came up here so I could be alone with my thoughts."

Her thoughts had given over to fear hours ago. She felt nearly panicked as she scoured the horizon, watching for the English to crest the ridge and head for the castle.

"You know ye need only ask, and I'll take you out or have one of my men do it. And as for being alone, we're done with that. You're my wife. You're not alone. You cannot leave me out of whatever is bothering you. I won't have it."

"Oh? And what will ye do? Shake it out of me?"

She took a step toward him, fists clenched, but her voice quivered with fear. She knew better than to be afraid of Cam, but she'd never been so full of rage. While it hadn't been caused by her husband, he was the only one she had to direct it to.

Unfortunately, he knew her well.

He held up his hands in surrender. "I'll not let you bait me into an argument or seduce me into distraction. I may not be bright, but I know what you're up to, lass, and I'm done. I've given you days to think things over, but still you won't come to me. Until you can speak to me as your true partner, you can keep your hands and your biting tongue to yourself."

"You didn't even want a wife!" she called after him.

"Maybe not. But I have one, and I'll thank ye to start acting like her."

He turned and left her. The breeze caused a chill as her tears overflowed. What had she done?

More important, what was she to do now?

That night, Cam stayed out until after she'd gone to sleep.

She was shaken awake by her husband. "Mari? You're dreaming again. He's gone. He cannot hurt you anymore," he attempted to reassure her.

"I know."

And she did know. It wasn't the duke she had dreamed of this time. It wasn't her past that had caused cold sweat to rise on her skin and triggered her panic.

It was her future that had brought on this nightmare.

In her dreams she was being chased by Sir Ridley and the other Scot, just as she had been the day she'd met Cam. The dogs were bigger than they'd been in reality, and foul-smelling venom dripped from their fangs as they tore at her dress, just out of reach of her flesh.

This time when she made it to the clearing, Cam wasn't

able to help her. She called his name, but he didn't turn to her. As she reached him, she grasped his bare arm. His skin was cold despite the warmth of the day. Her light touch caused him to topple over, and he fell on his back. An English sword stuck up from his chest, and his eyes stared blankly at the perfect blue sky.

Oh, God.

"Make love to me, Cam." She reached for him, needing to feel his skin warm with life. What had he called it? Battle lust. She was in a battle with fate, and she needed him.

"Nay," he said.

It wasn't like him to dissuade her. She touched him, trying to change his mind, but he pulled her hand away.

"I said nay, Mari. I will not allow you to use our joining to hide from what is worrying you. You can talk to me. You can tell me about your dream, if you like. But you will not push me away any longer. Do you understand? Whatever has upset you, it is for us to face together."

She burst into tears at his words. She wanted so much to confide in him. To tell him about the letter, and how she sometimes woke feeling a rope around her neck, unable to breathe.

But this *wasn't* something they could face together. This was her fate, and she'd not allow him to be dragged into it.

"Will you not hold me?"

"Of course." He pulled off her damp shift and tucked her in against his warm body. "You are safe in my arms, Mari. I'll not let anything hurt you. Even the demons that haunt you in your dreams. Tell me. Together we'll conquer them."

She would not tell him about the letter, but there was part of her dream she could share. "I dreamed of those boys, tying me up and throwing me in the cart to earn the reward. I can't help but think it could happen again. A hundred pounds is a lot of money to a crofter or a farmer in these parts. A person might turn in their own mother for that sum."

"Nay. Not a MacKinlay. We're loyal, and you are the laird's sister-in-law. No one would even dare consider it. 'Tis why it was mere lads who snatched ye up. No man would have done such."

But Mari knew it wasn't just the MacKinlays she had to worry about.

Soon enough the English would be here, and life as they knew it would be over.

• • •

Cam left Mari to sleep longer. She'd worn herself out crying and dreaming all night. She needed rest. He took a seat next to Kenna in the solar and scooped the babe into his arms.

"My, it won't be long until you're heavier than me," he said to the child, who looked up at him with Kenna's green eyes. The older boys looked the spitting image of their da, but this one had some of Kenna in the mix.

"I believe it," Kenna said with a smile. "He's an armful, I can tell you that."

"He has a bit to grow until he fills my arms." Cam smiled down at the bairn, who reached out and grabbed his lip. "Let me go, or I'll have no choice but to bite those fingers off." He made a chomping sound which caused the other boys to giggle and hold out their own fingers to be eaten by the giant. It was a game they often played.

"Is Mari well?" Kenna asked when the boys settled again.

"Aye. She's sleeping." He paused and thought of a tactic he hadn't yet tried. "Actually, Kenna, she's not well. She's worried into a frazzle and willna talk to me about it. I want to help, but she keeps me at a distance. I ken she's your sister, and she may have asked you to keep a secret. But I'm her husband. Should I not know what demons she battles?"

Kenna huffed out a breath and closed her eyes. "I'll not feel guilty for speaking to you about it. I've given her more than enough time to tell ye herself, and she's not done so. Very well. I'll do it."

Even after her defiant statement, Kenna looked around the hall as if making sure her older sister wouldn't catch her in the act of betrayal.

"She received a letter from her maid in London. It said that Ridley is questioning the servants at her old home. As soon as he forces one of them into signing a statement that they know she went to Scotland, he will have his order to come here and take her back."

"Is that why she paces the battlements? She's watching for his return?"

"Aye. Though she hasn't said what she plans to do if a river of red crests our hills. I'm worried, Cam. I think she plans to do something courageous—and therefore incredibly stupid."

"Thank you for telling me the truth. I'll see that she's taken care of."

With that, he went back to their room. He didn't wait for her to wake. Instead, he opened her chest and rooted through her things. When he found no letter there, he went to the other chest.

"What are you doing?" she asked, sitting up in bed.

"Where's the letter Lucy sent you? I want to read it."

"Kenna." Her sister's name crossed her lips like a curse.

"Aye. *Kenna* told me after I asked for her help. Asking for your help dinna work, so I went to someone more reasonable. And how do you like that? *The wild one* is the more reasonable of the two of you."

Mari stood and went to the blanket that had been on top of the chest. Folding over a corner, she retrieved the note and held it out.

His eyes scanned the paper twice before his mind made sense of the words written there.

"What do ye plan to do when he gets here?" Cam asked in a low voice.

"I'm not sure. But I can't have you risk your life or the lives of your men for me."

"That is not for you to decide."

Brushing aside that nonsense, he left their room and headed down to the bailey. Knowing Mari was in danger pushed him into action. He pressed the men harder and longer. When they protested, he challenged them.

"At this very moment, the English could be on their way. We have to be ready. We have to be better. They outnumber us and outarm us, so each of you must fight as three men, not one. Liam, Paul, Rufus, come forward." He waved at them to hurry. "If the three of you take me, we'll stop for the meal. If you canna, we keep going. Agreed?"

They all nodded and drew their weapons. They had youth on their side, but Cam was stronger and better trained. Soon Rufus dropped away and then Paul. Liam put up a good show. He was a strategist, and he'd grown in the last months. But eventually Cam deflected a lunge and forced the sword from his hand. Heaving in air, Liam lifted his head as Cam rested his sword tip at the lad's throat.

"We continue," he commanded, and everyone lined up again to go through the motions. Another hour, and another, as the noonday sun crested and slipped past its peak.

It was a warm September day and the men were drenched in sweat and growing weak, but still Cam pushed, even knowing he was dancing on the edge of sanity. The sun was moving toward the horizon, and they'd had no food or drink the entire day.

He sparred with Liam again, and the lad stumbled and reached out, raising his sword. The steel wavered, and the boy collapsed in the dirt, his pale blond hair soaked.

"Liam? Lad? Get up." Cam knelt beside him and touched his pale, clammy face, feeling his heart pounding. "Bloody hell." His skin was far too hot. He hefted the boy to his shoulders and headed for the loch. "We're done for the day. Go rest and get something to drink."

In the nearest shady spot he submersed Liam, making sure to keep his head above the water. When he finally woke, Cam handed over a flask of ale and sat with him as he sipped it.

"I'm sorry for my weakness," Liam said while resting his head on his knees. "I can't believe I disgraced myself in front of all the men."

His color was better, but Cam wanted to make sure he was well. "Nay. It wasna you who was the disgrace, but me. A warrior is only as strong as his body, and I didn't take care of yours. I'm sorry, lad, truly."

"You want us to be fierce, as would any war chief."

"Aye, but there's being fierce and there's being foolish. I've been something far worse than foolish."

"What's that?" Liam asked.

"Desperate."

Liam nodded, not needing any explanation. "You want to protect Lady Mari."

"Yes. Very much so."

"I understand. I'm in love, as well. And I'd do anything to keep her safe."

Cam gave him an indulgent smile. "I'm not in love, but Mari is my wife, and it's my duty to protect her."

Liam's brows pulled together. "Ye don't love her? I was sure you did. The way the two of you are always sneaking off to your room and the woods…"

Cam chuckled. "That's lust. I've got that aplenty. But I also have a responsibility to keep her safe. I don't want anything to happen to her."

Liam nodded. "I understand. I feel the same. Even if I only met her after she'd already been injured."

"The Stewart lass?"

"Aye. Evelyn." Liam's eyes got all dreamy in that way love made men lose their wits.

Cam wouldn't fall into that trap. "I want to protect my wife. But I'll not lose ye to do it. That was wrong. I won't let it happen again."

"I'd give my life to protect her, and be glad for the honor," the boy said, causing Cam's guts to turn.

He should have been pleased to hear the young warrior's vow of fealty. He should have clapped the lad on the shoulder and told him he was a brave man. But it didn't ring true. Giving one's life for another was an honorable thing. But what was one life saved if another was lost?

What made Mari's life more valuable than Liam's, or the rest of his men? For it was clear it would not be just one man to fall in protection of Mari when they faced the English, but many. Could he ask a warrior with a wife and children at home to give his life so that Cam could save his own wife?

"Go to the kitchens and tell Millie I said to give you some salted meat. It helps. And don't let any of the men shame you for falling over. Go on."

Liam nodded and headed for the castle. Cam watched him to make sure he was well enough to walk, then turned to watch the water lap against the rocks. He didn't need to look toward the sound of footsteps to know who soon approached him.

"If you've come to scold me for being too harsh on my men, I already know what an arse I am."

Lach sat next to him. "*Your* men? I thought they were *my* men."

Cam smiled and nodded, acknowledging the slip.

"Whoever's men they are, they'll be far more impressive if I don't wear them down to naught but bones."

"I don't think fighting is going to get her out of this." Lach kept his gaze on the water, too.

Cam knew his cousin well enough to understand he did not mean they should surrender.

"You think Mari and I should run, then."

Lach nodded. "We have ties to the Campbell clan through our mothers. Bryce is also a Campbell. Or perhaps it would be safer to leave Scotland altogether. Mayhap France?"

Cam swallowed back a refusal to leave his homeland. While it wasn't the best option, he knew he would do it if it meant protecting Mari as well as his clan.

"Wherever ye decide to go, you'll not speak of it with any of us. Afterward, there should be no letters or contact at all. Nothing that can tie you back to the clan. Don't even tell Mari until you're on your way. She'll tell Kenna, and Kenna will want to check on her sister."

Cam nodded, already feeling the chill of the self-imposed exile. "I agree. I'll make the necessary arrangements."

Chapter Twenty-Nine

Mari's nightmares continued and grew even worse. Cam hated feeling helpless and wanted to help. But he didn't think she'd shared all her fears. She was still holding something back.

When Lach gave orders for him to take his men to Skye to try to negotiate access to the sea through the McInnis lands, Cam asked the laird to send someone else.

"It is because of you we have no access to the sea through a McCurdy alliance. I need you to find us another viable port," Lach said with his brows creased. "Why do you fret? Your wife is safe here. We'll not let anything happen to her. Besides, you may find a way to board a ship easier if you make the connections beforehand."

"I know. It's just that she's been having nightmares of late. I'm afraid my leaving will cause her more stress."

"She's married to the war chief. She's going to have to face it sooner or later. Now seems to be the right time. And I have heard rumors that the McCurdy may try to take the McInnis clan. If we help them hold their lands against our common enemy, they may warrant an alliance. I'll ask Kenna to keep Mari busy, distract her from your absence, but I need ye to do this."

Cam let out a breath, knowing a protest would be in vain. He had a responsibility to his laird and clan. He had a responsibility to his wife as well, but his duty came first, whether his heart agreed or not.

Not wanting to upset her, Cam left the news of his departure until the night before he was to leave.

To his surprise, she only nodded. "I understand. I'll look forward to your return."

"That's it?"

"I said I'd not beg a promise from you in the future. I know you have little say in what awaits you on the road, so I'll not add to your burdens."

"Thank you. But just because you haven't asked for a promise doesn't mean I won't give you one." He kissed her. "I promise you, wife, I will do all in my power to come home to you. And if the Almighty calls me home, I will be waiting for you at the gates."

She kissed him again. "Thank you. I trust you to do what needs doing."

And as easy as that, his farewell was accomplished.

Or so he thought.

Later that night just after he'd drifted off, Mari began to mutter and toss. Another nightmare. He gave her a small shake to wake her from the horror.

She gasped in air, struggling to breathe.

"Are ye all right?" he asked worriedly.

She cried into his chest, and he felt her body tremble with sobs.

"Shh. Please just tell me what has you so upset. Please, Mari, I beg of you. Let me help in whatever way I might."

She looked at him, her eyes bright with tears in the dim

light, and blurted out, "I think I should turn myself in to the English."

Of all the words that could be strung together to form a thought, he'd never expected those to come out in that order.

"*What?*" he said, thinking maybe he'd misheard. Praying he had.

"The fear of them coming for me and hurting everyone here has me tied into knots. If I turned myself in, it would all be over."

"Aye. It would. So would your life. We would be over, too, and I'll not have it. It's been months since you came to me. They have bigger things to worry about in London than a wee lass who stood up for herself against her bugger of a husband."

"But Lucy—"

"I know what Lucy's letter said. But even if Ridley badgers someone into saying you planned to come here, it might not get him an order from the crown."

She nodded, but without real agreement, so he decided to tell her of his other plan.

"If we get word that they are coming for ye, I have some things stashed away. Money and the like, to take us far away from here."

"Away? *Where?*"

"I'll not say, for it canna be shared with anyone here. It's safer if they don't have answers, should they be questioned."

She let out a breath but still didn't say anything to make him believe she'd given up on her plan to turn herself in.

"Mari, I'll have your promise you will be here when I return," he said sternly.

"Of course," she said, though he couldn't help but see how she'd worded it so she hadn't actually promised anything. Before he could press her into saying the actual words, she yawned and fell asleep.

He woke before dawn the next morning and kissed her forehead before leaving their room to start his journey. Lach was waiting in the hall to see him off.

"Mari is entertaining the daft idea of turning herself in to the English," Cam muttered. "You'll please make sure that doesn't happen while I'm gone?"

Lach's brows hiked. "Aye. I will. Why would she say such a preposterous thing?"

"I think it was no more than a desperate thought after a nightmare, but keep an eye on her. Don't let her leave on her own."

"We already have men with her at all times. She'll be safe. I'll make sure of it."

...

Rather than go down to break her fast, Mari went to the solar to sit by the window to watch for a line of soldiers wearing red coats to crest the hill. It hadn't happened yet, but it would. Someday.

Just as she'd seen in her dream.

Cam had tried to reassure her by telling her he had plans for them to escape, but how would that help the people here? They might not have answers to supply the soldiers regarding her whereabouts, but they'd certainly be questioned relentlessly if Ridley thought they knew something.

That would be just as bad as if she were found here. Perhaps worse. Soldiers given permission to do whatever it took to extract information would not stop until they had something to report back.

Kenna rushed into the room, then stopped and smacked Mari in the back of the head.

"Ow. What was that for?" Years of being the second-eldest sibling hadn't prepared Mari for such things from her baby sister.

"You told Cam you want to turn yourself over to the English."

"He told you?"

"Nay. I don't get up to see the men off when the bairns are sleeping. But Cam told Lach, and he told me. So what are you thinking? Have you gone mad?"

"I've grown weary of living in fear of what is coming."

"That letter. I knew I should never have given it to you. I tell you true, the MacKinlays will protect you, sister. You are one of us now. You have nothing to fear. Now here, I brought you a tart. Even though you speak like a muttonhead, you're my only sister and I love ye."

"I love you as well." And it was because of that love Mari would make sure her sister and the rest of the clan were never put in danger because of her past.

Kenna settled into the chair next to her and picked up her embroidery. She let out a sigh. "Thanks for fixing this."

Mari smiled. "It's not a problem. Go ahead and make another bunch of knots for me to fix tomorrow. At this rate, we'll have a fine linen in a year or two." Mari expected Kenna to offer a snappy retort, but instead she sat staring at the hoop in her hand. Mari placed a hand on her sister's. "I was only jesting, Ken. It's beautiful."

"It's not the embroidery—which is a far cry from beautiful—it's…" Kenna turned her head to one side as if listening for something. "I think I need to lie down. I feel a little off." With that, Kenna's face went even paler, and she melted onto the settee.

Acting quickly, Mari went to fetch a pitcher of water and some linens. She wetted one and placed it on Kenna's forehead.

"Sister?" She patted Kenna's clammy cheek. "Kenna?"

Kenna's eyes opened and she blinked. "Oh my. I'm sorry.

I—"

"I'll get Lachlan."

"No. I'm—"

But Mari was already out of the room. She nearly fell down the stairs and was out of breath when she burst into the hall. Rather than shout across the room, she walked as fast as could still be called walking and focused on the head table at the dais.

She must have looked like the devil was chasing her, for Lachlan jumped down to come meet her. She leaned up to whisper in his ear that Kenna had fainted.

His face went white, and he gave her upper arm a squeeze before rushing past her to go see his wife. With that task completed, she hurried to find Abagail, who was naturally not in her cottage. Her neighbor said she'd gone to another village to help a man who'd lost his leg.

As Mari headed back to the castle, she noticed one of the men staring at her as if she were a tasty ham. It was then she realized she'd left the safety of the castle without a guard. And she remembered she wasn't just a tasty morsel. She was a walking hundred pounds sterling.

Back in the safety of the castle, she rushed upstairs.

Kenna glared at her over Lachlan's shoulder as he knelt in front of her.

"I'm sorry. Abagail is not available at the moment. What can I do to help?"

"You could have kept your mouth shut until I'd had the chance to explain that I hadn't had the chance to eat yet, and that I often get light-headed if I don't eat early enough."

Mari winced. "Oh."

Lachlan took charge despite still looking shaky. "I am having a meal brought up for you. In the meantime, I think it best you stay away from the children. Just in case."

"I am fine. You'll see, once I've eaten."

"I'll check on the food." Lachlan paused when he passed her. "Could she be with child again so soon?" he asked.

Mari smiled. "I'm afraid you would know that better than me."

"Good God, what have I done?" he murmured. "I hope she just needs to eat."

He left them alone, and Mari apologized again.

"You've done it now," Kenna said with a laugh. "He'll be hovering and watching over me for days to make sure I'm not ill or increasing. Lord, I hope I'm not increasing already." She gave a good-natured groan.

"Is it so bad to have a husband who cares about you and sees to your every need?" Mari asked.

"You tell me. You don't seem to be enjoying it from Cam."

Mari let out a breath. She hadn't been fair to him. He'd only wanted to share in her worries. She wasn't used to such a thing from a husband.

Unfortunately, what worried her was something she needed to take care of on her own.

• • •

Cam arrived at the McInnis castle on a bright, sunny day. The salty smell of the sea put a smile on his face as he greeted the laird and explained the reason for his visit.

While he was greeted warmly, the McInnis laird made no promises that they'd be able to strike an accord. In fact, during the evening meal, the McInnis laird began to explain the predicament of their small port.

"I fear we've not an easy access, despite being so close to the water." He went on to tell how a large portion of a cliff had fallen into the sea and cut off the small beach. They'd not yet found a way to navigate around the new obstacle and he was doubtful it would ever be feasible for more than small vessels.

Cam was almost glad for the news, for it meant he'd be able to start his return to Dunardry the next morning. But he knew Lach would be disappointed if he didn't try to come up with another way to make it work. So, the next morning they went down to the water to see the devastation. As the laird had said, large boulders and rocks filled what once had been a modest harbor.

The McInnis shook his head in despair as Cam studied the line of rocks. None were of the same height, but the shortest one was of fair size. He reckoned the others could be cut down to match, then the stone that was cut away could be used to fill the gaps.

Before he realized it, he'd opened his mouth and started talking.

"It would be similar to a curtain wall," he clarified. "You'd need to pile up the rock in the crevices so it would provide support against the force of the sea even during storms. You're protected here, but you'll want to plan for the worst nature has to offer."

An hour later, Cam had requested paper and had drawn out formal plans for their path to the sea.

"With a taper here toward the shore, you'd be able to ride carriages and wagons right up on the wall to aid in loading cargo." Cam walked the laird to the best place to start the structure.

The McInnis followed, making comments and pointing out things as they went. When Cam was done explaining his plan, the man looked a bit overwhelmed.

"This will not be an easy feat," the laird said. "Especially with the reduction to our coffers because we've been unable to trade. We also lost ships and some good men." The man grimaced. "But it sounds like it can be done, and doing so will give us back our freedom. When we're on solid ground again, I'll be sure to reach out to the MacKinlay to see if we can come to an agreement. Thank you for your help."

Cam and McInnis clasped arms to solidify the future possibilities. They were leaving the coast for the village when they were approached by a half dozen British soldiers.

"What may we do for you?" McInnis asked with a slight edge to show his displeasure with their intrusion on his lands.

"We're looking for this woman. It's thought she might try to board a ship. There's a reward of one hundred pounds sterling for her capture."

McInnis smiled. "That would certainly help us pay for our repairs." He laughed and took the notice.

Cam remained calm despite being able to see Mari's likeness from where he stood. This was worse than he'd ever imagined.

"My, a duchess wanted for murder," the McInnis murmured. "You sure do breed your women to be malicious in London."

"She is a Scot, sir," the sergeant pointed out, which drew a scowl from the laird.

"Are you traveling all the coast of Scotland?" Cam asked the sergeant.

"Yes, three squads have been dispatched to visit all ports. We'll find her soon enough."

Cam hoped desperately that wasn't true.

Chapter Thirty

"Might I have a word with you, my lord?" Mari hovered by Lachlan's door. "Kenna is well, that's not why I'm here," she added when his face went pale. The poor man had watched over Kenna for days, only to see she was fine and had only needed to eat when she'd fainted.

Mari's brother-by-marriage looked surprised at the request, but he nodded and stood to help her to her seat like a gentleman.

"What can I do for you today, sister?"

She smiled at his words. Despite his not-so-welcoming greeting that first day, Lachlan had since made her feel as though she were truly part of his family.

"I'm afraid I've come to ask a favor of you."

"I'll hear it," he said. She hadn't expected him to agree without hearing her request, but it would have made things easier if he had.

"I know you're aware I received a letter some weeks ago from my maid in London. I know she would have sent it with the utmost discretion. However, it speaks of danger."

"From London?"

"Yes. It seems they have not given up on their search for me. As you can imagine, when someone murders a peer of the realm, the English are sticklers for justice. Even as we speak, there may be trackers on their way with a warrant for my arrest."

His brows pulled together. She could see he was trying to come up with a solution, as good lairds did. "And if that is so, what would you have me do?" he asked.

"You have guards posted at the borders to alert us when the soldiers arrive. We should have a few hours' warning at minimum, yes?"

"Aye. A day probably. You would have plenty of time to escape." He nodded once. "We could spare some money, and Cam will find you a new home. He's already made provisions—"

She shook her head. "Dunardry is Cam's home. You are his family. I cannot ask him to give all that up for me."

"I do not think you would get a chance to ask him. He would leave with you the instant you were in danger."

"Yes. He promised to protect me with his life. Which is why I'm willing to do whatever it takes to protect him with mine. They won't stop looking for me. We would have to keep moving forever. Keep running. That's no life. Always waiting, wondering if today will be the day I'm found. And when they finally do come upon us…?"

Lachlan pressed his lips together for a moment before turning back to her. "What would you have me do?" This time the question was asked with a hint of desperation.

"If the time comes, I would like you to send Cam on an errand in the opposite direction. I do not wish him to be here when they take me away."

"Cam would draw his blade across my throat for even considering such a thing."

"You are the laird."

"And as Kenna points out, it means nothing if I don't have the respect of my people behind me. Turning you over to the English is a sure way to lose their loyalty."

"Perhaps it seems as if I'm a coward, wishing to give up. But if they come here looking for me, they will question everyone in the clan. It's unrealistic to think something wouldn't slip. And when that happens, the interrogations would become dangerous for everyone."

It was clear from his expression he had not considered this. "You've thought this through."

"Every night. It fills my mind constantly. This clan has become my family, and I need to do the right thing to protect them, or live with the guilt and sorrow forever. That is no way to live, my lord. Neither is forcing Cam from his home to spend the rest of his life roaming the earth on the run." She swallowed and looked away, blinking back tears.

"Your husband—"

"Cam's promise to protect me with his life will come to fruition, and he will be killed trying to save me. My death is inevitable. But his isn't." She stood a little taller, having come to terms with it. "I truly believe I would have died that night at the duke's hands had I not acted to protect myself. I had never seen the duke so angry. Having lived long enough to come here and spend these last months as Cam's wife and being part of Clan MacKinlay was more than I ever hoped to have."

Lachlan did not look happy. "As you've said, you are one of us. And Clan MacKinlay protects its own. When you married Cam, it wasn't just his promise of protection you acquired."

A tear ran down her cheek. "I appreciate that, and it is because you have all become my family that I could never bring a fight with the English to your gates. When the time comes, I ask you to deliver me to them without resistance."

"I think your sister is going to have something to say about that." Lachlan rubbed the back of his neck.

"Which is why you cannot tell her."

He laughed once. "You ask me to keep this secret from my wife?"

"I do. I know you have given her a promise of protection. Delivering me to the English is keeping that vow in the best way you can. I am sorry you are caught in such a situation. She will be angry with you, I'm sure. But when she calms, she'll see you did the right thing."

"It's the *when she calms* part that has me worried." He rubbed his jaw. "Let me consider all of our options. Mayhap there's still a way to protect ye without such an extreme plan."

She nodded and went to the door, hoping he could come up with something she hadn't thought of.

Hiding here wasn't a viable option. The soldiers would rip the village and the castle to shreds looking for her. If she wasn't found, that wouldn't be the end of it. Surprise inspections and searches would be ongoing and relentless. She'd thought of every possible outcome, and the only one that ensured the people she loved remained safe was turning herself in.

"I ask that when the English arrive, you at least let me know, so I can be part of your decision."

He gave a reluctant nod. "I will discuss it with you, if ever they arrive."

• • •

Cam went to find Mari as soon as he arrived home. He was filthy from travel, but he needed to see her. He'd only made it into the hall before she slammed into him. Her arms looped around his neck and he bent to kiss her, not caring who else might be in the hall to see them.

"God, I've missed you. It's only been a few weeks, but it's felt like years since I kissed you."

"It feels the same to me." She laughed and kissed him again. "I'll have a bath brought up."

"Nay. I must see Lach first, because once you get me in our rooms I'll not come out for a few days." She blushed, and he pressed a kiss to her head. "You haunted my dreams, wife."

"You were in mine as well."

"Do I take that to mean your nights weren't filled with terrors?"

She frowned, and he saw the truth.

"We're safe. I'll make sure of it."

"And what about your safety?" she asked.

He let out a breath and pulled her to his chest. He couldn't lie to her, but he wasn't ready to tell her of the soldiers he'd encountered. He needed to speak with Lach and determine their options first.

"Get us some food. I'll meet ye upstairs shortly."

She nodded and left. He watched her until she was gone, then went to find the laird.

"Nay, like this, Roddy. Hold it like this," Lach instructed his child as Cam walked into the solar.

"Isn't he a bit young for swords?"

"Do you remember the first time you held a sword?"

"Nay. I thought I was born with one strapped to my hip. My dear mother complained my birth was a horrendous battle."

They laughed as Lach slapped him on the back in greeting. When he released his cousin Cam took up a small wooden sword and tapped it against the matching one in Roddy's hand. The boy laughed and made a move to stab him.

Cam fell to the floor and moaned in a display of pain, causing the other twin to jump on him as Roddy struck him again. Both boys dissolved into giggles when he lurched up from his fake death to grab and tickle them.

Once they'd settled, the nurse arrived to take the children away. Cam gave them each a smacking kiss on the cheek before handing them over.

"You'll make a good father someday," Lach said when they were alone.

Cam nodded. "I don't fear it like I once did, but it's not something I wish for right now. Not with what we may be facing."

"Something's happened?" Lach guessed.

"Aye. Squads of English soldiers are visiting every port with a notice about Mari, including a likeness. In a matter of weeks, every sailor and dock mate will know her face. We'll not be able to board a ship without encountering someone who wishes to earn the hundred-pound reward for her capture."

Lach drew in a long breath. "We'll think on it and come up with something."

Cam noticed the man's bleak expression and knew the laird had been worrying over this since Cam had brought Mari home.

"I'm sorry this will fall at our door."

"We do what we must to protect our kin," Lach said. Cam nodded in agreement and went to find his wife.

• • •

Mari already had the bath prepared for Cam's arrival. She expected him to want to sit and relax in the tub while he told her of his trip, but he didn't. Instead he washed quickly and came to her naked, without so much as drying off.

"If you don't want your gown drenched, you should remove it."

She laughed and clutched at the laces as he reached

around her, making her clothes wet as he helped. Once she was naked, he kissed her and led her to the bed, where he laid her back and covered her with his body.

The way he touched her scared her. It was as if he knew it was the last time they'd lie together, or he was worried it would be. When they finished making love, he drew her against him, holding her tightly.

"What's happened?" she asked, her hand continuing to trail up his chest. She felt his breath catch before he uttered the lie.

"Nothing."

She wanted to push him to tell her, but doing so might force the truth from her own lips.

"Let's agree to take each day as it comes," he finally suggested. "We'll not think about what may or may not happen in the future. Just today. And then the next."

"For how long?"

"For as long as we can."

She nodded in agreement. "Very well. We won't speak of what might happen."

"We won't."

It seemed a foolish thing not to prepare for the inevitable, but she latched onto his offer with both hands. She'd said her piece to Lachlan. The laird would either give her the chance to save Cam and the clan, or he'd launch them into a battle they couldn't win.

The decision was out of her hands for now.

She and Cam spent every night in each other's arms, making love with that same conviction. *Live for today. Don't look too far ahead.*

For a month, their plan worked. They lived their lives without the worry of tomorrow.

But as tomorrows tended to do, the one day she'd dreaded for so long finally arrived.

Chapter Thirty-One

Mari woke to the sound of Scottish grumbling. She smiled and stretched, remembering the night before. Remembering all the nights before. All the ways Cam had loved her and she'd loved him back.

"Come back to bed," she pleaded, missing his warmth in their chilly chamber.

It was still dark. There was only so much practice he and his men could subject themselves to.

"I canna. I'm sorry I woke you." He leaned down and kissed her. "But I'm not sorry you're awake now."

She laughed and sat up, grabbing her wrapper and pulling it on.

He slipped his cold hands inside, causing her to jump and shiver. Autumn was giving way to winter. Each day the sun came closer and closer to losing the battle.

"I'd love nothing more than to crawl back into bed where it's warm and take you again, but Lach has ordered me to take a message to the McCurdy. I'm not sure when I became a messenger, but he worries there could be trouble. So I must go."

It took a moment for her sleep-muddled mind to catch up with his words…and the meaning beneath them.

"How long will you be gone?"

"Should only take about five days, a week and a half at the most."

Lachlan was sending Cam away on an errand. It was possible he truly wanted Cam to speak to the McCurdy laird, but it was more likely this was the distraction she had requested so Cam wouldn't be here when the English came for her.

Oh, God.

This was the last time she would ever see her husband.

When she tensed in his arms, he pulled away to offer a smile. "I'll make good time and maybe I'll be back in four. Don't worry. If another lass comes running up to me and tries to marry me, I'll tell her I already fell for that trickery."

He winked and kissed her on the nose before turning to pick up his sword.

"Cam." Her voice shook, and she swallowed to get control. It wouldn't do for him to see her heightened anxiety. She needed to play the part of a wife seeing her husband off for a few days, not a desperate woman saying goodbye forever to the man she'd come to love.

He hadn't wanted love between them, and in fact, she hadn't realized how she felt until this very moment. But she couldn't tell him now.

He stepped back and placed his arms gently on her shoulders. "Are ye well, lass? You look pale."

"I'm fine. I'm just going to miss you," she said as tears welled up in her eyes.

"What's this?" he teased. "Am I so fine a lover you don't think you can make it a few days without me?" He kissed her tears away and pulled her close, then his tone turned serious.

"It's hard for me to leave you, too. I never understood before. I'd heard people talk about being bound to someone, but I feel it now. As sure as if we still had that piece of your dress tying us together."

It sounded as though he felt the same way she felt about him, but she was too afraid to ask.

He kissed her again, and she couldn't help the way she clung to his shirt.

"I must go." Another kiss and he turned for the door. "I'll see ye soon."

She couldn't speak. She was torn between begging him to stay and run away with her, and screaming with the unfairness of it all.

He smiled and closed the door behind him. A second after he was gone, she lurched for the chamber pot to cast up her accounts.

...

The barest hint of light illuminated the sky as Cam mounted his horse and headed off on his mission to the McCurdy lands.

A smile claimed his face as he thought of the night before. The smile dimmed slightly when he remembered the uncertain future he and Mari faced. While their months together ensured she did not fear his touch any longer, he knew well what kept her from having true peace in their new life.

They'd been living in a dream pretending they didn't have anything to fear, when he knew the English were searching for Mari. It wouldn't be long before they showed up at Dunardry and the war would begin.

She'd killed a duke. The crown would demand justice. Especially when it was a Scottish lass who was to hang for it.

It was long past time for Cam to take her away to safety. He needed to find a new place for them to live. She'd been a duchess, so he wanted to offer her some luxury. Living in the rough, constantly moving, was not an option if they planned to have a family someday.

He'd need to gain a piece of land and build a house. Unfortunately, his soldier's pay didn't allow for much. His wife had once lived a life of opulence. While she'd adjusted without complaint to castle life, he couldn't have his wife living out of a cave.

He frowned up at the sun when it occurred to him that living out of a cave would be far preferable to being hanged.

If she was ever caught, she would be killed.

He must make sure that never happened.

...

Mari dressed quickly and hurried down to the hall as soon as Cam had left. She found Lachlan pacing in front of the fire.

"Are they coming?" she asked after checking the room to make sure Kenna wasn't there.

"Aye. I got word late last night. I sent Cam away as you asked of me, but I don't think I can see through on the rest of the plan. Kenna—"

"My sister will be angry, to be sure, but she and your children will be safe, along with the rest of the clan you're responsible for." She swallowed, hoping she wouldn't embarrass herself by being sick again. Her stomach was a knotted mess of worry and fear. "Would you see me out to meet them so they don't get close to the castle? If you'd rather not, I can go by myself. But I promised Cam I'd not venture beyond the castle walls unescorted by a warrior."

Lachlan gave a humorless bark of laughter. "I doubt he'll appreciate your attempt at following his orders, but I'll not have you face them alone. I will escort you. It's the very least I can do."

She nodded and reached into the satchel she'd packed long ago for this eventuality. Pulling out the letters she'd written to everyone, she handed them to her brother-by-marriage. "Will you see that everyone gets my letters?"

"Of course."

"Then I'm ready."

That was a bald-faced lie. No amount of planning could prepare her for this moment. She had looked at Cam for the last time. She only wished she'd realized how she felt about him before it was too late. Somehow, never saying the words "I love you" seemed her greatest betrayal.

Lachlan bit his lip and shook his head. "I'm not sure *I'm* ready. You have become my sister in heart, and I truly don't want to lose you. My children will only remember you from stories, and I fear I will always feel responsible for that loss."

She hadn't expected this from the normally practical and hardhearted laird. But she'd known there must be something under his shell that her sister had found appealing and worthy of her love.

Mari gave Lachlan a quick hug and stepped back. "Let us be off." *Before we are not strong enough to go.*

• • •

The English were in the process of breaking camp when Mari and Lachlan arrived.

She wasn't sure her legs would hold her as he helped her down from the horse.

Sir Ridley came forward with a sly smile on his face. "Didn't I tell you this would be easy, Felix?" He turned toward a large man. "The Scots claim to be fearless warriors, but they would turn over their own mother if it meant avoiding unpleasantness and claiming a reward."

The men laughed, and Lachlan released her to take a step forward, his hand on his sword.

She looped her hand through his arm to hold him back. "Don't. They're trying to rile you," she whispered.

"Your Grace," Sir Ridley said, bowing formally. "We meet again."

She gave him a single aristocratic nod. Since she wasn't certain she was calm enough to speak, she handed over her satchel and turned to the laird as Ridley stowed her bag in a waiting carriage.

"I wrote a letter for you as well, my laird," she said, holding it out to Lachlan.

He scowled at the letter, then snatched it from her fingers. "I don't think you understand the wrath I'll face back at Dunardry when your husband and sister find out what I've done this morning. This is so wrong. The duke deserved his death for mistreating you so badly."

"Thank you for your escort, Lachlan. The situation is not fair, but you are doing the right thing as laird. I know what this will cost you, and I'm sorry for it. In time, they will forgive you. I truly believe that."

He handed over a bag of food. "For your trip. I doubt the bastards will provide for you." He gave her a fierce hug and stepped back with a firm nod. "It was a pleasure knowing you, my lady. I will tell my children what a brave woman you were." He wiped a tear from his eye. "Far braver than I."

With that, he walked back to the horses and mounted. She watched as he rode away with her horse following behind him.

"Your Grace, we are ready to leave for home," Ridley said, holding the door to the coach with his other arm held out to her, waiting.

Her feet wanted to run away. But the three pistols hanging

from his belt made it clear she wouldn't get far. With another regal nod, she accepted his offer and allowed him to help her inside her dead husband's coach.

The sun rose as the horses were whipped into movement. She looked back toward the castle and saw the grove of trees and the field where she'd first met her husband.

She was right back where she'd started. But she'd been forever changed.

She'd face whatever came next knowing she'd had this time with Cam to remember. Those all-too-short months had made all the coming pain worth enduring.

...

Cam knew something was wrong as soon as he rode into the bailey.

The feeling of unrest he'd had the whole trip had increased until he'd found himself racing his horse the last hour to get home and see his wife.

But she wasn't waiting for him. Instead, he was faced with a grim-looking Lachlan.

Cam passed his horse over to a waiting groom and greeted the laird. "Lach." He nodded. "I'm honored you came out here to meet me, but if I can be honest, you're not really the person I wish to see."

"I know, but I didn't want you to wonder why she wasn't here to greet you."

Unease snaked around Cam's stomach, squeezing uncomfortably, far worse than the fear at the first cry of battle when his body lurched into action. This was cold, numbing. He was unable to move.

"What's happened?" he asked, knowing he couldn't bear to hear the answer.

"She's gone."

"*Gone?*"

"The English came for her."

Cam looked around the keep in confusion. "I missed the battle? We lost?"

"There was no battle. She went willingly. It was why you were sent away. So you wouldn't be here to make it bloody."

Cam stared at his friend in horror, unable to swallow the profound betrayal. "You tricked me into leaving the castle so you could turn over a woman—*my* woman—to be hanged? *Your own wife's sister?*" He couldn't hide his disgust. "What kind of man have you become?"

"The kind who honors the wishes of my wife's sister, despite feeling strongly otherwise." He held out a folded parchment.

"What is that?"

"The letter she wrote you. She wrote one to all of us."

"I don't want a bloody letter. I want my damn wife!" Cam brushed his hand in the air, refusing to take the parchment as he walked in a circle. "How long ago did she leave? I can still catch them."

His horse was spent, but surely he could borrow another and be on his way.

"You were not yet off MacKinlay lands to the west as she was leaving in the carriage to the southeast for London."

"Four days. I can catch up to them." It would be a struggle, but he'd make it work.

Lachlan shook his head. "And then what?"

"I'll fight whoever's holding her and steal her back."

"They'll only send others in their place. Don't ye see? You'll never be free. She killed a bloody duke. They won't just turn a blind eye to murder. Especially when the killer is a Scot. She'll swing, if only to show their bloody power over us."

"Nay!" Cam roared and took a step toward the stables.

He'd get a fresh horse and leave this instant. He'd get Mari back and they'd run. Somewhere far away. He wasn't sure where yet. They'd figure it out when he had her in his arms once again.

He got to the stables and found his way blocked by Bryce, Liam, and four of his other men.

"Stand down," he ordered, but they didn't move.

In fact, they stepped out toward him, creating a half circle. He spun to see Lachlan close in with three other warriors.

Cam pulled his sword. "I don't want it to come to this. But I'll strike you down if you don't get out of my way so I can go claim my wife and bring her home."

His voice cracked on the last word. He knew he'd not be able to return to Dunardry. He wouldn't bring the English down on his clan.

"Cam, take the letter. I'm sure she explained her decision—"

"No!" He pulled his dirk so both hands held weapons. He was one man facing down ten warriors. Most of them trained by him. All his brothers, his kin. "Please," he begged, knowing he'd not win against them all. Not at the same time. "Help me get her back. I beg you."

Lach swallowed and shook his head. "I canna. She didn't want it. She chose to go in peace rather than risk harm to those she loves. You would have done the same. You know in your heart it was the bravest thing to do. The only thing possible."

Cam let out a sob and fell to his knees, his weapons scattered in the mud.

The men gathered around him, placing hands on his shoulders and head, some whispering prayers, some wordlessly telling him they hurt for him. The icy rain on his neck added to the chill in his bones as he wailed, his cries echoing off the stone walls of the courtyard.

When the pain had exhausted him, the men helped him to his feet and led him off. He didn't bother to look where he was going. He knew wherever it was, there would be whisky.

Even when he was locked in the dungeon, he barely noticed. He was numb from pain and longed to become even more so with drink. Through the grates of the cell, his men plied him with whisky, and all sat near to drink with him. It wasn't until the next morning when he woke feeling like hell itself that he realized he was locked up.

His cell was clean and covered in fresh straw, but it was the dungeon.

What the bloody hell?

"Why am I in here?" he demanded of Lach, who sat against the wall outside his cell. He looked as if he'd been there all night.

"I couldn't be sure all the warriors in the clan would be able to stop you if you decided to go after her. I don't want anyone hurt, least of all you." Lach stood and let out a sigh. "And I don't know that any of us truly wants to stop you. For everyone's safety, you will remain in there until we hear that it's been done."

Been done.

With horror, he realized Lach meant that his wife had been hanged and was dead.

"What would you do if it were Kenna?" Cam asked, tears of anguish blurring his vision.

"I'd hope you would be the one sitting out here making sure I dinna do something that would endanger the whole clan."

"I wouldn't," Cam declared gruffly. "I'd be on the horse next to yours as we rode like the devil himself to go get her back." That thought brought on a different question. "Does Kenna know what you've done?"

Lach frowned. "Why do you think I spent the night down

here with you instead of in my bed with her? She's spitting mad. I'm not sure she'll ever forgive me."

It was small consolation. "I know I never will," Cam spat out. "In my heart, it's the same as if you'd tied the rope around her neck yourself."

Lach's eyes, already bleak in the low light, shimmered. "Mayhap if you read her letter—"

"I'm not reading the damned letter. If she wanted to say something to me, she should have bloody well been here to tell me herself. Not snuck off as soon as I turned my back." Cam's chest was on fire. The slash he'd suffered in battle and the broken ribs had been nothing compared to this pain. He couldn't breathe.

Lach had already dropped the parchment through the grate. It lay on the stone floor at Cam's feet.

"I'll hate you forever for this, Lachlan MacKinlay." Cam's voice was calm as he stared at the man he'd once loved like a brother. He would have to move to another clan, for he'd never respect his laird again.

Lachlan let out a breath and nodded. His head hung in despair. When he finally turned to leave, Cam saw unshed tears in the man's eyes, but he didn't feel the slightest spark of sympathy.

Despite the fire blazing in the hearth across from his cell, he began to shiver uncontrollably. Picking up the two heavy blankets he'd been given, he wrapped them around himself, but still he shook.

They brought food, but he didn't eat. They brought whisky as well, but he was past his desire for oblivion. He paced his cell, thinking and planning.

Surely there must be a way to get out of here. When he'd shaken every bar and tested every stone twice, he gave up and slumped onto his pallet. Other than the maid who brought his food, he hadn't seen anyone. No doubt they were giving him time to be alone with his thoughts. He wasn't sure if it was a blessing or a curse.

When the main door opened and he heard the soft footsteps of a woman, he assumed they had sent him more food. Was it already time for supper again? He'd lost track of time.

"Cam?" a familiar voice called.

Kenna.

He came close to the bars, and she reached out to take his hand. When tears filled her eyes, he gave in to his own grief once again. He hadn't cried since he was eleven and his dear mother died. But today he couldn't seem to stop.

"I have a plan," Kenna whispered, brushing her tears away.

For a moment, her words made no sense. Then they sparked, and hope began to stir. A plan? That meant doing something to get Mari back.

Kenna held up the key to his cell and glanced toward the main door.

"Come. We must hurry."

Chapter Thirty-Two

The stench of London woke Mari, and like many other times on their long voyage from Scotland, she was forced to pound on the roof so the driver would stop. She barely exited the carriage before being ill.

She'd not been one for travel sickness before, but her nerves were a jumble and had made her nauseous. Who could blame her? She was facing certain death.

Wiping her mouth, she took in the pale-pink sky of early morning. Would this be the last day of her life? Would they even bother with a trial?

Sir Ridley did a fair job of hiding his annoyance at yet another delay. No doubt he had a large bounty waiting to be claimed upon his return with her.

Admittedly, over the weeks as they'd traveled, the man had been a gentleman. Even his pointed comments had died down after a few days, and he'd spoken with her as a regular person. Once he'd even asked for her account of that night. She'd explained her terror, and how she'd been certain her life was at stake. It seemed ironic now. She hadn't saved her life at all. She'd only delayed her death.

But no. In that delay, she had made wonderful memories to take with her to the gallows. Memories of a large Highlander with a kind heart and a blissful touch. She would recall the tight hugs of her nephews and the soft smile of her beloved sister.

"I am taking you to Blackley House so you may change and rest in comfort. You'll be guarded heavily while arrangements are made to bring you before the lords for your trial."

"Thank you, sir."

He thought he was doing her a kindness, but in truth, she hadn't ever wanted to set foot in that house again. It had been a place of pain and fear, not comfort.

When she was brought inside, Lucy came to her in tears. "Oh, Your Grace. Are you all right?"

"Yes, Lucy," she assured the maid, though it was untrue. Nothing would be all right ever again. "I'm just tired."

"Of course. Let us put you in the blue room. The other room is…not ready for guests," she said.

Mari nearly laughed. First, because she wasn't a guest. And second, because she was doubtless the reason the room was unusable.

"The dowager duchess is here," Lucy shared as they walked upstairs to the blue room.

Mari gasped at this news. The Dowager Duchess of Endsmere had been an unhappy shrew even before Mari had killed her son. Lord only knew how much worse her attitude would be now. She'd never wanted her son to marry Mari.

At this rate, Mari might be begging the lords to end her sooner rather than later.

Lucy helped her into bed, where she closed her eyes, feeling the sway of the carriage even now that she was on solid ground. She squeezed her eyes tighter, but it didn't help. She vomited what little was in her stomach and sat on the floor.

Lucy came rushing back in, having not gotten far. "Are you ill, Your Grace?"

"It's travel sickness. I've had it since the morning I left." She blinked and shook her head. "Actually, I was sick before I got in the carriage. It's nerves. Facing death will do that."

Lucy looked her over critically. "Have you been eating more recently, my lady?"

Mari shook her head. "No. I could barely keep anything down the whole journey here. I've eaten far less. Though truthfully, I could stand a bite to eat now."

Lucy tilted her head to the other side thoughtfully.

"What?" Mari asked.

"As you say, you've eaten less. Yet, that nightgown is tighter across your bosom than it was before you left. Traveling sickness doesn't start before traveling. I believe, Your Grace, you're with child," Lucy announced happily.

Mari looked into the smiling eyes of her maid while she counted the days since she'd last had her courses. She counted a second and then a third time to confirm, and then swallowed.

"Good heavens. I think you may be right."

Sleep was hard found after that, despite her exhaustion. Mari worried what would happen to her child. Would they hang her despite her condition?

"I'm sorry, little one," she whispered into the darkness, tenderly touching her stomach.

...

Cam didn't want to stop, but he had to. He'd never run a horse to death and he wouldn't start now. His da always told him there was a special place in hell for those who mistreated their beasts. Cam was already living in hell, but he surely didn't want to make things worse.

While his horse rested, Cam stretched his stiff muscles. Blast Lachlan for confining him in a cell like a criminal. Cam would never be able to thank Kenna enough for releasing him. Though he knew it wasn't only for his sake she'd planned his escape. She'd wanted someone to go rescue her sister, and Cam was the only willing accomplice who would defy the laird's orders.

Lachlan would no doubt be enraged, but he wouldn't hurt Kenna. Cam wouldn't have left if he'd had any worry she'd be in danger for their actions.

As the days of travel wore on, the familiar mountains and valleys of the Highlands dropped away. He'd never been so far from home, but he didn't think Dunardry would ever feel like home to him again. Not without Mari.

He occasionally pulled out her letter, still sealed and unread, and wondered what words she'd left him. No doubt it was goodbye, and therefore he'd not open it. He wasn't ready to admit he would never see her again.

He might well be too late already, but he needed to go and at least try to bring her home.

...

After spending an hour being sick and then being dressed in one of her former fancy gowns by Lucy, Mari went down for breakfast. She was always famished after being sick.

She'd been at Blackley House for five days now, and so far she had avoided the other inhabitant. Mari rather hoped she would continue her run of luck for the entire duration of her stay, but she wasn't big on luck lately. It wasn't a surprise to find the dowager duchess sitting in the breakfast room with a plate of eggs and a scowl.

"Good morning, Mother," Mari said, her normal way to

address the dowager.

"Please don't feign familiarity with me."

"Well, a good morning to you anyway." Mari hadn't apologized to the woman for killing her son, because she wasn't sorry. The man had been a monster. But she only had a short time left, so she damn well wouldn't spend it arguing with the unpleasant woman.

Mari sat down and unfolded her napkin. How she missed eating in the great hall at Dunardry with her husband.

But the dowager wouldn't appreciate Mari's tears for another man. Dabbing at her eyes, she wondered how she hadn't wept herself dry by now. She'd cried herself to sleep each night since leaving home. She wondered if Cam had gotten back to the castle yet. Had he read her letter? Was he angry with her?

She was fairly certain she knew the answer.

"When will they be coming to take you away?" The dowager's rusty voice disrupted Mari's thoughts of home. Mari sensed concern in the woman's voice but decided she must have imagined it. Surely the dowager wouldn't worry about Mari.

"I'm sorry to disappoint you. I was taken before the court yesterday, and it was decided to postpone my trial until after I deliver."

The dowager's eyes widened in surprise. "You're with child? But how?"

"I remarried in Scotland. It was a bit of a misunderstanding, to be honest. I certainly hadn't planned to marry again, ever. However, it turned out to be a great blessing. He is a wonderfully kind man. And now we're having a child."

"A child you'll never see grown." The older woman frowned and looked out the window.

Mari would have thought she looked wistful if the crabby woman were capable of such an emotion. Or any emotion at all, save annoyance and bitterness.

"I understand you're angry with me. I can't imagine the hatred I would feel for someone who hurt my child, and I haven't even met my babe yet. But I am to stay here until I deliver and have been tried. If you do not wish to share the house with me, perhaps you could retire to the country estate."

"Richard, the new duke of Endsmere, was recently married so he can do his duty to produce an heir, and he is installed there. I'll not invade their privacy at this time."

The woman had always been cold. She'd not once come to visit here at Blackley House, no matter how many times Mari had extended the invitation.

"In case you're hinting that I didn't do my duty to procure an heir, it is clear *I* am capable of conceiving." She wouldn't go into the details and tell his mother how her son had hated his wife so much he could barely look at her, let alone lie with her.

"I do not *hint*. If I have something to say, I will say it straight out."

That was what Mari was afraid of. "As will I."

"I suppose the gaol was not suitable for someone of your station and condition." This was muttered into the dowager's tea. "They were unable to find another place for you?" she asked more directly.

Mari had never felt welcome here. It had been a living hell for her, but never had she felt so alone as at this moment. She gathered her pride and sat up straighter, donning her best fake court smile. "I'm afraid I'm not permitted to leave. We'll just have to get on as best as we can."

The dowager made an unhappy sound and pushed her plate away. "How unfortunate."

• • •

Upon his arrival to London, Cam was directed in circles, until he finally came to stand in front of a shiny black door at a fancy town house. He dropped the elaborate brass knocker, and the door opened almost instantly.

"Good evening, sir. May I help you?" The man was quite small, despite being full grown. His look of unease at the sight of him made Cam feel slightly better.

"I'm here to see Mari."

The man took him in from foot to forehead, then shook his head. "I'm afraid there is no one here by that name." He began to shut the door.

Cam threw out an arm to stop him. "Wait. I meant the duchess. *Marian*."

The man's eyes took him in again, hovering at Cam's dusty kilt. "I'm sure you can't expect to be let in..."

"Of course not." Cam frowned. "Will you go check with your mistress and see if she'll allow me to enter?"

The fact the man hadn't said she was dead gave Cam a feeling of hope he hadn't felt since he'd arrived home from his false errand with the McCurdy.

"Do you have a card?" the man asked.

"I'm afraid I do not. You'll just have to tell her my name."

"Which is?" The man's nose went into the air.

"Cameron MacKinlay. War chief of Clan MacKinlay. Her Grace's husband."

The man swallowed before closing the door, which remained firmly shut for a few minutes. Cam was about to reach for the bloody knocker again when the door whipped open and Mari launched herself into his arms.

It was like that day in the field, except now he knew how precious she was. As on that day, she clung to him as if the hounds of hell were yapping and snapping at her bare feet. But instead of fear, she cried and showered Cam with kisses.

He set her down so he could look at her and wipe the

tears from her eyes, and he nearly collapsed in relief right there on the front step.

"Please, Your Grace," the skinny butler urged. "Come inside so the door can be closed. We wouldn't want the neighbors to witness your reunion."

Mari laughed and allowed the man to pull them inside and close the door.

"You're alive," Cam whispered, and kissed her again. A medley of feelings rushed through him. He'd been numb since he'd heard the news of her surrender, but suddenly he was able to feel again.

At least for now.

• • •

As much as Mari had not wanted Cam to be there when she turned herself in, she was grateful for his presence now. She had gained a reprieve until she gave birth, and she could think of no one she'd rather spend her gift of time with. She had missed him so much.

"We must speak. In private," he said when he released her from the kiss. He eyed the butler, who was attempting not to stare at them and failing.

Mari knew what would happen when they were alone. Cam's happiness to find her alive simmered with an undercurrent of anger. He was very angry with her for leaving him. Maybe it was the house and the horrible memories that lurked in nearly every room, but she shivered as she nodded and led him to the parlor and closed the door.

Lucy's eyes went wide when she and Cam entered. "Should I stay, Your Grace?" the maid asked.

"No. That isn't necessary. Please excuse us. I'll make introductions later."

When Lucy was gone, Mari turned to Cam with her best

smile. "You must be famished. Let me order a tray of food."

"I'm near starved, but I don't want food this minute. As I said, we need to talk."

Mari nodded and let her gaze drift to the floor.

"Look at me," he ordered. "I thought to find ye dead. The least you can do is look me in the eye for the hell you put me through."

She met his gaze to see his whisky-colored eyes shimmering with tears. It was enough to bring her own as she reached for him.

Instead of allowing her to touch him or take her in his arms again, he held her wrists, keeping her apart from him. "Why? Why would you have made a plan that dinna include me?"

"You know why."

He shook his head. "I know you made a decision that destroyed me without telling me. Do I mean that little to you, wife? Do ye not care at all that my heart nearly shattered into pieces so small I never thought to gather enough to make it work again?"

Tears continued to stream down her cheeks, dripping off her chin. She'd known he would hate her for her decision, but she'd thought—in time—he'd understand and think her courageous for protecting their people.

"Can you really look at Douglas, or Roddy, or wee Cameron, and condemn them to death in exchange for me?"

"There had to be another way. This...this is madness." Running a hand through his hair, he turned back to her. "When will it happen?" he asked, his voice dropping in anguish.

"Excuse me?"

"I was sent all over this goddamned place to find you. The whole time I expected to do nothing more than retrieve your body to bring it home for a proper burial. In a way, I thought it a blessing not to have to see it done. But I'm here now and find you're still alive. I'll be there with you. Whatever you face, I'll not leave you here alone." His voice caught, and he swallowed heavily. "How much time do we have? We'll relish every minute together."

She wished there was a better way—a better time—to tell him, but there wasn't.

She took a deep breath and plunged right in. "My trial has been postponed until after I give birth to our child."

Cam looked at her, blinking. Then his eyes went wide. "A child?"

She was immediately grabbed up into his large, strong arms. As quickly as she'd been drawn against him, she was forced back a few steps. He held her firmly to keep her steady on her feet. "Tell me you didn't turn yourself over to them knowing you carried our child?" He looked as though he would break in a thousand pieces.

"No. I didn't know until after I arrived here." She let out a breath and twisted her fingers. "I wish I could tell you it would have made a difference. That maybe I would have stayed, but I don't think that's true." She shook her head. "The babe and I are but two people compared to the lives of the entire clan. Everyone who lifted weapons in our defense would have been struck down. The ones left would have been starved out or worse. Don't you see? I will lose no matter what choice I make. At least this way, I will face what is to come knowing I've protected those I love. You and our child will be safe. That is what matters most."

Cam's eyes had gone dark, and it was clear he wanted to argue. Instead, he reached for her again and held her close, gentler this time. "You are a brave woman, Mari. We have been given a great gift, along with more time together. Let's not waste it in discord."

She leaned back, resting her chin on his broad chest

so she could look up at him. Gone were the darkness, fear, and worry in his face. Though, she knew they simmered just under the surface of the wide smile he offered now.

"I'm going to be a father." The smile faltered slightly. "Do ye think I'll do it well?"

Placing her hand over his heart, she spoke the truest words she'd ever spoken. "You'll be the best father in all the world."

Chapter Thirty-Three

Cam and Mari had been granted a reprieve, and he promised himself he wouldn't waste a single moment with sadness over what was to come. The months would go by fast enough, and soon the time would come to face what came next. They could grieve and cry and rail against it then. For now they would celebrate the joy of impending parenthood.

Cam had never wanted to be a husband or a father, but he found both to be comforting. Life had a way of giving a person the things they should have rather than what they thought they wanted.

He placed his hand on Mari's belly, sending wishes of health and happiness.

"Let's live these days as if we have a hundred years to follow. We'll not speak of a future beyond the next day, and the next."

It had worked for them in the past. Those days they'd been happy together and had put their fears aside so they could focus on their love.

She nodded in agreement. "Yes."

Before he'd had a moment to request a bite to eat or a place to wash, she'd launched herself at him. With her arms around his neck and her legs around his waist, she kissed him so hard he stumbled from the attack.

Then a different hunger took over. "Where do you sleep in this place?"

She pointed toward the stairs and he took them two at a time. At the top, she gestured toward the end of the hallway. "Last on the right."

He made his way down the never-ending corridor, vaguely noticing the stern faces on the paintings along the way. Apparently, the previous dukes of Endsmere didn't approve of a man ravishing his wife in their corridors. They could all go to the devil.

He sat her on the edge of a fancy bed draped in the finest fabrics. She already had his belt undone and was tugging at his kilt when he stayed her with a hand on hers.

"This isn't the bed you shared—"

"No. I never stayed in this room until I returned."

That was all he needed to know. He gave in to his growing desire and rose over his wife as she wriggled under him. He rested at her entrance and then stopped.

"The babe?"

"Will be fine." She shifted, pulling him down, and he went gladly.

The first time was rushed and frantic. He was just so overjoyed to find her alive and carrying his babe. He couldn't contain his happiness. The second time, he was able to make it last. He treasured every touch and smile between them.

Afterward, lying there with her in his arms, he had no choice but to face the reason he had fled his home to come to this godforsaken place for this woman.

Cameron MacKinlay—the war chief of Clan MacKinlay—was in love with a tiny duchess on trial for murder.

Fate had a cruel sense of humor.

Later, after they rested a bit, Mari requested a tray be brought up for their dinner. The meal they received was hardly enough for him, let alone to share with a woman who was increasing. Even so, he'd pushed more of the food on her, wanting to keep her healthy. Now, as dawn made its claim on the day, he silently gathered his dusty clothes to go forage for breakfast before he grew weak with hunger.

He didn't know how to go about a meal in London. He hoped to find the kitchens and gather what he needed himself. He'd take enough to feed Mari as well, so they could keep to their bed as long as possible. There in her room they were safe from the truth of the situation. It was easy enough to pretend they were back in Dunardry, despite the fancy bedclothes, the fabrics on the walls, and the elaborate bed.

At the bottom of the stairs he encountered a man standing next to an open door. In Cam's haste to be with his wife, he'd forgotten to ask if she was alone in the house.

The man was impeccably dressed, with a haughty demeanor. His eyes remained straight ahead. Cam looked down at himself and decided he looked a mess. It was no wonder the man didn't care to glance his way.

He opened his mouth to say something. Maybe explain to the snotty Englishman that he was in a shambles because he'd been kept in a dungeon for days by a man he'd once loved as a brother. Then he'd ridden like hell for London, and even so he had looked fairly decent…until his wife got her hands on him the night before and dragged him to her bed.

"Good day, sir," the man said with a bow. "Would you care to take breakfast? It's been set out."

A servant. The man was dressed better than all the lairds he'd ever seen in Scotland. Cam's brows creased, but the smell of meat made his feet move forward.

"Aye. That would be fine. Thank you."

A brief shift of his eyes was the only sign the other man was surprised by Cam's crude Scottish tongue.

Following the man's gesture, Cam entered a room and gaped at the amount of food sitting ready on a large sideboard.

"How many people live in this house?" he asked before the servant could leave.

"Two—or rather three, now that you've arrived, sir."

"I see." Cam frowned at the feast before him that would rival a celebration at Dunardry. "In that case, I'd best not let it go to waste." Grabbing up a plate, he helped himself.

He was finishing his second plate when the sound of small approaching feet called his attention to the door. With a smile in place, he waited expectantly for his wife to enter.

The gray-haired woman who stepped into the room was clearly not his wife. Even if Mari had aged forty years in one night, she would never look so shriveled and dour.

The old lady gasped and clapped a hand to her chest. "Parkes!" she called in a frantic voice. The man who had escorted Cam into the room stepped closer. "We've been set upon by barbarians!"

"I'm to understand this is your daughter-in-law's new husband, Your Grace," the man said formally, casting an unsure glance toward Cam.

Cam stood and took a step closer to introduce himself, but the small woman scurried behind the servant as if Cam planned to finish off his meal with her leathery flesh. Another step from him forced a squeak of worry.

Good God. He wasn't *that* fearsome.

"Thank ye for your hospitality, Your Grace. I am Cameron MacKinlay, Mari's husband. It is a pleasure to make your acquaintance." He attempted a bow, since it seemed to be the way of things here. Damn if he knew whether he'd done it correctly.

"I assure you, the pleasure is all yours," she said harshly, taking another step backward.

Cam smiled at the old biddy. Being orphaned at the age of eleven, of necessity he'd mastered the art of charming the older women of his clan into giving him treats. Occasionally, he'd gone so far as to lavish compliments on them to win a coin here and there. He'd always been able to bring them around to thinking him sweet.

He wasn't certain the dowager duchess of Endsmere had ever been charmed in her life. If so, it was surely six hundred twenty years ago, judging by the creases of her permanent frown.

But he was a war chief, and not one to back down from a battle. Even when the enemy was a formidable old goat with a scowl so intense she put some of his warriors to shame.

He stifled a chuckle.

This was going to be great fun.

• • •

Mari woke to the sound of screaming. Not wishing to give in to the nightmares of her past, she snuggled deeper into her warm blankets and reached out for Cam.

He'd loved her well the night before, but she was far from done. Kenna had mentioned how the cravings of pregnancy weren't limited to those for food. At the time Mari hadn't understood, but she surely did now. Though an egg and a bannock wouldn't go amiss as well.

When her hand found the end of the bed without encountering the warmth of Cam's skin, she opened her eyes. She was in London, not Dunardry. And the yelling she'd heard wasn't a dream from her former life, but real and now.

The harsh scrape of the dowager duchess's voice was followed by the low rumble of Cam's.

"Oh, dear." Mari jumped out of the bed and searched for

something to put on. After she knocked on the door to her maid's chambers, Lucy rushed into the room.

"Oh, dear," Lucy repeated Mari's thoughts exactly.

"Hurry. I must get down there before she hurts him."

Lucy laughed at the thought but swiftly laced Mari's dress. "Did you sleep well, Your Grace?" Lucy asked with a sly smile.

A blush warmed Mari's cheeks. "You shouldn't call me that. I'm no longer a duchess, and the dowager won't take kindly to hearing you refer to me as such."

"The dowager can go suck an egg."

Mari didn't scold her, because she felt the same way.

"I'm so glad to see you happy," Lucy said, quickly looping Mari's hair up and pinning it.

"Yes. Being with Cam is worth whatever comes."

Lucy's lip quivered and Mari clasped her maid's hand. "All will be well. You'll see. And if not, I still wouldn't have changed a thing."

The maid nodded and bobbed a curtsy as Mari left the room, hoping to stop a domestic war.

Parkes stood by the door to the dining room looking uncomfortable as his mistress clung to his arm. When Mari got closer, she realized the dowager was pushing the poor man into the room.

"Get him out of here, Parkes, or by God, you'll be out on your ear!"

"What's amiss?" Mari interceded and placed a hand on Parkes's shoulder to keep him from moving farther into the room. She didn't think Cam would hurt Parkes, but it was clear the poor footman would faint if pressed into moving any closer to the looming Highlander...who was peacefully eating breakfast.

"What's *amiss*?" The dowager laughed harshly. "It's not enough I must share my home with you, but that you bring your brute of a husband here as well. I'll not live under the same roof with that scoundrel."

"And I told *ye*, a brute I may be, but I'm not a scoundrel," Cam called from the table. He winked at Mari, looking incredibly rumpled and every bit the scoundrel. "Very well. We shall miss you when you leave."

"How dare you?" the dowager sputtered, and Mari had to hide a smile.

"What? I will live where my wife lives."

"Please, both of you," Mari interjected. "I'm sure we can come up with a plan that works for all of us."

"I want him out," the dowager said obstinately. The poor woman obviously had not experienced the will of a stubborn Scot.

"I'll not be going anywhere without my wife," he said calmly.

"Then by all means, take her with you. I was happy here on my own."

Mari didn't understand how anyone could be happy being as alone as the dowager always was. It was as if the old woman had imposed her own prison. She could go anywhere, be with anyone, but the dowager always chose to reside in whatever house the rest of her family wasn't inhabiting at the time.

Until now.

"As I'm sure you recall," Cam pointed out, "she is being forced to stay here by the court."

Mari put on a smile. "Perhaps you would be more comfortable at one of the country estates, Mother."

"I've told you not to call me that!" the dowager snapped.

Mari thought she saw a flash of pain across her face, but it was gone before she could be sure.

"And I will not be forced out of my own home by the likes of Scottish heathens."

"I believe I've mentioned that I prefer brute or barbarian over heathen," Cam said, finishing up the food on his plate.

"You're not helping," Mari said crossly.

"I'd argue that I am, since I'm giving instruction on the proper epithets for Scots." He held out his large hands in innocence.

God, he was infuriating. She'd deal with him later.

"Please consider going somewhere else more comfortable for the time being," Mari advised the one woman here who could actually leave.

"I'm sure you'd be happy to send me traveling at this time of year. I'd no doubt catch my death in this weather."

Mari felt a stab of guilt. It was true that the chill of winter was upon them. She sighed in defeat. "All right then, we'll stay here together. It's nearly Christmastide. We should all try to find a charitable spirit for the holiday." She eyed her husband.

He took her hand and drew her closer to him. It wasn't uncommon for a man to be protective of his wife. But she thought the gesture odd when faced with an aging woman who wasn't even as tall as Mari, partnered with a frail house servant.

She patted Cam's hand and tried again. "Perhaps we can start by sharing the breakfast table together. May I get you something to eat, Moth—I mean, Your Grace?"

"I think not. I'll stay in my rooms until *he* is gone."

"It will be quite a long exile, Your Grace," Cam offered. "Mayhap you should take some sustenance first."

"You're really not helping," Mari repeated in exasperation.

Cam laughed as the old woman sniffed and quit the room. "Aye. That time I wasna trying to."

• • •

"I must admit, I like having a library," Cam said while pouring whisky into a fancy glass. Good whisky, at that.

"You like to read?" Mari asked from her seat across from him. "Wouldn't the dowager be surprised you are capable of such a civilized thing."

They shared a smile.

"My parents used to take turns reading stories aloud to us each night. It was my favorite time of day."

"And not just because your belly was full from just eating supper?" she teased.

"That might have been part of it." He glanced around the room and inhaled the smells of paper and leather. "I've always enjoyed being around books. Being in this room, I can almost feel them tugging me toward their secrets. All the things they already know that are just sitting there, waiting for me to learn them, too."

Mari smiled and rubbed her stomach. "I hope you will continue the tradition and read to our child each night."

Cam nodded. "Aye. I will. I promise." Neither of them spoke of the immediate future, but he knew they both thought about it often. That he would be reading to their child alone because she would be gone.

Perhaps it wasn't too late. He hadn't been enough to make her fight to stay. But maybe their child would be. Maybe…

It was time to tell her of his plans.

He took a seat across from her. "I want to tell you something. Though it hardly matters now, but it was a plan I'd wanted to share with you."

She reached for his hand. "Tell me."

"I asked Lach for a place for us. That field where we first met. I had planned to build us a proper home there. Nothing as extravagant as what you were used to here, but a home of our own. I didn't want you living in a cottage or in my chambers in the castle. I wanted to give us a place that was just ours."

She swallowed. "It sounds lovely."

He let out a breath and flashed a smile. "I'd planned to have a library, too, for all the fancy houses have them." He stood again and walked to the window, allowing his finger to trail down the glass. "It would have taken me forever to afford it. We would have been gray and wrinkled before we'd have been able to live there. Our children would be grown with their own little ones, no doubt." He clenched his fist. "I'm grateful for this place and the time we have, but at times…my heart fills with rage at the unfairness of it all."

She went to him and wrapped her arms around his waist, resting her cheek against his back.

"Pretending everything is wonderful isn't working," she whispered. "It was unrealistic to think we could keep all of our fears inside and not be affected by them. I think it's better that we are honest with each other and ourselves."

He nodded and shifted to hold her. "Are you scared?" he asked quietly.

"Yes. Terribly."

Chapter Thirty-Four

Cam had gone on errands early the next morning and still arrived first for breakfast. He filled his plate and had just taken his seat when a woman's scream had him running out of the room.

"She fell down the stairs," Parkes said from the foyer, clearly upset.

Cam raced to get to his wife. The baby. But it wasn't Mari lying on the floor at the bottom of the stairs, but the dowager. The prideful biddy was attempting to get up, using her cane to support herself and failing at the attempt.

"Be still, woman, until we assess how badly you're injured. Parkes, send for a healer," he ordered.

"At once, sir."

"I'm fine," the dowager barked, but winced and whimpered as the final word crossed her lips.

"Aye, I see that. Let's check you over." As he did on a battlefield with wounded soldiers, he went about checking her legs and arms.

"Unhand me, you savage! That is not the proper way to

touch a lady."

"Trust me, Your Grace. I well know the proper ways." He winked at her to make sure she was thoroughly offended by his remark. When he could see she was in no great harm, he continued his campaign simply to ruffle her, now that he had the opportunity.

"Please just go back to your meal and leave me my dignity, so I might get back on my feet."

"That will not do at all. Your foot is broken. I believe your wrist is, as well."

As if to challenge him, she turned her foot and promptly hissed. Then she moved her wrist and winced.

"It's back upstairs with you, Your Grace."

He slipped his arms under her frail body and lifted her up, being careful because she might have lesser injuries in other places.

"Put me down, you brute!"

"I'll do so soon enough." With a nod to Parkes to lead the way, Cam carried the dowager up the stairs she'd just fallen down and into her elaborate suite of rooms at the farthest side of the house away from his and Mari's.

He settled her in bed and removed her slipper, noticing how the skin was already turning purple.

"Well, you've gotten what you wanted," she snapped at him when he propped an extra pillow behind her back so she could sit up.

"Nay, hardly. You didn't break your neck, did ye?" Cam laughed so she knew he was teasing. It was so easy to rile her up, he couldn't seem to help himself.

As expected, he was awarded a glare of surprised disgust.

"What has happened?" Mari rushed into the room.

"I stumbled on the stairs and your barbarian of a husband couldn't stash me away in my rooms fast enough."

Mari blinked at him as he chuckled. "Her foot and

her wrist are most likely broken. A healer is on the way to confirm. I merely wanted her to be comfortable."

"He wanted me out of the way," the dowager muttered. "And we don't have healers, we have physicians."

"Ah, I'm sorry." Cam crossed his arms. "A physician will have to do, I guess."

Her lips pulled up tighter, and he hid a smile. He really couldn't help himself.

"I'll bring up some breakfast for you," Cam offered.

"I'll not eat anything you've touched."

"I'm not planning to touch it."

"Please stop." Mari raised a hand at each of them. "I'll bring you your meal—"

"Nay." Cam shook his head. "I'll not have another lass fall down those stairs. Especially not the one carrying my babe in her belly. I'll get the food, and you will eat it, you miserable old crow."

With that he left. He passed the *physician* on the stairs as Parkes led him up to the dowager's room. The man's eyes went wide, and he moved to the far side of the steps so as not to risk brushing against Cam's kilt.

Bloody English.

Cam offered the man a menacing smile, and he practically ran the rest of the way up the stairs.

Had Cam known being in London would be so much fun, he might have visited sooner.

・・・

Mari sat with the dowager as the physician checked her over. Cam had been correct. Her foot and wrist were both broken.

Her former mother-in-law looked close to tears when the man told her she would need to stay in bed indefinitely. "People who stay in bed never leave them," she complained.

"You'll be up and around soon enough. Sooner if you mind what I say and stay off that foot until it's healed properly," the physician scolded.

"These people—"

"I used to live here," Mari reminded the woman stiffly. "And I can assure you I have no need for any of your fancy possessions. I'll not be able to use them where I'm going."

That shut them up.

The dowager looked away and let out a breath. "Very well. I'll stay up here and hope for the best."

"I'll make sure you're taken care of," Mari promised.

She didn't know why she felt the need to see to the woman's health and comfort. The dowager had been nothing but nasty to Mari every time they'd ever shared the same space.

But there was something about facing death that made Mari want to treasure every bit of life while she had the chance. She would make sure she had no regrets over how she'd lived her life at the end. Caring for people—even surly dowagers—made her feel needed. As though she actually served a purpose here on Earth.

She rubbed her stomach as she remembered her true purpose.

To love her husband and child for as long as she drew breath.

• • •

"I feel sorry for the dowager," Mari told Cam a few days after the witch had been settled in her rooms.

Cam's eyes widened. "You must be joking."

"No."

"Then ye have the kindest heart imaginable, to care for someone so prickly." He kissed the top of her head, knowing his words were true.

"I think she is deliberately mean. It's her way of keeping people at a distance so she doesn't have a chance to care about them."

Cam thought about it and realized Mari might be right. No one could be that hideous unless they were trying hard to be. "Or mayhap she's just a miserable crow, as I've said."

"No doubt we're both correct. But my guess is she wasn't born this way. People seldom are. I think she grew to be this way from experiencing constant hurt and disappointment. I know her son, the late duke, never treated her well. The new duke, Richard, doesn't seem to want her around, either."

"Can you blame them? I think you may be putting the chicken before the egg. Mayhap they didn't like her because she's a miserable crow, rather than she became a miserable crow because they didn't like her. You see?" Cam held out his hands to make his point, earning a laugh from his wife.

"Still, a little kindness on our part might help her see she doesn't need to be nasty with us. That she's safe. Maybe once she realizes it, she'll be nicer."

"We have been forced to live here, so I'll do my best not to cause you distress by fighting with the old crow. But I think you are setting yourself up for disappointment if you expect friendly conversations between me and the dowager. She hates me as much for where I'm from as for who I am."

"You get enjoyment from pestering the woman, Cam, and I'm asking you to stop."

He dropped the innocent smile on his face, since it hadn't served him well, and reluctantly agreed to stop antagonizing the biddy. Though it was a rare bit of entertainment in this place.

"Fine. I'll relent."

"Thank you. Now, why don't you bring her down so she might eat with us this evening?"

He stood and bowed. "Certainly, wife."

He left the room and went upstairs. After knocking on the door twice before he entered, without a word he went to the dowager's bed and picked her up.

"What are you about?" she complained in alarm and squirmed in his arms like a slippery pig.

"I'm taking ye downstairs so you can sit at the table and eat like the civilized lady you are."

"Put me down at once!"

Of course he did no such thing but instead carried her down to the dining room so they could share a meal together. He didn't do it just because his wife had asked it of him, though that would have been reason enough. He did it because he understood why a person might want to wrap themselves in bitterness and not allow anyone else to enter.

When his Mari was gone, he could see how such a refuge might offer him protection from those who wanted to force him to move on when he didn't wish to.

He was in a perfect position to become just like the dowager. He only hoped if he did give in to the pain and anger, someone would try to help him find his way back to life.

The days turned into weeks. He and Mari visited the dowager daily so she wasn't alone all day. She wasn't much for conversation, but she thanked him each time when he left.

Eventually she was well enough to leave her bed and regularly join them for dinner. Sometimes she'd even stay as they sat next to the roaring fire enjoying an evening together. She always said it was because of the warmth, but he thought it was a different kind of warmth that drew her.

"Tomorrow is Christmas," he said to test the waters a few days later.

As expected, the dowager's head shot up and her eyes went wide. "You can't possibly think to celebrate in this house."

Cam chuckled at having prodded a response from her. "I'm an unwanted war chief married to a murderess. Do you not think I'd risk Cromwell's rule to ensure a good pudding?" He laughed harder when she just glared at him.

"While it's true there's to be no public celebration for the holiday, you must be aware that every house on the block is secretly planning private festivities," Mari said. "Even the duke demanded goose for dinner on Christmas Day."

"I forbid it." The dowager went back to cutting her food into the tiniest of pieces. Cam wondered if she even had a need to chew.

He said nothing else. He planned to do as he wished, regardless. As for ordering the meal, if he and Mari had to stay in their room to eat it, he didn't see that as such a terrible idea. Having her near a bed was always his favorite thing.

But Mari was upset. While she was not usually one to push things with the dowager, she did this time. "I plan to have a proper Christmas meal and share stories in front of the fire tomorrow," she declared resolutely. "If it's my last holiday on earth, I'll bloody well celebrate it the way I see fit. What will they do? Hang me?"

Cam couldn't help but smile at her joke. He loved to see his wife all afire. She'd spent too many years being subdued. The fact that she felt safe enough to rant in her displeasure gave him much joy. Especially since, for once, he wasn't the cause of her annoyance.

But as she went on, he feared this outburst was more than simple irritation. His wife cried more than normal now that she was with child, but he thought the tears he currently saw lurking in her fierce eyes were something other than a maternal shift in her emotions.

The dark thing they tried not to speak of still lurked on the edges of their lives, finding small ways to wear them down and destroy their fleeting happiness.

"I don't understand why you stay here if you hate us so much." Mari's voice trembled as she spoke. "You have the means to go back to Sussex or Chiswick, or lease a different house here in town. Why do you tarry here? You never stayed here before. Not once in all the years I lived here in this hell with the duke." Mari halted her tirade and looked at the other woman as a bird might examine a worm.

And then her face cleared, as if she'd had a major epiphany. Which, perhaps, she had.

"You *never* stayed here," Mari repeated as her eyes went wide and accusing. "You never stayed here because *he* was here. Isn't that true?" she demanded.

"I have no idea what you're babbling about. I've been in this house many times."

"You occasionally visited for a few hours, but you never stayed. And come to think of it, I cannot help but notice you never once asked me *why* I killed the duke." Mari narrowed her gaze on the dowager. "Because you knew all along how he was. *What* he was."

The dowager's thin lips pursed in displeasure, but she didn't refute Mari's claim.

Was it really possible the woman knew what a violent bastard her son had been?

Cam reached for Mari's hand, suspecting she would need his strength to get through the rest of this conversation.

"Could you not have warned me, so I'd not be put through hell as his wife?" she accused.

The older woman laughed without humor. "You came here with bright eyes and dreams of being a duchess. I tried to save you. I tried to stop the marriage. But your parents were blinded, too enamored of an alliance with such a prize."

"But if you'd come here to help me, maybe he wouldn't have—"

"Oh, he wouldn't have stopped on my account, I can assure you."

"But if you'd been here, I wouldn't have felt so all alone." With that, Mari burst into tears and fled the room.

Cam would give her a moment before going to her. For now he needed to deal with the prideful, unfeeling woman before him. So, she hadn't ever visited while her son was alive. Cam didn't think it had anything to do with Mari. If so, the dowager wouldn't be staying here now.

Something else was the cause.

Someone else.

"Did ye fear him?" Cam asked quietly. "Was he so far into evil that he'd raise a hand against the woman who bore him?"

The dowager said nothing, just sat there looking at him as her eyes glistened. But no tears fell, even as she clenched and released her fingers.

"I see," he said and reached over to place his large hand over both of hers. She flinched, but he kept her gaze. Her backbone seemed to be made of steel, the way she sat there so stiffly.

"Tomorrow Mari and I will gather down here by the fire," he informed her. "We'll have breakfast and share stories until the day grows late, and then we'll eat a wonderful meal. You are welcome to join us or not. It's your choice. But I *will* do this for my wife, because she wants it. We're not blind as to what lies ahead for us. We know we have only a short time. That is why I'll not lose the chance to make this new memory."

He let out a breath and swallowed against the tightness in his throat.

The dowager watched him carefully, her face a mask of neutrality.

"Can you give us this?" he asked. "I ken I have no right to ask anything of you. We don't get on all that well, and it's true Mari and I have invaded your home. But I beg you to let her enjoy this one day."

When she said nothing, he squeezed her hand, surprised she hadn't flung him off.

"Next Christmas I'll be in Scotland with our child. And Mari…"

He couldn't finish. The horrible words wouldn't come out of his throat.

The frail woman before him pulled one of her hands out from under the weight of his, and to his utter shock, she rested it on top of his hand in a gesture of comfort. She cleared her throat in that regal manner of hers and straightened her already stiff spine. "I suppose we can share a meal. However, I'll not tell any stories."

"Of course," he agreed, and leaned over to place a kiss on her gnarled knuckles. "Thank you, Your Grace."

Knowing she wouldn't want the attention, he gave a quick bow and left the room to go comfort his wife.

Chapter Thirty-Five

Mari sat in the seat next to the window and tucked her feet under her. It was raining, but even as she sat there, the sound against the glass changed to the faint tinkle of ice.

Eventually the door opened, and Cam came in to sit next to her.

"It's all worked out. She's agreed to allow our celebration."

"It was never about that."

"I know." He pulled her tight against him. "But it's the one thing I can do, so I'll thank ye to pretend to be impressed that I've done it."

She let out a laugh despite not being in the mood for levity. That was Cam. He always knew how to make her happy. Even when she didn't want to be.

"You're going to be a splendid father."

"Well, if I've managed to win over the miserable old goat, I should have a fair chance at earning the respect of a more reasonable person."

"You think a child from your stock would be reasonable?"

He laughed once and kissed her temple. "Vixen."

She placed her hand on his face and looked into those honey eyes. "Thank you. For taking care of it. The day means more to me than it should."

"I understand." He took her hand and placed a kiss to her palm before putting it back on his cheek. "I'll do anything for ye, love. You have only to ask."

"I know. I'm so glad you're here."

He nodded but didn't say anything.

She knew he didn't want to be there. He would rather be back at Dunardry preparing the great hall for the holiday feast. The strength it must take for him to remain silent was more impressive than watching him wield his sword or move a pile of large rocks with his bare hands.

That night he held her close, and she asked what they would be doing back home. He went into great detail, sharing tales of the preparations at Dunardry, past and present, until she fell asleep.

The next day they spent as others in the city were doing, quietly celebrating the holiday in the privacy of their homes. After a hearty dinner with the quiet dowager, they sat and read stories in the library in front of the fire.

Mari closed the book she'd been reading, and Cam set something on her lap. It was a horribly embroidered handkerchief that could have only fallen victim to the hands of her sister. "Kenna surely sent this," she said, overwhelmed with love and amusement.

He laughed. "Aye. She made the handkerchief, but the thing inside it is from me. I wrote and had her send it to me."

Mari unwrapped the bundle to find a silver locket shimmering in the light by the fire.

"It belonged to my mother."

She wanted to tell him to keep it, that it was a waste to give it to her, but she didn't. There was no place for sadness on this day. Instead, she smiled and happily fastened it around her neck.

"These are not for you, but for the babe." He held out a wooden box. She opened it to find an assortment of wooden animals. Some were smoothed and painted. A few were still raw wood, and it was clear they weren't completed.

"I still need to finish the cattle. And the wee mouse."

Mari picked up a rabbit and smiled at the detail, including a tail and a pink nose. "An elephant!" she exclaimed. "I saw one two summers ago."

"Do I have it right? I remembered you telling me of seeing it. I thought it fascinating and wondered if it was a real creature."

"It's just so." She held it to her chest. "They are wonderful, Cam. Truly." She placed a kiss on his cheek, and for once the dowager didn't make a disgruntled sound at their affection.

He picked up another package and took it over to the older woman. Bending down, he placed it on her lap.

Mari had never seen the woman so startled. Cam had shocked the perpetual frown right from her face. It brought a smile to Mari's lips.

"What are you about?" The frown was back, but Mari could tell the woman was touched.

"Open it and see."

A wooden carving tumbled out into her lap.

"I know you like to watch the birds in the mornings. You have a special place for the red ones," Cam noted.

"It's a horrible likeness," she said, though her lips were pressed into an indulgent expression. Cam laughed, unaffected by her words. "Really, you shouldn't have bothered."

"Well, I did, so you'll just have to like it."

The woman tried her best not to, but a slight smile tugged up her lips when Cam bent to kiss the top of her head.

"Impertinent brute." She swatted at him.

"Miserable goat." He winked at her.

As promised, Cam launched into the tale of how his father had taught him to carve, and from there the rest of the evening was spent with them sharing stories.

"Your sister sounds like a hoyden," the dowager said matter-of-factly.

"That is a right description, Your Grace," Mari agreed. "But she is the most wonderful person imaginable. She told me once that when she reaches the end of her days, she will have no regrets, for she will have lived fully." Mari let out a breath, missing her sister dearly.

"Would that we could all live in such a way. But some of us have obligations. Duties to fulfill."

"Surely you don't still feel obligated to the Endsmere name?" Cam asked, no doubt insulting her yet again. "'Tis not even a real person, but merely a title. What has it ever done for ye?"

The dowager turned the little red bird over in her fingers. "It's not just a title. It's my very existence."

"He didn't mean to say—" Mari began.

"No, I heard him clearly. And he's right. When I'm gone, I'll be but a portrait in the gallery, whereas your sister will be talked about for ages as the woman who faced down the English army and invited them for tea."

Mari smiled at the story she'd just told. The observation was true enough.

"There's still time to create some fine stories about your own life," Cam offered the dowager. "In fact, we're doing so right now. They'll all tell tales of the brave dowager duchess who was forced to spend her holiday with a Scottish war chief."

If Mari didn't know better, she might have thought the sound that came from the dowager was a laugh. It was a dry, rusty kind of sound. But the dowager rarely laughed, and when she did, it was never from joy or humor.

"Just so," she said, and cleared her throat before calling out for Parkes.

Mari expected the dowager wanted to return to her room and required assistance, but instead she remained seated as she doled out an order to the butler. "Bring it in now. Hurry along," she snapped.

The man left, and a moment later he returned carrying something bulky. It was placed on the floor at Mari's feet.

Suddenly, she realized what it was. A gasp left her as she gazed misty-eyed at the beautifully scrolled wood curving into the legs of a cradle. A large *M* had been carved into the headpiece.

Even Cam made a sound of surprise.

"It is indeed lovely. Thank you for such a perfect gift," Cam said. He must have realized Mari couldn't yet find words.

This was beyond anything the dowager had done for Mari in the past. It wasn't an heirloom brought down from the attic and brushed off. It was new and must have been ordered weeks ago.

"It's nothing more than a necessity." The dowager brushed off her generosity. "The child must have a place to sleep."

Mari went to her and offered a stiff hug. The woman patted her shoulder but didn't give more than that tiny bit of affection.

Mari had always thought the woman a frigid person, but now she could see there was more to her below the icy layer she'd created...most likely to protect herself from the truth of her son's evil.

"Thank you, Mother. It's wonderful."

The dowager opened her mouth, likely to scold Mari for calling her Mother, but she closed it instead and gave a stern nod. "I'll be off to bed now. It's been a tiring day." She stood stiffly on her still-healing foot and shuffled toward the door, where she paused. "Thank you for including me."

Before they could respond, she was out the door.

• • •

Cam hadn't ever expected to spend the holidays in London, but if he couldn't be at home, he'd be wherever Mari was and like it just fine.

They'd had a joyful holiday, but he found himself missing Dunardry. Not the castle, but the people in it. One person in particular especially weighed on his mind over the months as winter turned into spring.

He didn't know how he would get on with Lach when he returned. Perhaps after Cam ran away, Lach wouldn't even be willing to take him back. Kenna wouldn't allow her husband to cast out her niece or nephew, so he knew when he returned with the babe, he'd be granted access.

But would Cam be able to look on Lach as a friend after what he'd done?

"A letter has arrived for you, sir," Parkes announced, and delivered a sealed letter to him with a bow.

Cam still wasn't accustomed to the fuss and was about to tell the man to stop bowing when he noticed the seal on the missive.

Lachlan.

Rather than open it, he set it to the side to focus on his meal.

"Who's it from?" Mari inquired, rubbing her large stomach, where their child grew.

Since he'd been at Blackley House, he'd not received any correspondence other than the locket from Kenna, so it was natural she'd be curious. Mail was such a rare thing. It was always shared with others unless it was truly to be kept private. But Cam didn't want to share whatever words the letter held.

"No one."

Her frown spoke of her disappointment. "But you'll read it before you dash it into the fire?"

"I haven't decided yet."

"What if someone is ill?" She gasped in distress. "What if it's one of the boys—or Kenna?"

"Bugger," he grumbled while snatching up the letter and breaking the seal. He'd not be able to finish his meal now until he knew for certain his family was in good health.

Dear Cam,

I hope this letter finds ye well. Kenna shared the news of the babe, and I send my heartfelt wishes of happiness to you. Fatherhood is a great blessing. Ye shall make a fine father. My boys love you, and I know your child will as well.

I must warn you, the rest of this letter will be nothing more than a groveling mess. For I've no clue as to how to ask for your forgiveness when I don't deserve such a thing.

However, I must also say that I wasn't wrong. I know this is a sorry way to start an apology. I acted as a laird, and in that, I did what was best for my clan. But I should have also acted as a friend and brother, for that is what you are to me. At the time I wasn't sure how to unite the two, and I didn't see any way to be both the laird and your friend when faced with the options I was given.

I also acted as a brother-in-law to Mari. I'll not put

all the blame on her shoulders, for I was the one who honored her request when I needn't have. But when I put myself in her place, I knew I would have done exactly the same thing she'd asked.

What I neglected to do was put myself in your place, for I know if I had, I would have kept trying to come up with another plan.

I failed you, and for that I feel this whole letter and asking for forgiveness will be in vain.

As I see it, my only chance at redemption is to offer you what I withheld earlier. My sword. My men. My loyalty.

If you need us to march on London, you have only to send word and we'll be there, ready to stand with you in an attempt to save your family.

Your brother in honor,
Lachlan James Campbell MacKinlay
Laird of Clan MacKinlay

Cam swallowed the large lump in his throat.

What good would the MacKinlay army do him now, anyway? It was easy enough for Lach to promise things now that there was no need for it. An empty alliance wasn't worth Cam's time.

Not when he needed to focus on a way to save his wife.

Chapter Thirty-Six

When Cam set the letter off to the side of his plate and turned back to his food, Mari took it as an invitation and picked it up to read it herself. She'd expected it would be some sort of apology, and she was right. When she was done, she folded it again and put it back. Silence continued for a few bites as she waited him out.

"I'll not forgive him," Cam finally blurted.

"But you've forgiven me, and I'm the one who forced him into it." It wasn't fair that Lachlan should be punished for respecting her wishes.

"You're wrong," he seethed, not looking at her.

"It was me that went to Lachlan and asked him to escort me to the English when it was clear there was no other ch—"

Cam's fist slammed down on the table, causing the dishes to rattle and Mari to jump. "I dinna say ye were wrong about coercing my cousin into going along with your piss-poor plan. I'm saying you're wrong about me forgiving you. I haven't."

With that, he rose from the table and left the room.

She sat there in shock, expecting that her kind, gentle

husband would return and apologize for his outburst, but he didn't.

Instead, she heard the front door slam.

She rested her hand on her belly to comfort their child, who had shifted when she'd startled.

"It's fine, little one. He's just upset. He'll be back."

He'd been here for months and not once mentioned he still held anger over her role in her return to London.

She knew well what he was doing. He was building walls between them to protect himself. Distancing himself in a futile attempt to avoid the pain when the time came.

Part of her wanted to go to him and tear down those walls. Force him to let her in. But another part of her felt relieved, because those walls he built would serve to protect her as well. They didn't have much time left. Only a few weeks before the bairn arrived, and then the trial would begin.

It was late when Cam arrived home. She was already in bed, but she hadn't slept, and not just because the June heat made her restless and uncomfortable. She had not yet figured out what to say to him.

All these months, they'd walked side by side and hand in hand on a layer of ice. They'd been kind and gentle with one another so as not to break through the surface and face the frigid cold beneath.

It was time they confronted the truth. She just didn't know how to begin.

Cam's skin was warm and damp when he slid into bed and pulled her close. "I know you're awake. You're not snoring." His attempt at humor didn't work this time. They couldn't laugh this off any longer. He let out a breath and kissed her neck. "I'm sorry for what I said, and for scaring you."

"Then you have forgiven me?" she asked to see if he'd lie. They'd get nowhere if they couldn't speak the truth, as ugly as it may be.

"Nay. But I hadn't realized until it came out of my mouth. That wasn't the way to address the subject."

"I'm glad you're finally speaking of your feelings. It does no good to let them fester and become worse."

"I don't want to spend our final days angry with one another. But I am angry at you, Mari. And I canna even tell ye why."

"For leaving you."

"Aye, but I know why you did it. I gave you and Lach hell, but I would have done the same in your place. Still..."

"I left you."

"Yes. And you'll be doing it again sooner than we realize, and I hate you for it. I'll be alone again." He clung to her and kissed her hair. "I love you so much. You're my very soul."

His words filled her with both joy and sadness. He'd never said these things before. Hadn't wanted these feelings between them. But they had grown despite their mutual desire not to become attached.

She entwined her fingers with his over their child. "You'll not be alone this time. Our child will be with you."

"I've never been so eager for something yet feared it so deeply."

"I think that is true of all fathers."

He let out a deep breath and squeezed her closer. "When my father left me, I blamed him for not being a better warrior. For falling in battle because he'd not trained hard enough. When my mother left me, I grew angry because she'd given in to her loneliness. When you go, I don't want to feel that way about you. I want to hold on to the love I feel for you and the joy I know in your arms. But I fear I'm not strong enough to do so. Hate and anger are easier."

"Do you still hate your parents for leaving you?"

"Nay. In time I realized it was the way of things."

Such realizations came with age and maturity.

"Then perhaps, in time, you'll be able to put your anger aside and think well of me, too."

...

When Mari was asleep, Cam slipped out of their bed to go to the library for a drink. His mind wouldn't still, and his heart grew more frantic with every tick of the clock.

He loved his wife.

He'd known it. It was the thing that had driven him to tear off for London to try and save her. But he hadn't said as much. He hadn't admitted to her how he felt until now.

He poured a whisky and sat in the dark. He was well into his fourth glass when a ghost appeared before him. He jumped, then realized it was the dowager in a flowing night robe. Surely a specter wouldn't look so displeased.

"You're drinking all the good whisky in the house," she accused.

"Aye," he answered, noticing his tongue felt a bit numb. "It's almost as good as the MacKinlay stores."

She sniffed at that and sat next to him. "Why are you drinking? Mari could have the child any day now. You should be alert and ready."

He nodded, but his nod turned into a sway of his head the other way. "As soon as the babe is born, she'll be taken. And—" A sob broke free and he hung his head. "I wish to be hardened like you. My own mother was weak and succumbed to the pain of her broken heart, leaving me alone to fend for myself. I can't do that to our child. I need to find a way to go on, but I don't see how, loving her the way I do."

"You don't want this either, Cameron," the dowager said, placing a hand on his arm. "Hiding behind walls this thick means there's no escape from the hell you create for yourself."

She took the glass from his slack fingers and set it aside.

"I wasn't prepared for the pain, so I didn't know any other course but to wrap it around myself and wear it like armor. You have a choice. You can do better for your child than your mother did for you. Better than I did for mine."

When Cam awoke, he wasn't sure she'd ever been there. But her words remained, and with a groggy head he got up to face whatever the day would bring.

At one in the afternoon, Mari cringed with her first pain.

Cam's heart shattered.

Their time was nearly over.

...

Mari gazed down at her daughter with a tumult of emotions whipping around her like winds on the moor. She felt all of them so much clearer than ever before.

The fear she'd felt before twined around her heart and grew to include her child. What dangers would she face in her life that Mari wouldn't be there to protect her from?

Other feelings emerged. Anger at the duke for condemning her to death by his own actions. Sorrow for the loss of her mother: she wished her baby had a loving grandmother to watch over her. Excitement for what their child would become.

In the mess of emotions racing through her, it was joy that washed everything else away as she was swept up in the love that took over her entire being. Tears of happiness streamed down her face as she looked up at her husband.

"You did well, lass. She's beautiful." Cam's voice shook as he touched their daughter's cheek. "Elizabeth."

They'd decided on the name only weeks ago. It was her sister's middle name, and they both hoped it carried Kenna's strength.

The babe looked even smaller when Cam took her in his

large hands. He placed a kiss on her forehead and walked over to the window where the sun was just beginning to light the sky.

At that moment, Mari could almost believe they were in a different place. Home, in Scotland. And that they would be free to live in peace. No Ridley or magistrate waiting to take her to the gallows. Just Cam and Lizzy living in the house they would have built in that field where she'd unintentionally married the large Highlander she would grow to love with all her heart.

Life would have been so wonderful.

As happened every morning, a knock came two hours later. Each day someone came to see her. They wanted to confirm she remained on the premises and ascertain if she'd yet delivered the child.

This time the runner, Adam, was shown into her room and blushed at the state of things. She was still abed with her hair down and unkempt.

"I hope I find you well, madam," Adam said. He was a polite young man despite the duties he was forced to carry out.

"As well as can be expected," she offered.

"She's lovely," he added with a genuine smile that faded from his face when he turned back to her. "I'll not say anything today, but tomorrow I'll have to report back that you're fit to stand trial. It will be a few days until they can prepare."

"Thank you, Adam."

"Please forgive me. I'll leave you to your celebration." He stood and left the room, taking her dreams for hope and a future with him.

The next few nights as Lizzy slept in her cradle, Mari went over every detail she could think of.

"Don't be too ghastly when she takes a liking to a lad," she told Cam.

"You jest. I'll not let a boy near her. I was a lad— I know what they think."

"You can't keep her locked in the castle forever."

"Aye. I can. I'm sure to be bigger than her."

"Cam, I'm being serious."

"I am as well." Though he winked at her.

"Do you not want her to experience love, as we have?"

Cam winced and glanced toward the cradle. "Mayhap when she's older I might come around to it, but right now I just want to protect her from everything that could possibly cause her sadness."

Mari understood. This was something that became more acceptable to a father later. But she didn't have later, so she needed to tell him everything she wanted for their daughter now. While there was still time.

"If she shows an interest in things that are not ladylike, encourage her anyway."

"Love, I don't have the skills to encourage the ladylike pursuits, so you can be assured I'll encourage the others."

"Kenna will help."

"She will? Are ye certain?"

"You read her last letter?" Mari guessed.

"The one where she told you she *wouldn't* help raise your child so you needed to stay to do it your own self? Aye, I read it."

"She'll come around. She doesn't have it in her to turn our daughter away when Lizzy needs a woman to guide her."

Cam didn't answer. For a moment she thought maybe he'd drifted off. When she looked up, she saw him staring at the ceiling. "What is it?"

"I'm sorry, Mari. I canna do this any longer."

"You can't do what?"

"Lie in bed with you and plan a future without ye."

"But there's so much I want you to know." And so little

time.

"Let's run away. Tonight. We'll be out of England before daylight."

She sat up and winced, still tender from giving birth. She'd never manage to sit a horse, even if there was a chance.

"Cam, we can't. The house is guarded. They'll see us leave, and you'll be arrested. We've talked about this."

"Nay, *you've* talked about it. If I can come up with a way, will you at least hear it?"

"And spend the rest of our time arguing over false hope?" She kissed him, and he kissed her back. "I'd rather lie in your arms and know that you and Lizzy will be safe and happy."

He let out a breath and nodded in agreement.

"Which means you'll need to remarry," she said.

"Marian MacKinlay, if you've any wish of not spending the rest of our time arguing, you'll not suggest such a thing to me."

"Very well. Just know that as long as the woman loves you and Lizzy, you have my blessing."

He kissed her hard. "I need to stop your lips from moving."

"I wish we'd been able to make love once more," she said when he finally relented.

"Do you think you would have been happy with one more time? Wouldn't ye just want another and another?" He took a deep breath.

"Yes. I would have." It was the truth of it. Even if she'd lived a hundred years, she'd never have enough time with him.

Chapter Thirty-Seven

When the men arrived to take Mari to Guildhall, Cam fought them. It was beyond him to stand there peaceably and allow her to be taken. It was only by the grace of Adam Reeves that he'd not been arrested and thrown in the gaol next to his wife.

Cam had always been large, even as a lad. He'd been a formidable warrior with a strong sword arm. But in this he was completely helpless.

He managed to get himself together the next morning to attend the first day of her trial. She'd tried to prepare him for what would happen, but no amount of discussion would have readied him for the drivel these bewigged fools spewed in court.

"You claim self-defense, madam, however there is no prior claim that your husband injured you beyond his rights in the past."

Cam's stomach turned because as her husband the man had had the legal right to beat her. She was no better or worse than a horse to them. He'd heard of men who beat their horses to the ground without any repercussions. He could only imagine what went on in private with that type of man.

Cam had been born into a union joined by love and respect. He'd never so much as heard his father raise his voice to his mother. Yet she respected him.

"Correct, my lord, but I'm sure you understand why a woman in my position felt unsafe to file such a claim without a guarantee of protection."

"Could you repeat that? I'm having difficulty understanding your heavy brogue."

A number of the people in the hall laughed.

Mari's English was flawless. They were making a joke of her.

Cam clenched his fists, ready to grab these weak men and pummel them until they no longer needed to worry about understanding things. But his gaze met Mari's, and she shook her head.

Her mouth formed the word, "Please."

He knew she didn't want him to get thrown out of court. She needed him to be there. So he would stay. Even as she repeated her words, enunciating every sound.

The questions continued, though it was clear the magistrates were going nowhere but in circles.

"Perhaps if you'd been more obedient, he wouldn't have needed to punish you so severely."

"Could it be that you were jealous because he wasn't paying attention to you? A man is entitled to take a mistress."

"The duke's crime was selecting a wife who was unable to bear up to her responsibilities."

Round and round they went, accusing his lovely wife of being a shrew, a spendthrift, and a whore. Each time she remained calm and disputed their claim, but it made no difference. These men could not hear her words. They weren't even ashamed that one of their class had hurt a woman, much less terrorized her to the point that she had no choice but to turn to murder.

When they were done with their relentless interrogation for the day, Mari was escorted back to her cell. Cam was permitted to visit her.

"This is madness," he said when they were alone. "They ask questions but don't let you answer, or listen when you do. This isn't a trial."

"It's a formality. They need to do this so they can justify my punishment and send a message."

"A message that a woman does not warrant the law's protection and respect? Or that of her husband? I'm a father of a lass now, and I'll not abide such things."

"I thought this would go on a week or so, but at this rate, it will most likely be over in a matter of days. Perhaps you should bring Lizzy tomorrow. I want to see you both one last time. Then I want you to leave for home."

"Nay. I canna let you go, Mari," he said. "Lizzy and I need you. I'm going to get you out of here. I don't know where we'll go, but we'll be together. We'll make it work."

She shook her head. "No, Cam. You promised. If you're locked up or hanged next to me, who will take care of Lizzy? Please let this go. Just take her home and live a good life with her."

"*Live a good life?* How the bloody hell am I supposed to live a good life without you? You think I'm just going to take the babe home to Dunardry and wish you well?"

"Yes."

"No! I'll not leave you here to face this alone." He let out a breath. "There has to be some way out of this. Some way to save you so we can all go home and be a family. I can't do this without you."

He now understood how his mother felt, being the one left behind with a broken heart.

He'd always thought he'd be the one to leave someone else

to this kind of empty existence. He'd avoided love precisely so he wouldn't cause anyone pain. It seemed like a mockery of his plans that he was the one left behind once again.

His voice faltered, but he needed to be strong for her.

"I'll not run," she said firmly. "I'll not risk you or our daughter, and I'll not force you into a life in constant fear of discovery. I committed this crime. I shall pay for it, just as I knew I would since the moment I looked down at my bloody hands."

"I'm not leaving," he insisted.

"I don't want you there at the end. I don't want you to have that awful sight to dwell on. I want you to always remember me alive and happy. Please? When you think of me, think of us laughing and smiling and making love."

"You ask too much, Mari. I'm only a man. I promised to protect you with my life. I can't just walk away."

"You aren't just a man, Cam. You're also a father. And I expect you to do what you need to do to make sure you can see that task through. Protect Elizabeth. Keep her safe and give her a happy life. That's all I ask. And give her this." She placed the locket he'd given her in his hand. "I snipped a bit of my hair and put it inside so she'll have a small piece of me with her always."

"I don't want her to have a small piece. I want her to have all of you, alive and well to love us both. Please, Mari." He tried to give it back, but she wouldn't take it.

How was he supposed to keep Mari alive for his daughter with naught but a few stories and a lock of her hair?

"We both knew this day would come. We've lived the last months with happiness in our hearts, but the shadow has closed in. The day has come, and now we must face it bravely."

"I've been trained to fight my entire life. And now, for the biggest battle of my life, you ask me to lay down my sword and walk away in defeat?"

"Yes. That's what I'm asking you to do. Leave tomorrow night with Elizabeth. Take her home."

Cam wiped at the tears on his face. "I love you. God knows I tried not to, but I couldn't help it."

"I love you, too, husband."

They managed a kiss through the bars. He reached for her hand and squeezed it.

"Goodbye, Cam," she said.

"I'll not say goodbye. I can't." With that, he turned and left.

...

Mari felt numb as she lay on her filthy pallet that night, listening to the sounds of dripping water and small rodents scurrying to find food.

Somehow she'd managed to still have hope when she'd walked into Guildhall that morning. Despite what she'd said to Cam, she'd told herself there was still a chance they would hear her and one of them would have compassion for a woman who only did what she'd had to do to survive.

It was a crushing blow to be so wrong.

She shivered from the chill and closed her eyes. Pushing out the reality of the prison, she recalled the beauty of the MacKinlay lands. The hills, the flinty outcroppings of rock. The grove of trees and the stream that ran through it. The field where she'd met Cam.

Home.

She was surprised when the guard arrived to wake her.

As she'd predicted, the trial went on in the same manner as the day before. She tried her best to remain calm, but as they continued their attack on her reputation she finally reached her breaking point and railed at them for their behavior.

If she was destined to be executed, she might as well

unleash her fury on them. Unfortunately, all it served to do was to exhaust her and make her seem unreasonable. When it was over for the day, she nearly begged them to just be done with it.

As on the day before, Cam came to see her. But this time he brought Lizzy, as she'd asked.

"Hello, love." She greeted their daughter with a smile. "I'm so happy to see you."

Her daughter fussed and Mari longed to hold her. It wasn't possible through the bars, but she reached out to touch and caress her daughter.

"Please, Mari. I beg you," Cam said quietly as tears slid down his cheeks.

"I was afraid to love you, too," she admitted. "I feared that if I loved you, it would be too difficult to leave you when the time came. But love made it easier to leave, in order to protect you. Love makes it easier for me to say goodbye now, too. Because I love you so much, I want only happiness for you. Always know I loved you with all my heart."

"I'll not forget," he said so softly she barely heard him. Then he turned and walked away with their daughter.

When he was gone, Mari curled into a ball and cried herself to sleep.

...

Cam could not sleep. His body was tired, but his mind continued to search desperately for a way to save his wife.

She'd made it clear she wouldn't approve of an illegal rescue. She didn't want to condemn them to a life on the run. But she would be alive, and it would be a life together. It might not be easy, but he wanted to try.

Except it wasn't just about him anymore. He was a father. He needed to do the best thing for Lizzy. And if he ended up in an English prison, he wouldn't be there for her.

He couldn't take both of her parents away and condemn her to grow up alone, as he had.

It was an impossible situation. One that couldn't be solved with his brawn or a sword. Maybe if he weren't so exhausted, he'd be able to come up with a smart way out of this.

He was distracted from intense contemplation by his daughter's cries. He rose to go to her, but before he managed to get to the door, the crying stopped. Worried as to the cause, he hurried into her room.

There he spotted the dowager leaning over the crib. She raised Elizabeth in her arms, and Cam gasped. What did she plan to do to his child? He could only imagine the worst.

"Please, don't hurt her. She's all I'll have left after tomorrow," Cam begged, knowing he couldn't make it across the room if the woman chose to drop the babe on the floor.

His hands were raised in a nonthreatening manner as he stepped closer.

She looked at him aghast. "I wouldn't hurt this child."

"You don't seem to like bairns all that much, especially ones spawned by two Scots."

The dowager made a noise that would have been a snort if it weren't coming from someone so aristocratic.

"I don't care who her parents are. She's an angel." The dowager rocked the babe and smiled down at the infant in her arms.

Cam relaxed a little, though still a trifle wary. "I have to be honest and say it's because she looks like me."

"Arrogant wretch," the dowager said without her usual bite of distaste.

"I think she is the most beautiful babe ever created," he said, serious now.

"By Scots," the dowager amended.

His jaw dropped. "Did you just make a joke, Your

Grace?"

"Aye," she answered, using his own word.

He laughed and stepped closer, completely at ease now. When she made to hand Lizzy over to him, he shook his head. "Go ahead, if it pleases you." He even pulled the rocking chair over from the corner so she could sit. "Does your foot still bother you?"

"It's much improved. Thank you." She sat and rocked the baby with a stiff smile on her lips. She wanted to say something else. He could tell. It was the time of night one needed to unload worries and often sought out a place of peace to leave them.

"Is something bothering you?" he asked.

"I think you have enough worries of your own than to take on mine, as well."

"I need a rest from my own. I canna do anything for them."

"I'm sorry this is happening. I wish now I'd done more." Her face softened with sadness and regret.

Cam understood. She probably thought she might have helped her son if she'd known of his problems. It was Cam's experience that some people were inherently evil and couldn't be helped.

"You didn't know."

"That's just it. I did know." She frowned. "I once had a daughter named Elizabeth."

Startled, he cocked his head at her. "Is that so? I wonder why Mari didn't mention it when we chose the name."

The dowager pushed out a shaky breath. "She didn't know. My daughter died many years ago."

A prick of sympathy went through him. "I'm sorry. Mari's sister lost a babe once, and it haunts them still."

"Children have so many things stacked against them. It's a parent's job to protect them. That's why I'm the one to blame for my Eliza's death."

He studied her thoughtfully. He'd never before seen such emotion touch her expression as now. "I doubt that's true," he said kindly. "I think we often take on more guilt than we've truly earned."

She shook her head. "Sometimes. But not in this case."

She seemed to want to tell her story, so he gave her the opportunity. "What happened?"

She was silent for a long moment, then she began in a voice thick with emotion, "After having five boys, my husband and I were blessed with a girl. Her older brothers doted over her. She was their princess, always cheerful and happy. But when she reached about ten, she became quiet. Not having experience with little girls, I thought it normal. But nothing about the situation was normal. It was only a few months after her eleventh birthday that I found out she was with child."

Cam gasped in shock. "Good lord. I'm so sorry," he said, knowing his words were inadequate. He almost hoped she wouldn't finish the story. There could be no happy ending for this beastly tale.

"Of course I made her tell me who had touched her. I expected her to name a servant or a visitor. I would never have guessed it to be her own brother. Mathias was nineteen, heir to the dukedom."

Mathias. Cam had never heard the duke's given name before.

The dowager paused to gather herself, and Cam was grateful for the moment to put his thoughts together.

Good God. Mari's former husband had defiled his own sister. A mere child. Cam knew the man had been a monster, but he'd never realized he was this vile. Not just cruel and violent, but truly depraved.

The dowager's eyes closed. "We needed to do everything

possible to mitigate the scandal and protect Eliza. I sent her off to our country house while I stayed behind to deal with my son. My husband wanted him charged. I wanted to protect my daughter, and I knew a trial would end with her ruined and no real punishment for Mathias. He was a future duke, after all. So I forbade it."

Cam remembered the scars on Mari's breasts, and how she'd told him her husband didn't like her body, saying her breasts were too large. He'd been unable to perform. He hadn't liked her body because it belonged to a woman, and he was attracted to—

Cam swallowed down bile and once again wished the sick bastard had still been alive so he could bloody his sword on him. Surely there was a special hell for that kind of beast.

The dowager continued with an unsteady voice. "I sent Eliza away with one of the maids. When I arrived at the estate a day later, I learned my little girl had fallen over the second-floor banister and died."

The old woman didn't cry. No doubt she'd cried endless tears over the years and had finally made what peace she could from the scraps of truth. Cam felt great sorrow for her. It made sense now why she'd built those thick walls around herself. Holding a foul secret like this inside for all these years would eat away at a person's soul.

But a small part of Cam wished she'd done things differently. If she'd allowed her son to be arrested and charged, maybe Mari would have been spared her ordeal.

He understood the dowager had done what was needed to protect her family.

In the end, at the expense of his own.

He didn't speak for fear he would end up yelling at her and getting kicked out of the house. It was much too late to take his wee daughter away to find another place to stay for the rest of the night.

"I wasn't able to protect Eliza," she said quietly. "Nor was I able to protect Marian." Her breath caught on a slight sob. "But by God, I will not fail this little one. I'll do whatever I must to make certain my son doesn't hurt another innocent person."

She pressed her thin lips to Lizzy's head and held her up for him to take.

He scooped up the baby and held her close, using his other hand to help the older woman out of her chair when she struggled.

"For a Scottish brute, you've been ever so kind," she said without meeting his gaze, and left the room.

When he heard a door close down the hall, he looked at his daughter. "She's a touch batty, but I can't say I blame her for it. If someone hurt you, I'd have their head removed from their body, as well as a number of other parts."

He took the chair and rocked his already sleeping daughter. It would have been safe to place her back in her cradle, but he wanted to hold her a little longer.

"I'm still not ready to give up," he said softly. "I have to keep thinking."

Chapter Thirty-Eight

Through the night while holding his baby daughter, Cam's sadness faded and was overrun by intense anger. How dare Mari ask him to give up on their life together? How dare she not fight to be with him and their child?

She was ready to stroll up to the gallows and face death without protest.

It would be easier for her. She'd be gone. One more day and she'd not know this pain—the intense pain Cam would feel for the rest of his life. Or the empty spot in Lizzy's life where her mother should be.

"No. No. No!" He slammed his fist on the breakfast table, making the dishes rattle.

The dowager hadn't come to breakfast, which was good. In this mood he would most likely call her out for not stopping her son from taking a second wife and hurting her as much as he had his first wife and his young sister.

But as mad as Cam was, he wouldn't lay any more guilt at the poor woman's feet. He'd seen the torment in her eyes. She had been imprisoned by it for nearly her whole life. She'd punished herself enough.

Unable to eat, he stood. After seeing that Lizzy was safe with the nurse, he left Blackley House for the trial. Mari had asked him not to come back. But he couldn't stay away. He needed to be there for her. He might have a chance to spirit her away, and he needed to be ready.

. . .

Mari awoke only a few hours after she'd managed to finally fall asleep. She'd always had trouble sleeping over the years, whether from excitement or fear. But last night was different.

It was difficult to spend the precious little time she had left in sleep. Today she would be found guilty and ordered hanged for murder. And those few hours she'd spent sleeping could have been better spent thinking of her husband and daughter. Or her sister and her wee nephews.

It led her into thinking of all the time she'd wasted. Such as all those nights after she'd first come to Dunardry. If only she'd known how short their time together would be, she would have spent it loving Cam from the very first minute.

She knew there was no sense worrying. What was done was done. And in several hours, her life would be over, too.

Cam would take care of their daughter. As would her sister. She trusted them both to do the right thing for Lizzy.

As Mari was led into the chambers to face her punishment, she'd expected to feel somewhat at peace. There was nothing else she could do, after all.

But that wasn't the case. She found herself wishing she'd made plans to escape with Cam. She wasn't ready to give up. She wanted to be alive, to have a life with her husband and daughter.

It wasn't fair. She'd only done what she had to do to survive. But to those who judged her, that meant nothing.

She gasped when she saw Cam's head towering over the rest of the crowd.

He was still here. He hadn't left her as she'd asked.

Which meant there was still hope. A chance he might come up with some miracle to get her out of this.

She met his gaze and nodded, wishing they had a moment to speak in private. To plan.

She wanted to apologize for giving up. If only there were time…

The booming voice of the head magistrate cut through the air. "If there are no other witnesses to be heard, we shall—"

The justice was cut off by a single word from the back of the room. It was much too soft and feminine to have come from Cam, and it came from the opposite side of the courtroom.

The crowd murmured and parted until a small, regal woman made her way toward the front, her head held high and her lips pinched. Her cane clicked against the floor as she approached the men who were to decide Mari's fate.

"I will be heard," the dowager duchess demanded, and stepped closer. "Bring me a chair. This will take some time."

Mari sat there in shock. This woman she'd finally befriended—or so Mari had thought—the person they'd just months ago shared a warm and companionable Christmas with, had come to put the final nail in Mari's coffin. A sliver of betrayal sliced through her heart.

But Mari had killed her son. So she couldn't rightly blame her.

One thing Mari knew, now that she had a child of her own, was that she would punish anyone who harmed her daughter.

But as the dowager began to speak, it soon became clear she was not there to condemn and convict, but to defend

Mari.

Mari felt dizzy with surprise and gratitude. Even if it came to nothing, she felt humbled and thankful for the dowager's support— She was so incredibly brave, sitting there in public court in front of everyone telling her grim tale.

Mari wept for the mother who chose to spill her family's darkest secrets in order to help Mari. The pain the woman must have lived with all these years!

As Mari listened, so many things began to make sense. She felt vindicated, certain in the knowledge that she hadn't done anything to earn her unhappy marriage or her terrible fate. The man was sick and twisted. It wouldn't have mattered whom he'd taken to wife; that woman would have ended up one of two ways—dead at his hands, or a murderer herself. Just like Mari.

When the dowager had finished, the whole room hovered in silence for a few moments, then erupted in an avalanche of outrage. Mari didn't hear all of what was being said, only snippets.

"Disgrace to his title—"

"Monster—"

"Beast—"

"—should be thanking her for ending him."

And then, booming out above everything else, she heard the words she hadn't ever dared to imagine.

"Marian MacKinlay, you are free to go."

Mari was escorted out of the main room into a side chamber. The dowager followed close behind. When they were alone, she hugged the woman. "Why did you do this for me? You've brought scandal down on your family to save my life—someone you've always hated."

The dowager's lips—always pulled into a scowl before this—relaxed as her sharp eyes landed on Cam, who stood nearby, making arrangements for their departure.

"I attempted to stop him when he was leaving the house to come here today. He was very angry, and I knew he'd do something…manly and unwise. He finally confessed his plan to run off with you—a terrible life for a woman and a baby, mind you. Then he asked for my help. He told me swords and bravery could not save you. *He* could not save you. He didn't try to bully me into coming forward. Instead, he went to his knees and simply asked me to save his life, and Lizzy's life, by saving yours."

To Mari's surprise, the dowager reached for her, pulling her into an embrace with more strength than expected for a woman of her age and size. "Oh, Mother. Thank you."

"I'm ashamed to admit, at the time I told him no. I let him go off to put into motion his ridiculous plan to rescue you. But I couldn't sit there and let him sacrifice his life. Not when I knew you were innocent."

Mari shook her head. "But I'm not. I did kill him."

"Only because he left you no choice. I didn't hate you, Marian. I never have. I hated the helplessness you made me feel inside. I knew I couldn't save you from Mathias any more than I was able to save Eliza. It was easier to ignore you, so as not to feel responsible for your fate. I'm so sorry."

Tears brimmed over Mari's lashes. "I understand. I forgive you."

The dowager swallowed. "My dear, I may have shared my awful story to save you today, but in truth, you freed me when you killed my son. Freed me from worry that it might happen yet again. And today you saved me from the guilt of living with that terrible secret. A debt was owed, so a debt was repaid."

Mari pulled the other woman close as they cried together, both in joy and sorrow, and from all the other emotions swirling around them.

They were both free to live again.

And to love.

• • •

"Wife. Your Grace." Cam gently interrupted the embrace his wife was sharing with her savior.

Mari turned to him, and he scooped her up when she sagged into his arms. He was glad he was there to catch her. She'd been through so much in the last months. They all had.

"You saved me with wits rather than brawn," she told him with a wobbly smile. "I knew you would find a way."

He laughed. "Do not tell anyone about my wits, lass. It will undermine my intimidating disposition."

"You are quite imposing." Her smile lit up his heart. From the moment she'd come tearing out of the woods on that first day, she'd softened him…and he was a stronger man for it.

When she released him, he turned to the dowager and hugged her, careful not to squeeze too tightly.

As expected, she voiced her complaint. "Let go of me, you brute." But when he released her, she was smiling. Not much, but he could see it was a valiant attempt. "Take care of them," she whispered, and squeezed his hand fiercely.

This woman, frail, aged, and surly, had turned out to be a formidable warrior. She'd proven herself on the battlefield today. As with any other warrior he'd fought next to, Cam felt great respect for her. She should be honored for what she'd done.

"Will ye come with us?" he asked, clearly surprising her as much as himself. "To Dunardry?"

"Yes," Mari added immediately. As always, she understood him. "There is nothing left for you in London but scandal and loneliness. Please come with us. Join our family as Lizzy's grandmother."

When she shook her head, Cam tried again.

"This place is nothing but darkness and the memories you use to punish yourself. No more. Your daughter would be proud of what you did for us this day. It's time to let go of the past and start fresh."

"With us," Mari added, her eyes bright.

He was glad she was accepting of this plan, since they'd had no time to discuss it first.

"I appreciate your offer, truly, but I am an old woman. I cannot make such a long trip and start my whole life over."

"You are a spirited old crow, and more than capable of making such a trip if you decide it is something you want to do." He held up his hand to stop her rebuttal. "Consider it an open invitation."

She gave a nod and a sigh. "Thank you."

He smiled down at her. "I will not try to intimidate you into agreeing, because I know an impenetrable wall when I run into one and your head is thus. Just know this, Your Grace. Whether you stay here or come with us to Scotland, you are part of our family. We will write to you and tell you tales of Lizzy's growing up until you tell us to stop."

"I'll never tell you to stop." The old woman wiped a tear from her eye.

After allowing the dowager to fuss over Lizzy for a few moments longer, Cam helped his family into the Endsmere carriage, and they set off for home.

For Scotland.

・・・

Lizzy was a fair traveler for their fast-paced retreat from England. She only fussed on the occasion when her father—cramped from riding in the carriage—spent a few hours on a horse instead of inside with them.

It was late in the evening a few weeks later when the carriage finally crossed over into their homeland. Lizzy was sleeping in Cam's strong arms as he gazed down at her in awe, as he often did. It was at these times Mari knew with certainty that this was the life she was supposed to have. Not that other one. This was the man she was meant to be with.

Remembering the dowager's parting wish, Mari sat up and searched for the letter she'd been given. Taking their sleeping daughter from him, Mari handed him the sealed missive.

"What is this?" he asked, puzzled.

"I don't know. The dowager told me to give it to you once we were in Scotland."

Cam opened it and gasped as he read through the letter.

"What does it say?" Curiosity got the best of her when her husband's eyes continued to dart from side to side. She shifted closer so she could also read it in the low light from the lantern.

Dearest Highland Brute,

I've instructed my man of business to forward to you the sum of two thousand pounds, which was the amount of Marian's dowry, paid to my late son upon their wedding. However, the man was never a suitable husband to her, only a monster. I have witnessed the love you have for Marian, and I believe, as her true husband, you are the rightful recipient of these funds.

I thank you for doing what needed to be done with elegance and kindness.

The best to you and yours,
Wilhelmina

Cam glanced up and chuckled, though he was clearly

bewildered. "Well, I'll be damned. Did you notice she signed it with just her name?"

Mari was still trying to process the news. "I never knew her name. I was only permitted to call her 'Your Grace' or 'Lady Mother.'"

He handed her the letter. "She honors me with such a generous gesture, but it is your money, earned with your own blood. What will you have us do with it?"

Mari looked at their daughter, thinking over the possibilities. Part of her wanted to throw the blood money into a hole in the ground and never think of her past again. But Cam was right. She'd earned it through years of abuse and fear. And she was able to use it now for something that would make them all happy and safe.

She smiled at her husband. "It looks like we'll be building a manor house, after all."

Cam smiled back. "Aye. We can use these funds to build a fine home for my beautiful family." His large finger caressed Lizzy's cheek as he leaned in close. "As big as it may grow."

Then he kissed Mari in that gentle yet demanding way of his. Indomitable strength tempered with love. She knew her new life with this man would be filled with safety and happiness…not to mention passion and excitement.

Epilogue

"I see you're back to digging up rocks," Lach said, approaching as Cam tossed a large boulder into the cart.

Cam smiled at the laird and wiped the sweat from his brow. It had been easy to forgive him once Mari was safe and back at Dunardry. Cam knew Lach had done the best he could with the options he'd been given. It was not an easy thing to be a leader.

"Aye." Cam dropped another stone into the cart. "Though this time it's by choice." Every rock he plucked from the earth was going to building a home for his family. Complete with a suite of rooms for the Dowager Duchess of Endsmere, who had changed her mind and joined them unexpectedly a month ago.

"Are you going to sit up there atop your horse, or will you get down and help me?" Cam asked, squinting up into the early March sky.

"Aye." Lach swung down. "I have others on their way to help, but before they arrive, I wanted to speak to you alone."

Cam came to stand next to him, knowing it must be

important.

When he'd returned home with his wife and child, he'd made the difficult decision to give up the duty of war chief, handing over the position to Bryce. While Cam would gladly raise his sword in defense of his clan, he didn't want to be on the front lines any longer. He had too much to live for.

Bryce had been happy to take over the duty, not having anyone at home to worry over him. Nor ever wanting another family.

After drawing up the plans for his home, Cam had been commissioned to draw up other plans as well. He had a skill for seeing the way things looked before they were built. With Mari's encouragement, he had sold a few drawings already.

"What's amiss?" he asked when Lach hadn't continued.

"I finally heard back from the McCurdy. It seems they're getting desperate and have agreed to an alliance for peace."

Cam's eyes went wide. "Finally. That's wonderful. We'll gain access to the sea."

Lach nodded but didn't look as happy as Cam would have expected. This seaport had been his father's lifelong dream for their clan, and they were finally getting it.

Lach grimaced. "The alliance will be through a marriage to the McCurdy's daughter."

Cam frowned. "Who do ye have to marry off? I thought he'd only agree to the laird or the war chief." His voice faltered on the last two words. "Oh, God."

"Right."

"Does your new war chief know you've bartered him away for marriage?"

Bryce had been happily married and lost his wife and child. The loss had broken his heart. He'd sworn never to wed again.

"Not yet. I'll tell him soon. We have a few months until the wedding will take place."

Cam snorted. "Good luck to you." He might have said more, but at that moment his wife stepped out from the trees. This time she wasn't running with terror in her eyes. She was carrying their daughter and smiling.

Lizzy reached toward him, and he ran to meet them, scooping her into his arms and swinging her above his head to make her laugh. "Da!" she squealed so he'd do it again. But he sat her on his shoulders, holding her in place securely as he bent to kiss his wife.

"You're making progress," she said, taking in the stone walls that lined the perimeter of their new home.

"Aye. And it looks like we're getting help."

A group of men crested the hill in a line, with Liam leading the way. Women followed along behind, bringing food and ale to keep the workers nourished.

With this much help they'd be under roof by the end of the summer.

"Make sure not to do too much," Mari whispered before leaning up to kiss him. "I don't want you to be too tired tonight." A saucy wink clued him in to what she had in mind.

He grinned. "The last time you met me in this field while I dug rocks, ye forced me into marriage. Now you're seducing me to your bed. You provide a fine argument for spending all my days at the task."

She playfully poked him in the chest. "Surely you'll be too busy for such things when the second bairn arrives."

"The second—" Cam swallowed in surprise, and then a smile that matched the one on his wife's face pulled at his lips. "You never cease to make me happier than I ever thought possible."

"And I'll never tire of trying," she promised with a kiss.

About the Author

One very early morning, Allison B. Hanson woke up with a conversation going on in her head. It wasn't so much a dream as being forced awake by her imagination. Unable to go back to sleep, she gave in, went to the computer, and began writing. Years later it still hasn't stopped. Allison lives near Hershey, Pennsylvania. Her contemporary romances include paranormal, sci-fi, fantasy, and mystery suspense. She enjoys candy immensely, as well as long motorcycle rides, running, and reading.

Also by Allison B. Hanson...

WITNESS IN THE DARK

WANTED FOR LIFE

WATCHED FROM A DISTANCE

Discover more Amara titles...

Highland Renegade
a *Children of the Mist* novel by Cynthia Breeding

Lady Emily has received title to MacGregor lands and she's determined to make a new start. She just has to win over the handsome Laird MacGregor whose family has lived there for centuries. Ian MacGregor aims to scare her away. But despite his best efforts to freeze her out, things between them heat up. Highlanders hate the Sassenach, so Ian must choose—his clan or the irresistible English aristocrat who's taken not only his lands, but also his heart.

Highland Conquest
a *Sons of Sinclair* novel by Heather McCollum

To finally bring peace to his clan, Cain Sinclair will wed the young female chief of their greatest enemy. Only problem: Ella Sutherland may be clever, passionate, and shockingly beautiful, but what she isn't is willing. Every attempt Cain makes to woo her seems to backfire. The only time they ever see eye to eye is when they're heating up Cain's bed, and the only thing Ella truly wants is the one thing he cannot offer her: freedom. But when a secret she's been harboring could threaten both clans, Cain must decide between peace for the Sinclairs and the woman who's captured his heart.

A Scot to Wed
a *Scottish Hearts* novel by Callie Hutton

Katie has nowhere else to go but MacDuff Castle and she refuses to bow down to the arrogant and handsome Evan MacNeil. She's through with men controlling her. Now that Evan must spar with a beautiful lass for the rights to the lands, he will fight to the end. This battle is nothing like the ones his Highlander ancestors fought with crossbows and boiling oil. They never wanted to bed the enemy.

How to Forgive a Highlander
a *MacGregor Lairds* novel by Michelle McLean

William MacGregor would die to protect his clan but when he kidnaps the wrong woman, he puts everyone in danger. Rose Thatcher wants to protect her lady but the Highlander who abducted her is not helping. To save their respective loved ones, they must stay together. Somewhere along the grueling journey to Scotland, their constant bickering turns into something more. Perhaps something worth fighting for? If they can't defeat the enemy they accidentally led home, they might not live long enough to find out.

Printed in Great Britain
by Amazon